STAR WARS™
ADVENTURES
SMUGGLER'S BLUES

Facebook: **facebook.com/idwpublishing**
Twitter: **@idwpublishing**
YouTube: **youtube.com/idwpublishing**
Tumblr: **tumblr.idwpublishing.com**
Instagram: **instagram.com/idwpublishing**

ISBN: 978-1-68405-344-5   21 20 19 18   1 2 3 4

COVER ARTIST
DEREK CHARM

LETTERER
TOM B. LONG

SERIES ASSISTANT EDITORS
PETER ADRIAN BEHRAVESH
& ELIZABETH BREI

SERIES EDITORS
BOBBY CURNOW
& DENTON J. TIPTON

COLLECTION EDITORS
JUSTIN EISINGER
& ALONZO SIMON

COLLECTION DESIGNER
CLYDE GRAPA

PUBLISHER
GREG GOLDSTEIN

Originally published as STAR WARS ADVENTURES FREE COMIC
BOOK DAY 2018, STAR WARS ADVENTURES issues #10–11, and
STAR WARS ADVENTURES ANNUAL 2018.

Greg Goldstein, President and Publisher
John Barber, Editor-In-Chief
Robbie Robbins, EVP/Sr. Art Director
Cara Morrison, Chief Financial Officer
Matt Ruzicka, Chief Accounting Officer
Anita Frazier, SVP of Sales and Marketing
David Hedgecock, Associate Publisher
Jerry Bennington, VP of New Product Development
Lorelei Bunjes, VP of Digital Services
Justin Eisinger, Editorial Director, Graphic Novels & Collections
Eric Moss, Senior Director, Licensing and Business Development

Ted Adams, IDW Founder

Lucasfilm Credits:
Assistant Editor: Nick Martino
Senior Editor: Frank Parisi
Creative Director: Michael Siglain
Story Group: James Waugh, Leland Chee,
Pablo Hidalgo, Matt Martin

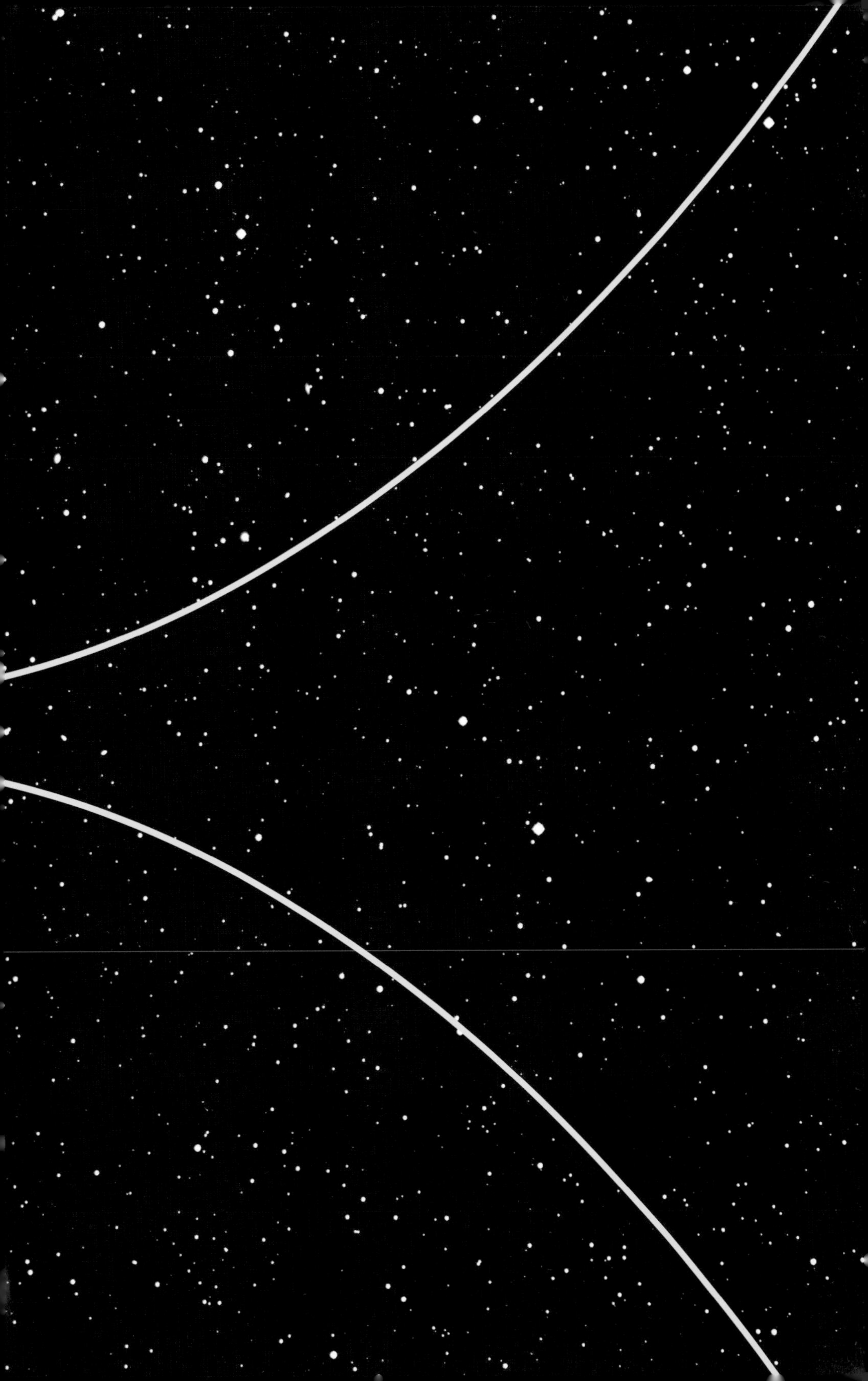

STAR WARS™ ADVENTURES

Powered Down

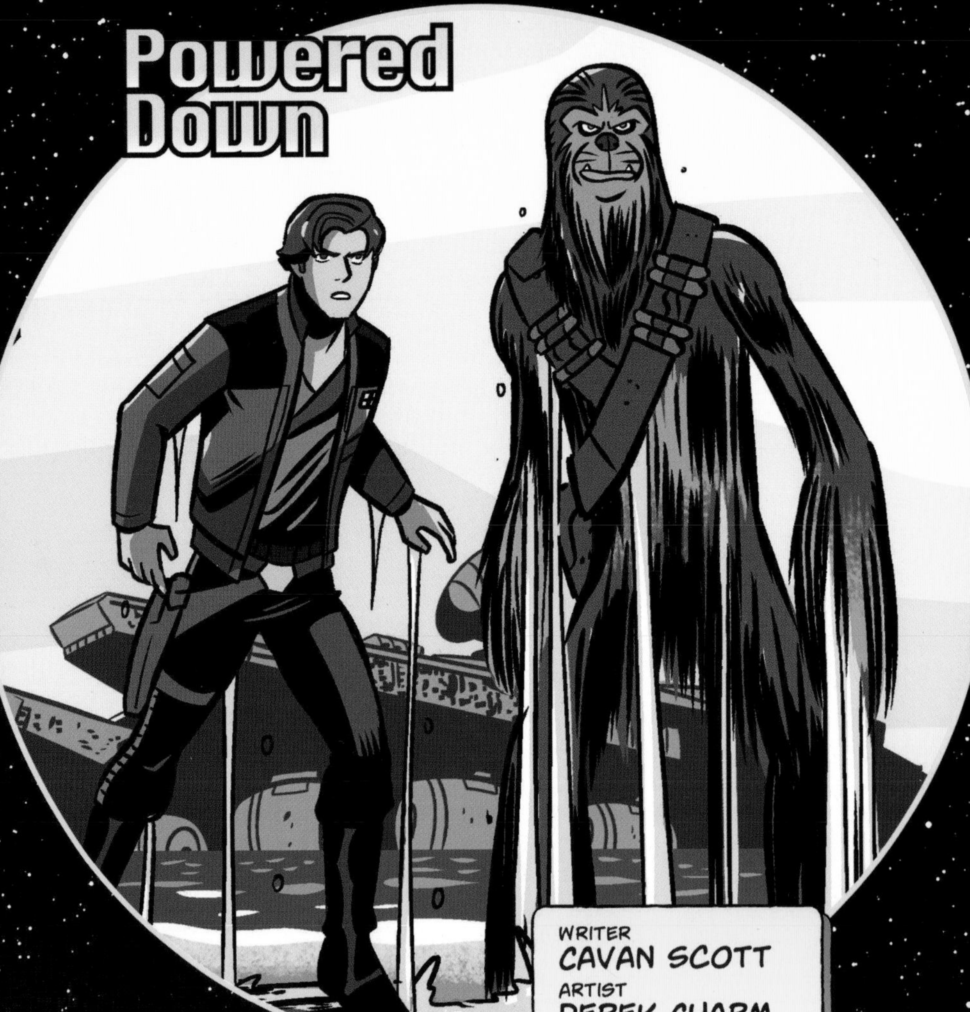

WRITER
CAVAN SCOTT
ARTIST
DEREK CHARM
COLORISTS
DEREK CHARM
& MATT HERMS

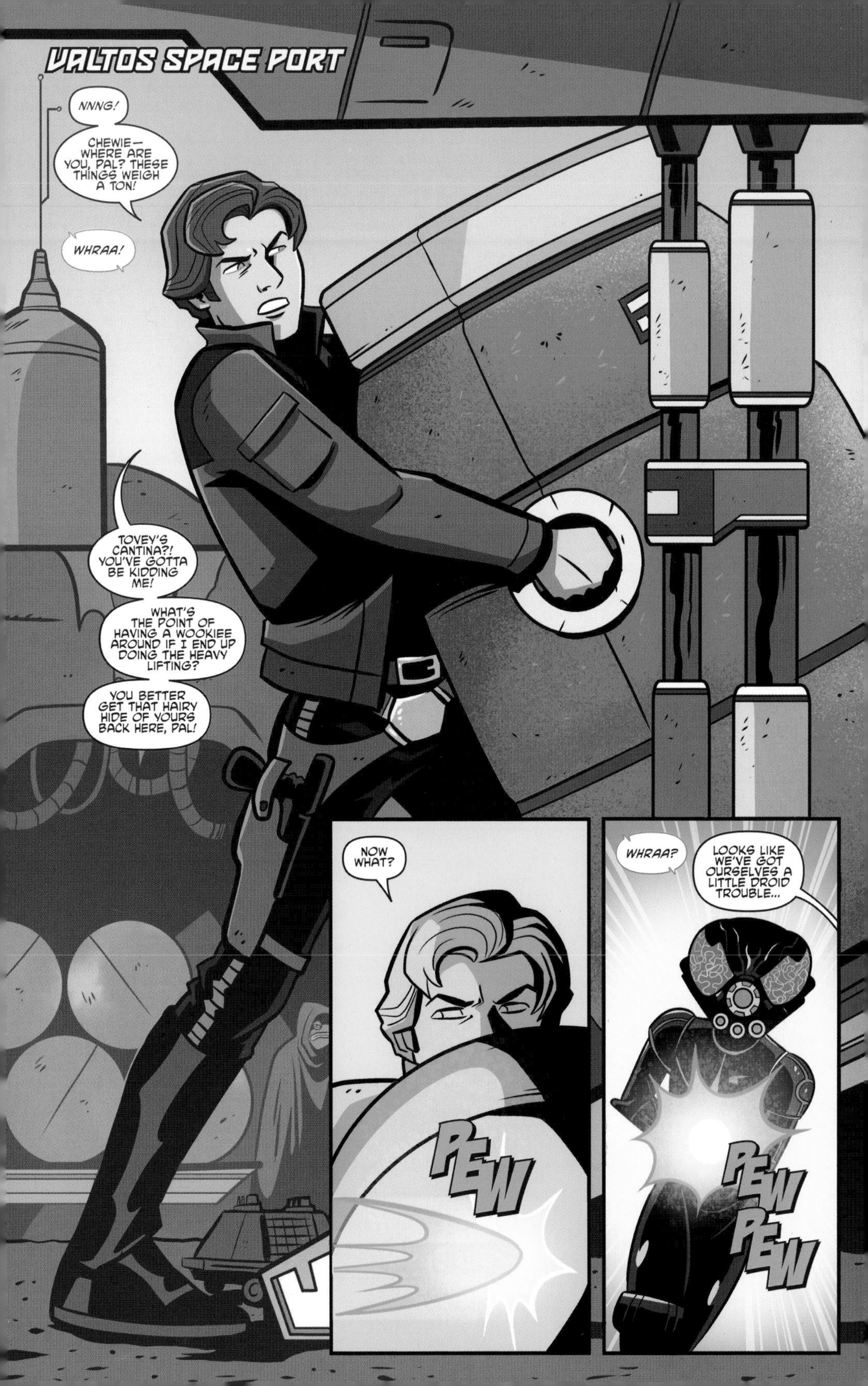
VALTOS SPACE PORT
NNNG!
CHEWIE— WHERE ARE YOU, PAL? THESE THINGS WEIGH A TON!
WHRAA!
TOVEY'S CANTINA?! YOU'VE GOTTA BE KIDDING ME!
WHAT'S THE POINT OF HAVING A WOOKIEE AROUND IF I END UP DOING THE HEAVY LIFTING?
YOU BETTER GET THAT HAIRY HIDE OF YOURS BACK HERE, PAL!
NOW WHAT?
PEW
WHRAA?
LOOKS LIKE WE'VE GOT OURSELVES A LITTLE DROID TROUBLE...
PEW PEW

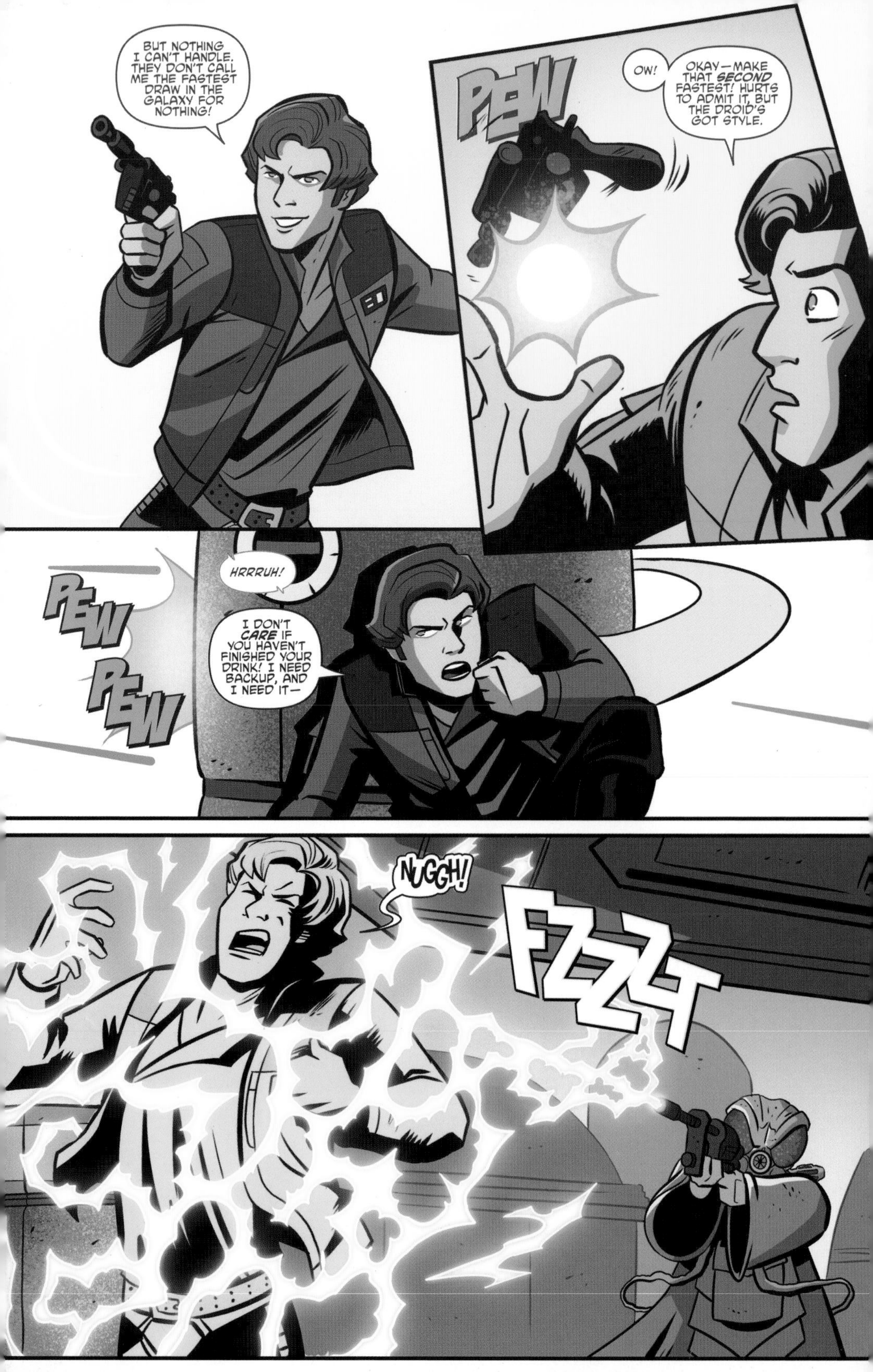

BUT NOTHING I CAN'T HANDLE. THEY DON'T CALL ME THE FASTEST DRAW IN THE GALAXY FOR NOTHING!
PEW
OW!
OKAY—MAKE THAT SECOND FASTEST! HURTS TO ADMIT IT, BUT THE DROID'S GOT STYLE.
PEW PEW
HRRRUH!
I DON'T CARE IF YOU HAVEN'T FINISHED YOUR DRINK! I NEED BACKUP, AND I NEED IT—
NUGGH!
FZZZT

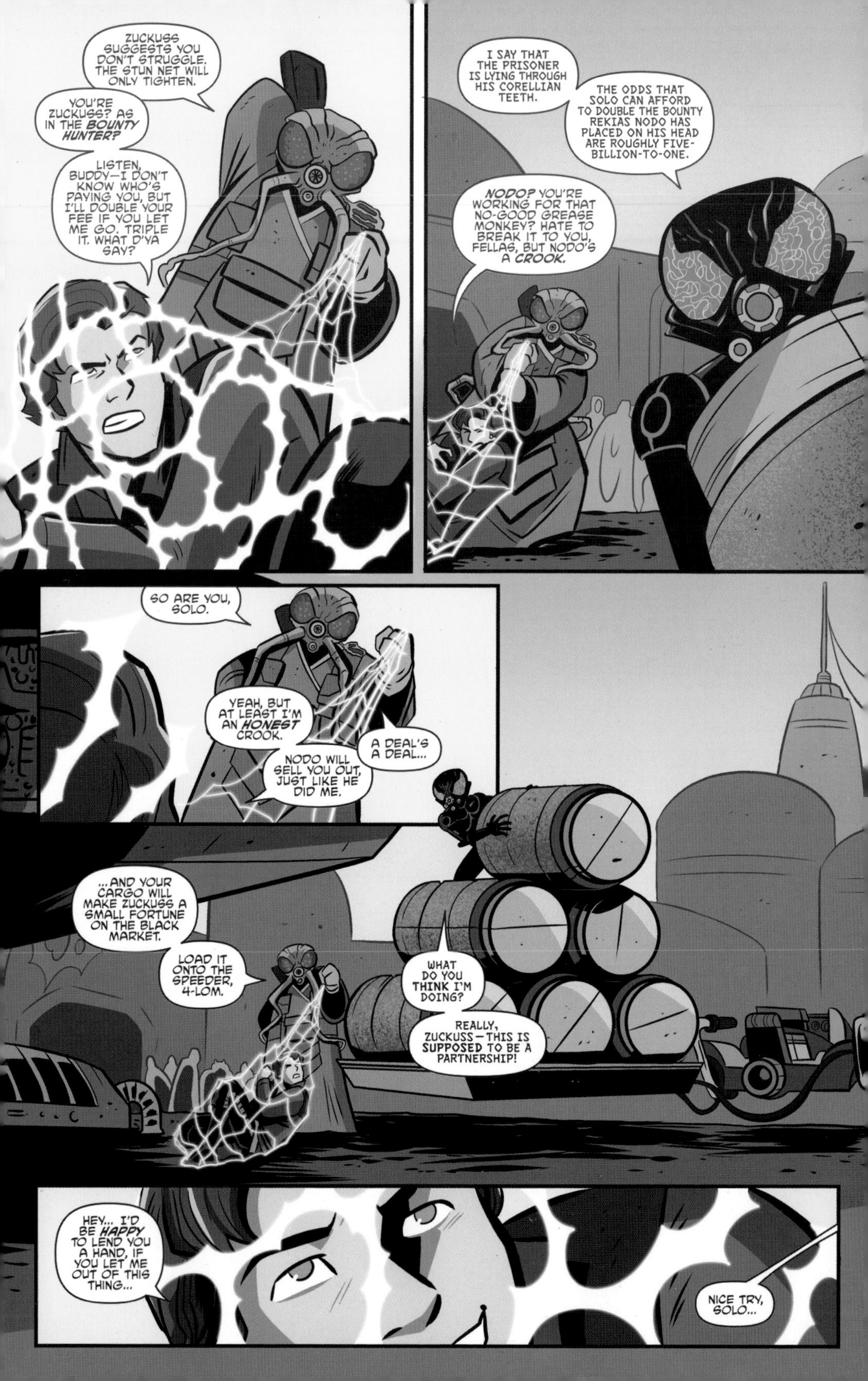
ZUCKUSS SUGGESTS YOU DON'T STRUGGLE. THE STUN NET WILL ONLY TIGHTEN.
YOU'RE ZUCKUSS? AS IN THE BOUNTY HUNTER?
LISTEN, BUDDY—I DON'T KNOW WHO'S PAYING YOU, BUT I'LL DOUBLE YOUR FEE IF YOU LET ME GO. TRIPLE IT. WHAT D'YA SAY?
I SAY THAT THE PRISONER IS LYING THROUGH HIS CORELLIAN TEETH.
THE ODDS THAT SOLO CAN AFFORD TO DOUBLE THE BOUNTY REKIAS NODO HAS PLACED ON HIS HEAD ARE ROUGHLY FIVE-BILLION-TO-ONE.
NODO? YOU'RE WORKING FOR THAT NO-GOOD GREASE MONKEY? HATE TO BREAK IT TO YOU, FELLAS, BUT NODO'S A CROOK.
SO ARE YOU, SOLO.
YEAH, BUT AT LEAST I'M AN HONEST CROOK.
NODO WILL SELL YOU OUT, JUST LIKE HE DID ME.
A DEAL'S A DEAL...
...AND YOUR CARGO WILL MAKE ZUCKUSS A SMALL FORTUNE ON THE BLACK MARKET.
LOAD IT ONTO THE SPEEDER, 4-LOM.
WHAT DO YOU THINK I'M DOING?
REALLY, ZUCKUSS—THIS IS SUPPOSED TO BE A PARTNERSHIP!
HEY... I'D BE HAPPY TO LEND YOU A HAND, IF YOU LET ME OUT OF THIS THING...
NICE TRY, SOLO...

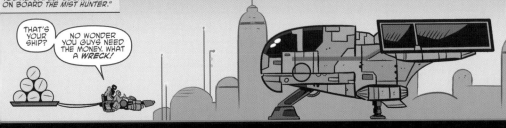

"...BUT YOU'RE NOT GETTING OUT OF THAT NET UNTIL YOU'RE SAFELY LOCKED UP ON BOARD *THE MIST HUNTER*."

THAT'S YOUR SHIP?

NO WONDER YOU GUYS NEED THE MONEY. WHAT A *WRECK!*

AND WHAT'S WITH THE *STINK?* THE PLACE SMELLS LIKE A BANTHA PEN.

THE GASSES REMIND ZUCKUSS OF HIS HOMEWORLD. YOU'LL GET USED TO THEM SOON ENOUGH.

WOULDN'T BET ON IT. THESE JOKERS HAVE HELD ME PRISONER FOR WEEKS, AND THE REEK STILL TURNS MY STOMACHS.

YEAH? AND WHO ARE YOU, KID?

VMMMM

BERIS FORD— A SMALL-TIME HOODLUM WITH IDEAS ABOVE HIS STATION. STILL, THE REWARD FOR HIS CAPTURE WILL PAY FOR OUR TRACTOR BEAM REPAIRS.

OH, AND DON'T TRY GETTING PAST THIS FORCE-FIELD. THE ODDS OF ESCAPE ARE ROUGHLY—

YEAH, YEAH. I GET THE IDEA, BUG EYES.

DON'T WORRY, SHORT STUFF. I'LL HAVE US OUT OF HERE IN NO TIME.

AM I SUPPOSED TO BE IMPRESSED?

YOU BET...

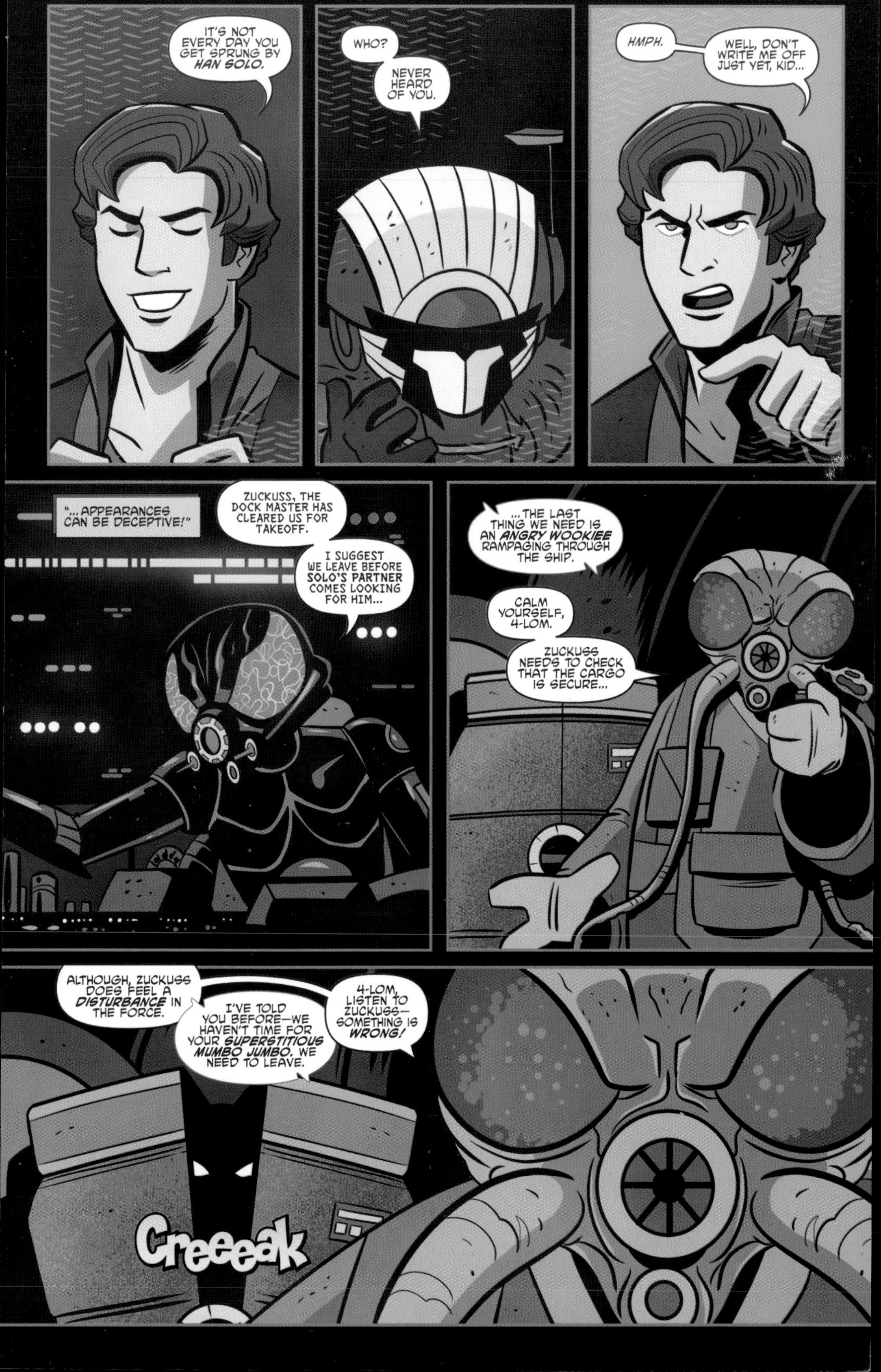
IT'S NOT EVERY DAY YOU GET SPRUNG BY HAN SOLO.
WHO?
NEVER HEARD OF YOU.
HMPH.
WELL, DON'T WRITE ME OFF JUST YET, KID...
"...APPEARANCES CAN BE DECEPTIVE!"
ZUCKUSS, THE DOCK MASTER HAS CLEARED US FOR TAKEOFF.
I SUGGEST WE LEAVE BEFORE SOLO'S PARTNER COMES LOOKING FOR HIM...
...THE LAST THING WE NEED IS AN ANGRY WOOKIEE RAMPAGING THROUGH THE SHIP.
CALM YOURSELF, 4-LOM.
ZUCKUSS NEEDS TO CHECK THAT THE CARGO IS SECURE...
ALTHOUGH, ZUCKUSS DOES FEEL A DISTURBANCE IN THE FORCE.
I'VE TOLD YOU BEFORE—WE HAVEN'T TIME FOR YOUR SUPERSTITIOUS MUMBO JUMBO. WE NEED TO LEAVE.
4-LOM, LISTEN TO ZUCKUSS—SOMETHING IS WRONG!
Creeeak

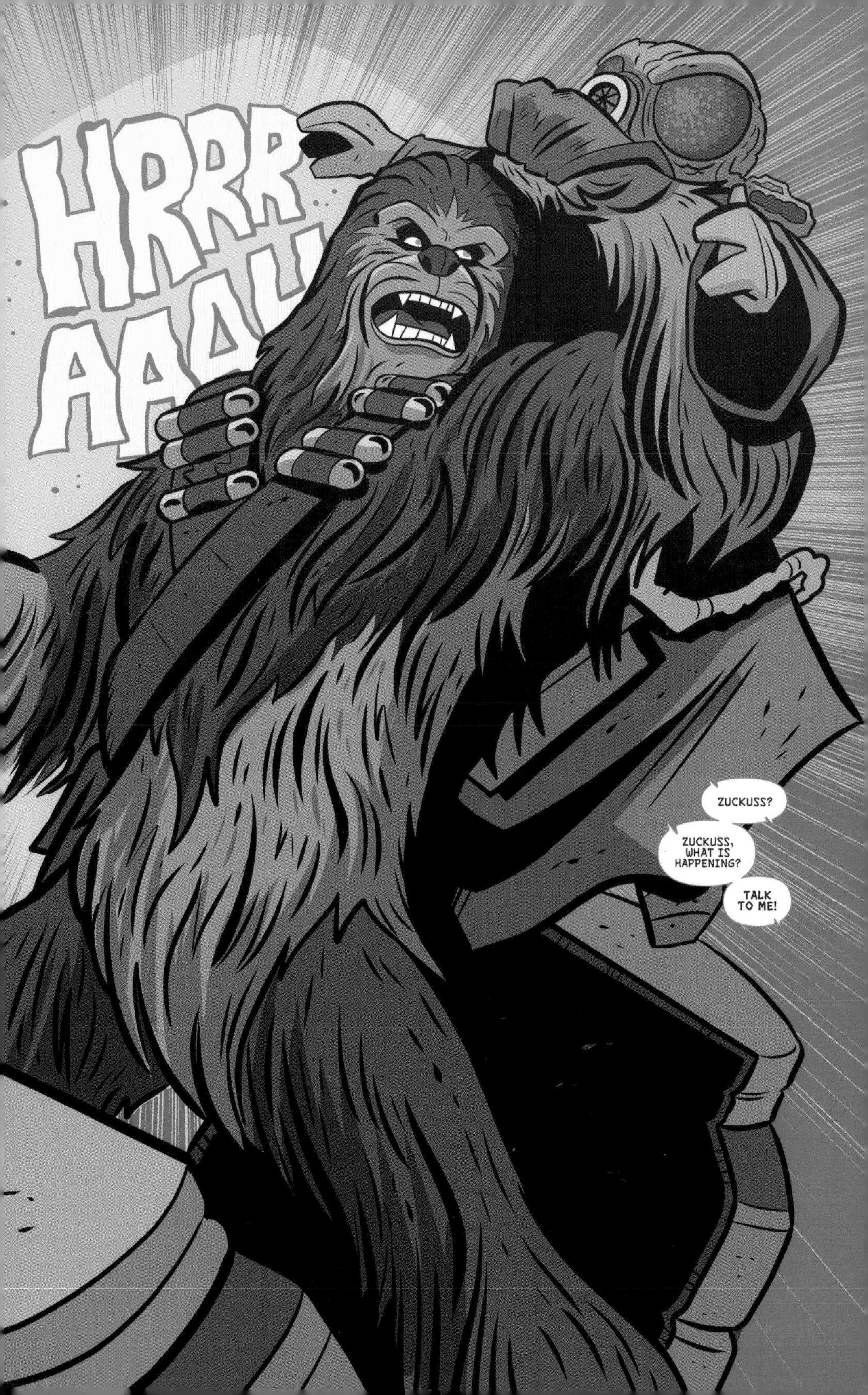
HRRR AAAU
ZUCKUSS?
ZUCKUSS, WHAT IS HAPPENING?
TALK TO ME!

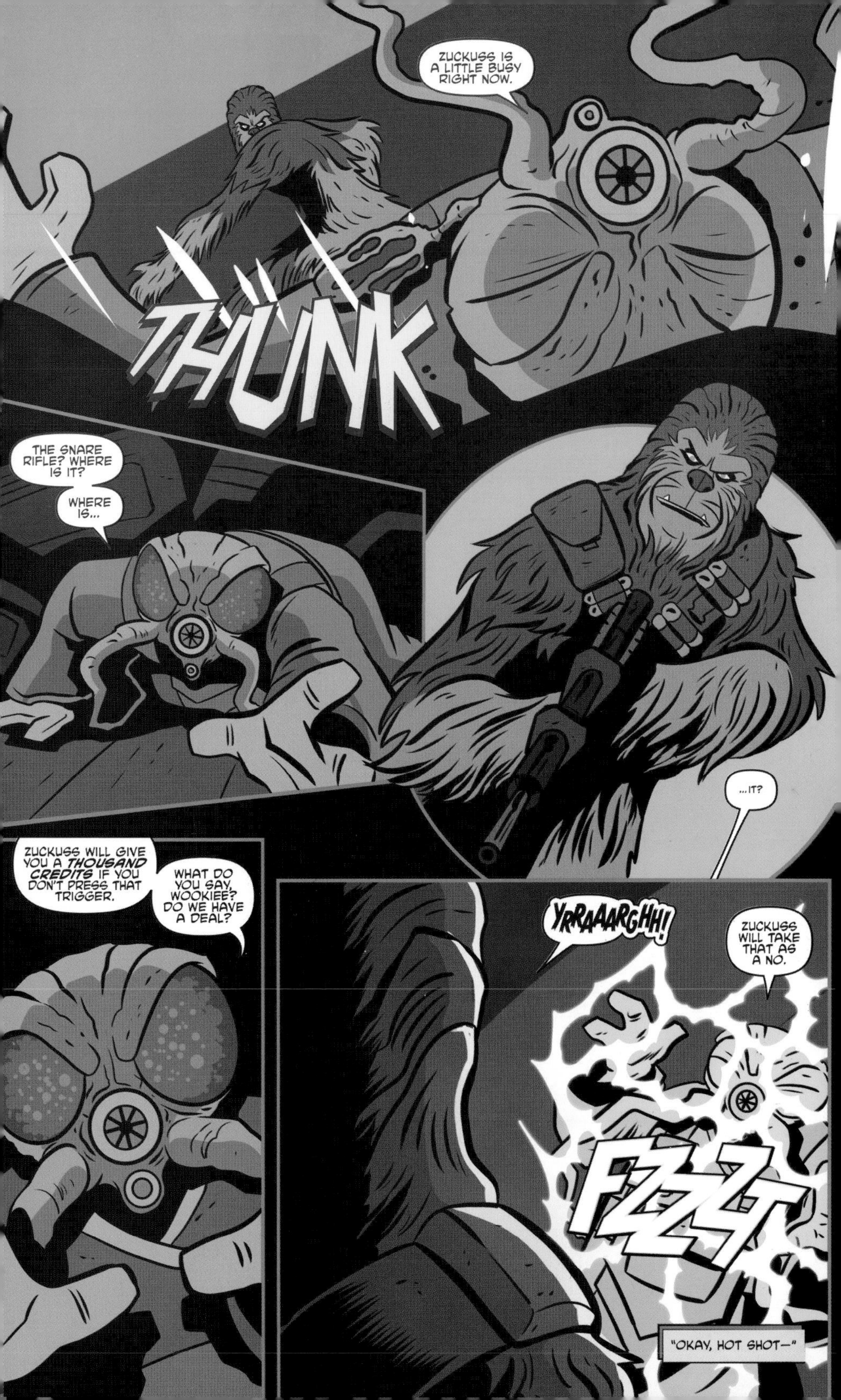
ZUCKUSS IS A LITTLE BUSY RIGHT NOW.
THÜNK
THE SNARE RIFLE? WHERE IS IT?
WHERE IS...
...IT?
ZUCKUSS WILL GIVE YOU A *THOUSAND CREDITS* IF YOU DON'T PRESS THAT TRIGGER.
WHAT DO YOU SAY, WOOKIEE? DO WE HAVE A DEAL?
YRRAAARGHH!
ZUCKUSS WILL TAKE THAT AS A NO.
FZZZT
"OKAY, HOT SHOT—"

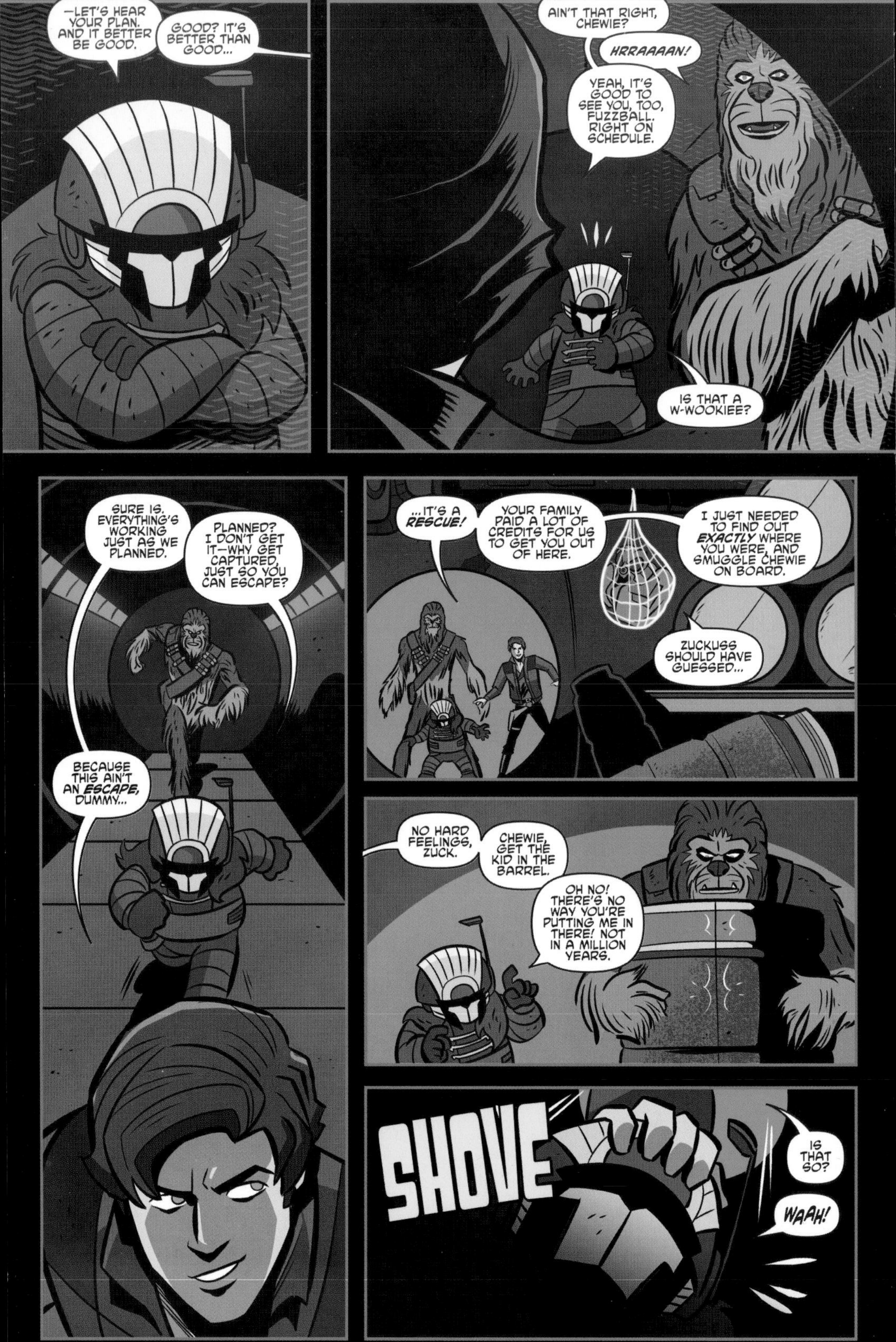

—LET'S HEAR YOUR PLAN. AND IT BETTER BE GOOD.
GOOD? IT'S BETTER THAN GOOD...
AIN'T THAT RIGHT, CHEWIE?
HRRAAAAN!
YEAH, IT'S GOOD TO SEE YOU, TOO, FUZZBALL. RIGHT ON SCHEDULE.
IS THAT A W-WOOKIEE?
SURE IS. EVERYTHING'S WORKING JUST AS WE PLANNED.
PLANNED? I DON'T GET IT—WHY GET CAPTURED, JUST SO YOU CAN ESCAPE?
BECAUSE THIS AIN'T AN ESCAPE, DUMMY...
...IT'S A RESCUE!
YOUR FAMILY PAID A LOT OF CREDITS FOR US TO GET YOU OUT OF HERE.
I JUST NEEDED TO FIND OUT EXACTLY WHERE YOU WERE, AND SMUGGLE CHEWIE ON BOARD.
ZUCKUSS SHOULD HAVE GUESSED...
NO HARD FEELINGS, ZUCK.
CHEWIE, GET THE KID IN THE BARREL.
OH NO! THERE'S NO WAY YOU'RE PUTTING ME IN THERE! NOT IN A MILLION YEARS.
SHOVE
IS THAT SO?
WAAH!

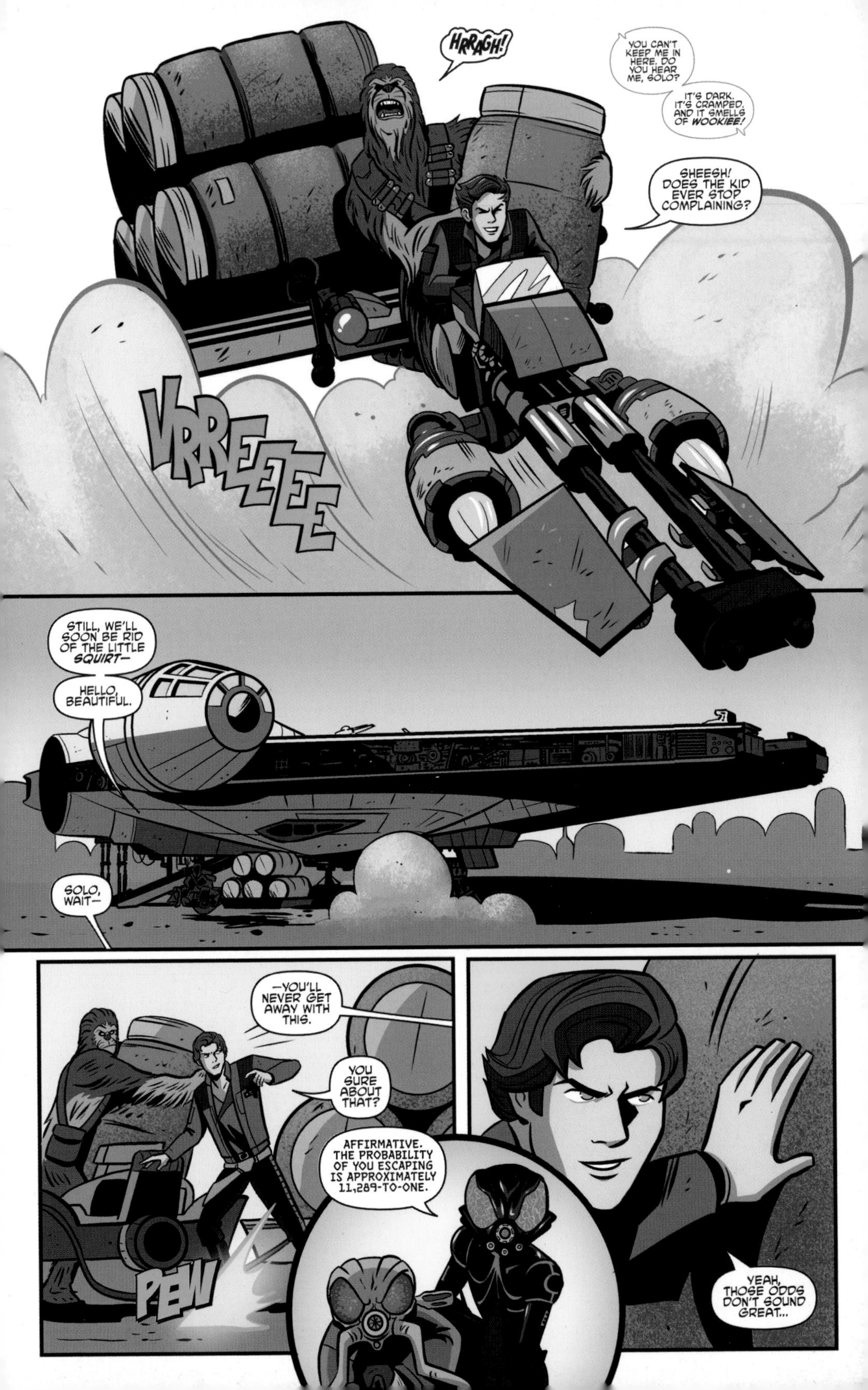
HRRAGH!
YOU CAN'T KEEP ME IN HERE. DO YOU HEAR ME, SOLO?
IT'S DARK. IT'S CRAMPED. AND IT SMELLS OF WOOKIEE!
SHEESH! DOES THE KID EVER STOP COMPLAINING?
VRREEEEE
STILL, WE'LL SOON BE RID OF THE LITTLE SQUIRT—
HELLO, BEAUTIFUL.
SOLO, WAIT—
—YOU'LL NEVER GET AWAY WITH THIS.
YOU SURE ABOUT THAT?
AFFIRMATIVE. THE PROBABILITY OF YOU ESCAPING IS APPROXIMATELY 11,289-TO-ONE.
PEW
YEAH, THOSE ODDS DON'T SOUND GREAT...

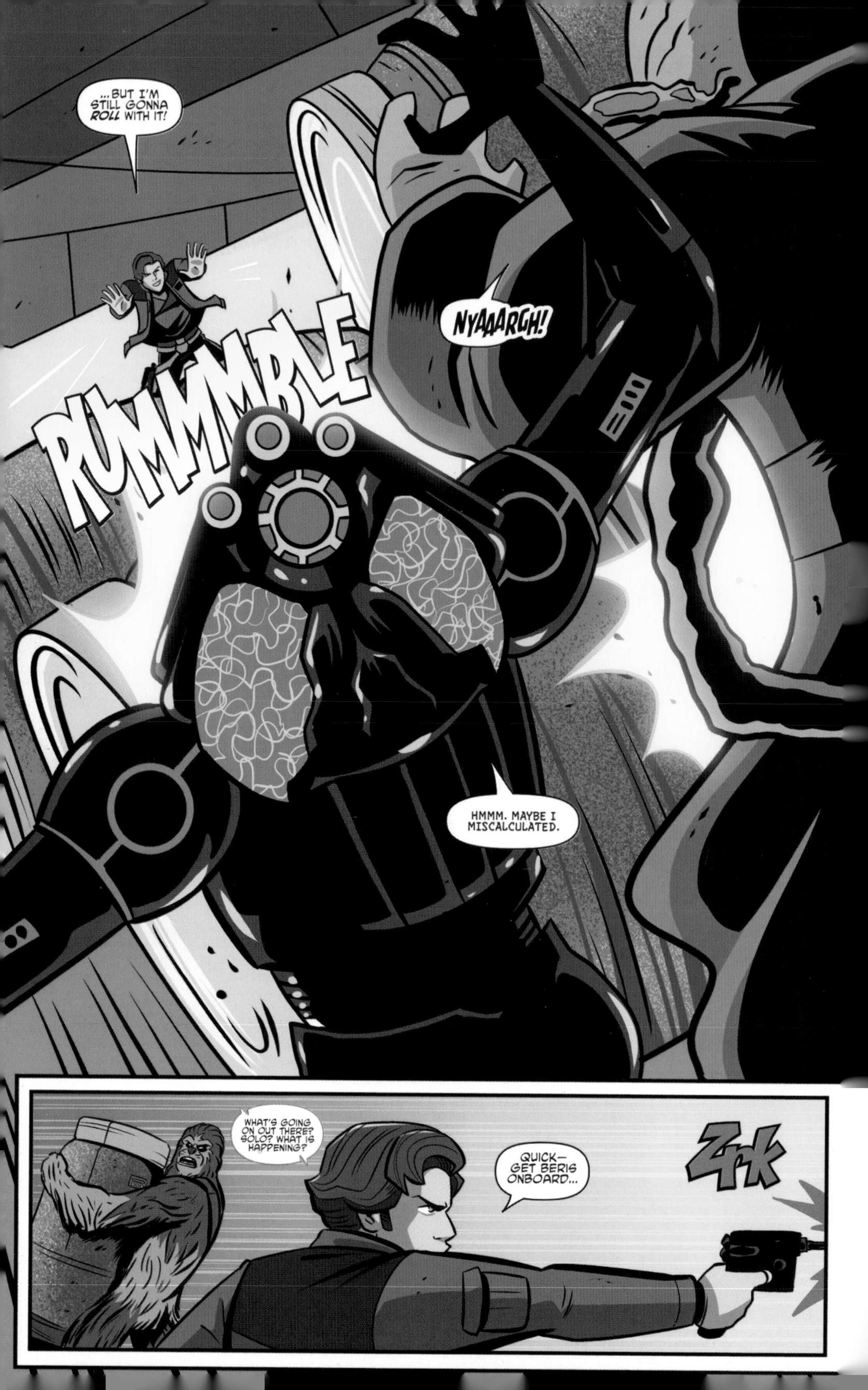
...BUT I'M STILL GONNA *ROLL* WITH IT!
NYAAARGH!
RUMMMBLE
HMMM. MAYBE I MISCALCULATED.
WHAT'S GOING ON OUT THERE? SOLO? WHAT IS HAPPENING?
QUICK— GET BERIS ONBOARD...
ZZK

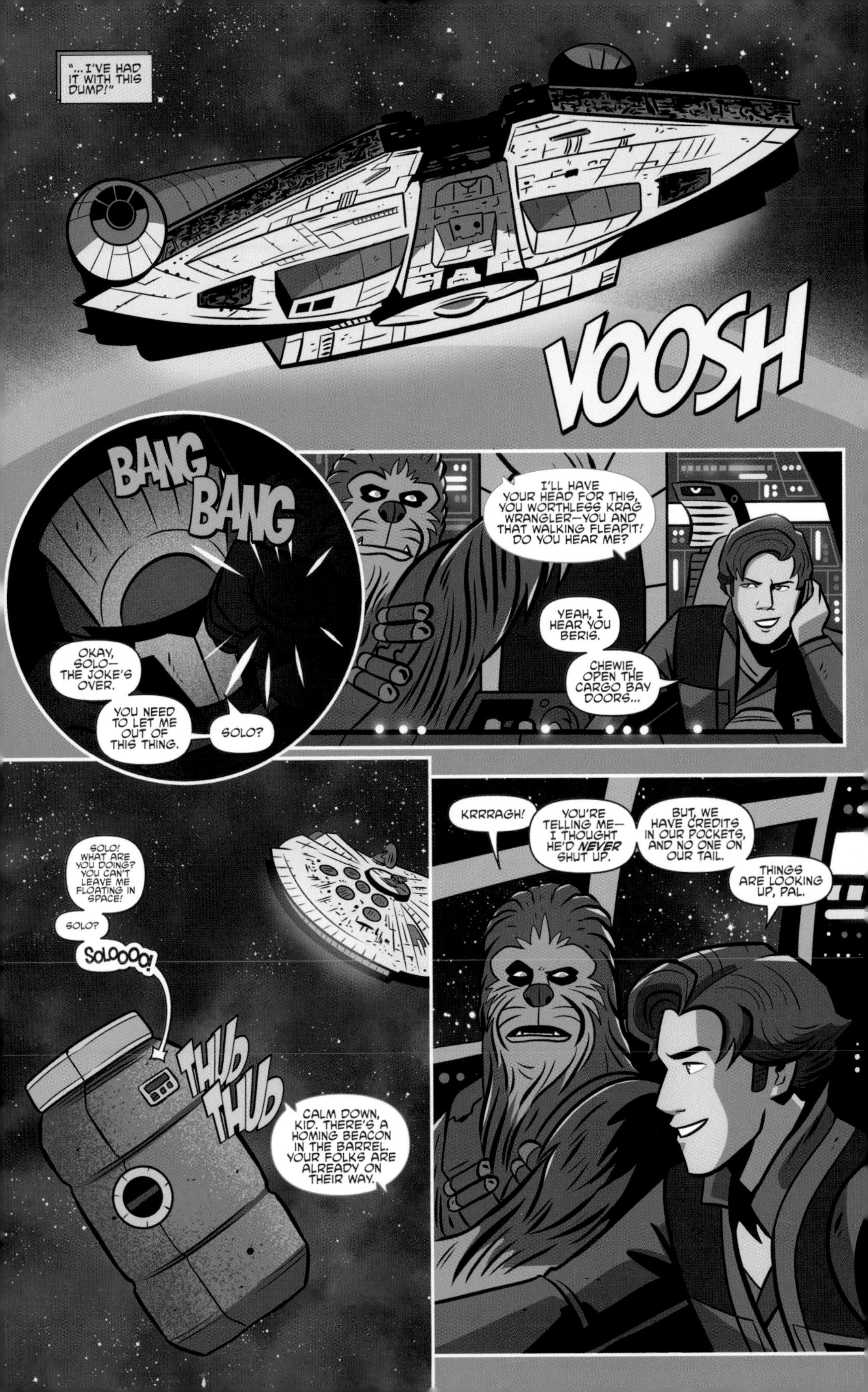
"... I'VE HAD IT WITH THIS DUMP!"
VOOSH
BANG BANG
OKAY, SOLO— THE JOKE'S OVER.
YOU NEED TO LET ME OUT OF THIS THING.
SOLO?
I'LL HAVE YOUR HEAD FOR THIS, YOU WORTHLESS KRAG WRANGLER—YOU AND THAT WALKING FLEAPIT! DO YOU HEAR ME?
YEAH, I HEAR YOU BERIS.
CHEWIE, OPEN THE CARGO BAY DOORS...
SOLO! WHAT ARE YOU DOING? YOU CAN'T LEAVE ME FLOATING IN SPACE!
SOLO?
SOLOOOO!
THUD THUD
CALM DOWN, KID. THERE'S A HOMING BEACON IN THE BARREL. YOUR FOLKS ARE ALREADY ON THEIR WAY.
KRRRAGH!
YOU'RE TELLING ME— I THOUGHT HE'D NEVER SHUT UP.
BUT, WE HAVE CREDITS IN OUR POCKETS, AND NO ONE ON OUR TAIL.
THINGS ARE LOOKING UP, PAL.

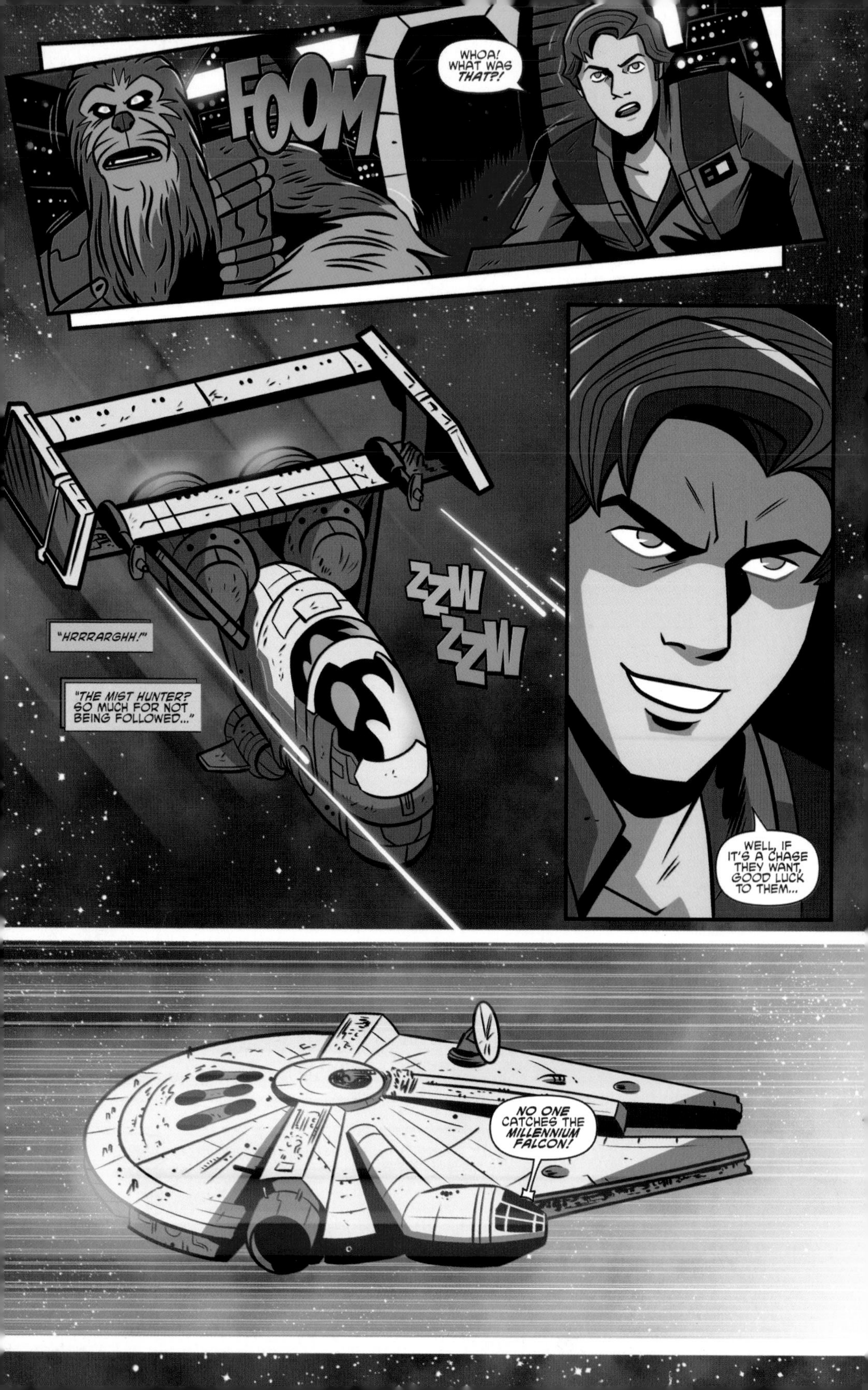
FOOM
WHOA! WHAT WAS THAT?!
"HRRRARGHH!"
"THE MIST HUNTER? SO MUCH FOR NOT BEING FOLLOWED..."
ZZW ZZW
WELL, IF IT'S A CHASE THEY WANT, GOOD LUCK TO THEM...
NO ONE CATCHES THE MILLENNIUM FALCON!

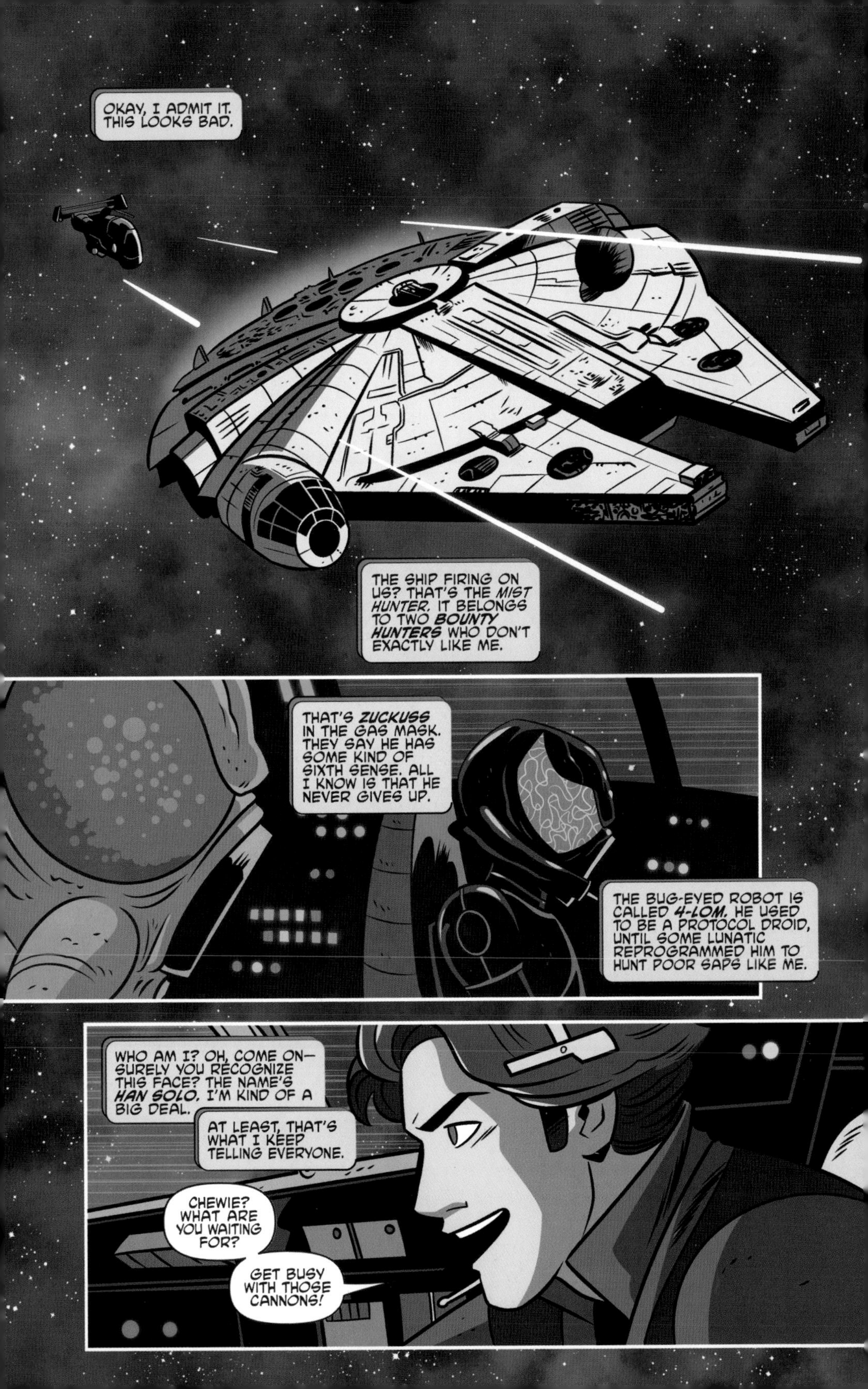
OKAY, I ADMIT IT. THIS LOOKS BAD.
THE SHIP FIRING ON US? THAT'S THE *MIST HUNTER.* IT BELONGS TO TWO **BOUNTY HUNTERS** WHO DON'T EXACTLY LIKE ME.
THAT'S **ZUCKUSS** IN THE GAS MASK. THEY SAY HE HAS SOME KIND OF SIXTH SENSE. ALL I KNOW IS THAT HE NEVER GIVES UP.
THE BUG-EYED ROBOT IS CALLED **4-LOM.** HE USED TO BE A PROTOCOL DROID, UNTIL SOME LUNATIC REPROGRAMMED HIM TO HUNT POOR SAPS LIKE ME.
WHO AM I? OH, COME ON– SURELY YOU RECOGNIZE THIS FACE? THE NAME'S **HAN SOLO.** I'M KIND OF A BIG DEAL.
AT LEAST, THAT'S WHAT I KEEP TELLING EVERYONE.
CHEWIE? WHAT ARE YOU WAITING FOR?
GET BUSY WITH THOSE CANNONS!

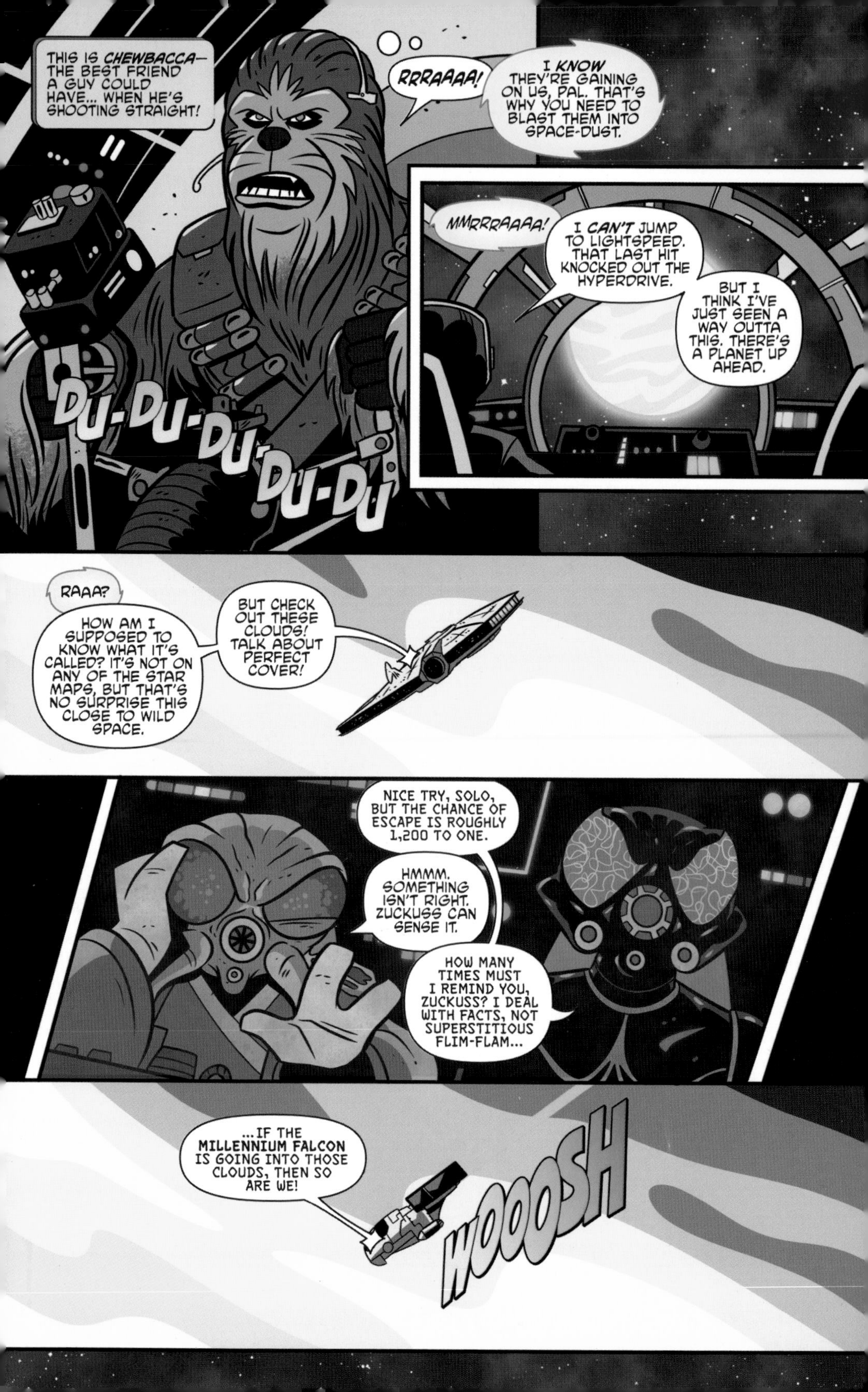

THIS IS CHEWBACCA— THE BEST FRIEND A GUY COULD HAVE... WHEN HE'S SHOOTING STRAIGHT!
RRRAAAA!
I KNOW THEY'RE GAINING ON US, PAL. THAT'S WHY YOU NEED TO BLAST THEM INTO SPACE-DUST.
DU-DU-DU-DU-DU-DU
MMRRRAAAA!
I CAN'T JUMP TO LIGHTSPEED. THAT LAST HIT KNOCKED OUT THE HYPERDRIVE.
BUT I THINK I'VE JUST SEEN A WAY OUTTA THIS. THERE'S A PLANET UP AHEAD.
RAAA?
HOW AM I SUPPOSED TO KNOW WHAT IT'S CALLED? IT'S NOT ON ANY OF THE STAR MAPS, BUT THAT'S NO SURPRISE THIS CLOSE TO WILD SPACE.
BUT CHECK OUT THESE CLOUDS! TALK ABOUT PERFECT COVER!
NICE TRY, SOLO, BUT THE CHANCE OF ESCAPE IS ROUGHLY 1,200 TO ONE.
HMMM. SOMETHING ISN'T RIGHT. ZUCKUSS CAN SENSE IT.
HOW MANY TIMES MUST I REMIND YOU, ZUCKUSS? I DEAL WITH FACTS, NOT SUPERSTITIOUS FLIM-FLAM...
...IF THE MILLENNIUM FALCON IS GOING INTO THOSE CLOUDS, THEN SO ARE WE!
WHOOOSH

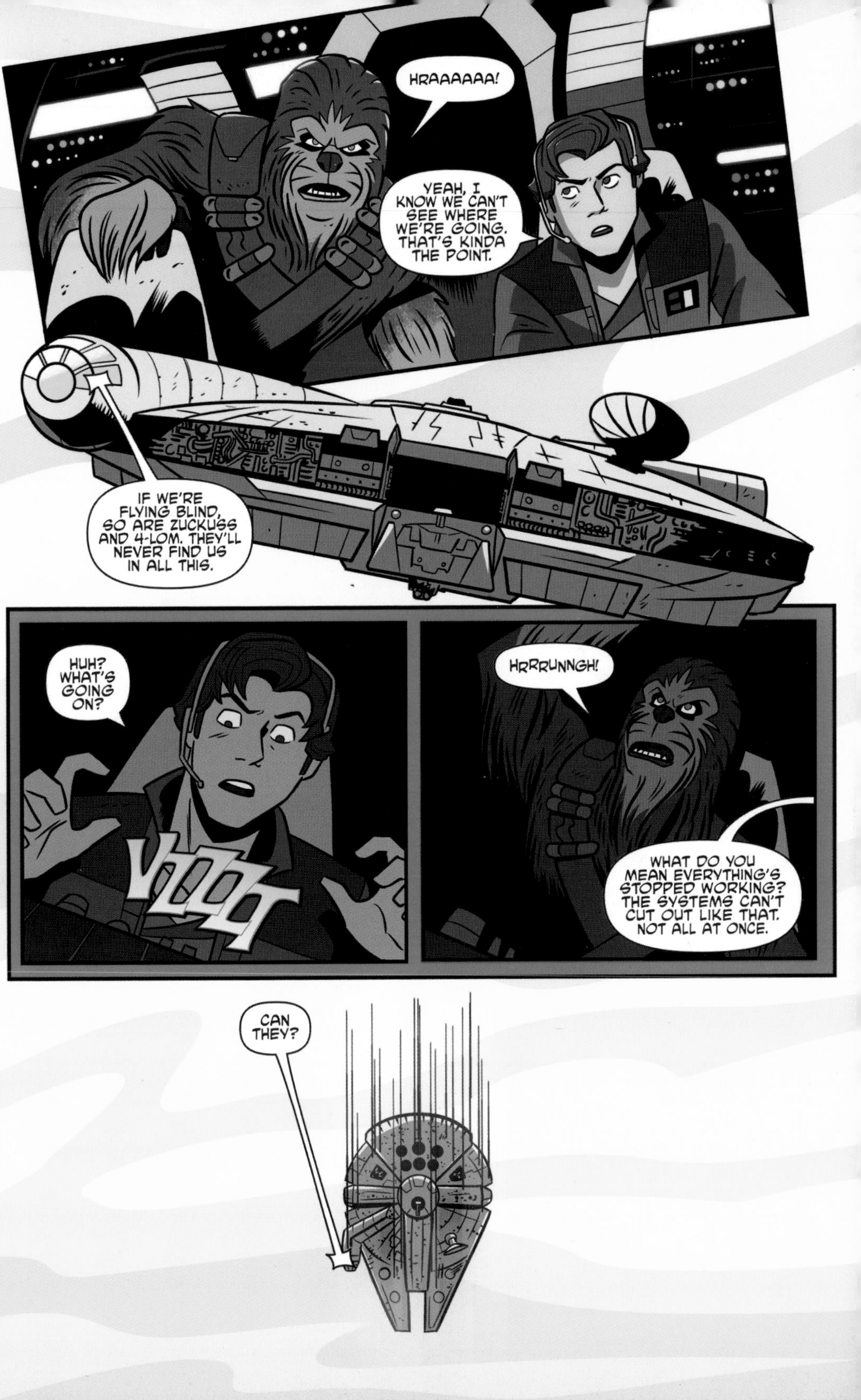
HRAAAAAA!
YEAH, I KNOW WE CAN'T SEE WHERE WE'RE GOING. THAT'S KINDA THE POINT.
IF WE'RE FLYING BLIND, SO ARE ZUCKUSS AND 4-LOM. THEY'LL NEVER FIND US IN ALL THIS.
HUH? WHAT'S GOING ON?
VLLLT
HRRRUNNGH!
WHAT DO YOU MEAN EVERYTHING'S STOPPED WORKING? THE SYSTEMS CAN'T CUT OUT LIKE THAT. NOT ALL AT ONCE.
CAN THEY?

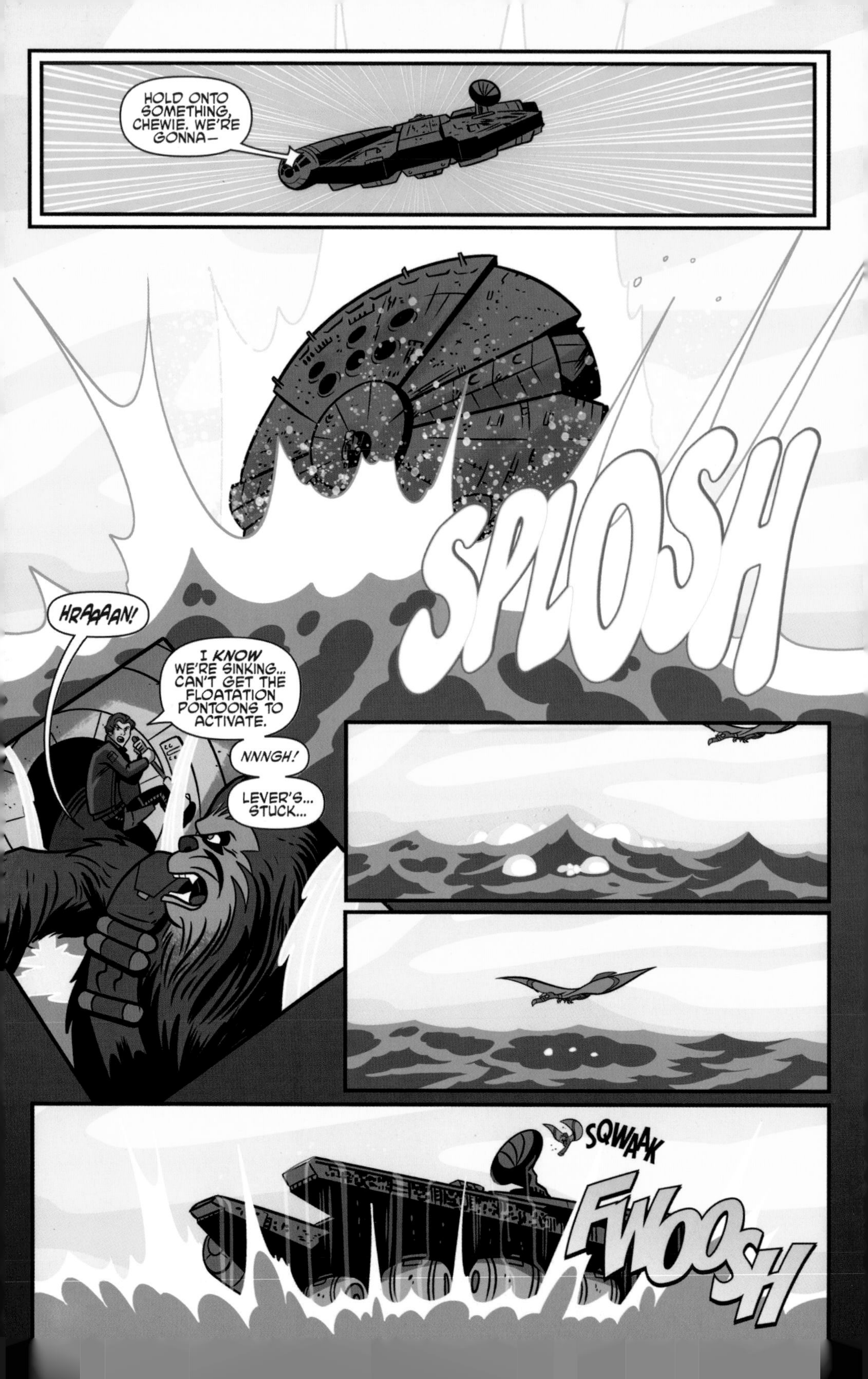
HOLD ONTO SOMETHING, CHEWIE. WE'RE GONNA—
SPLOSH
HRAAAAN!
I KNOW WE'RE SINKING... CAN'T GET THE FLOATATION PONTOONS TO ACTIVATE.
NNNGH!
LEVER'S... STUCK...
SQWAAK
FWOOSH

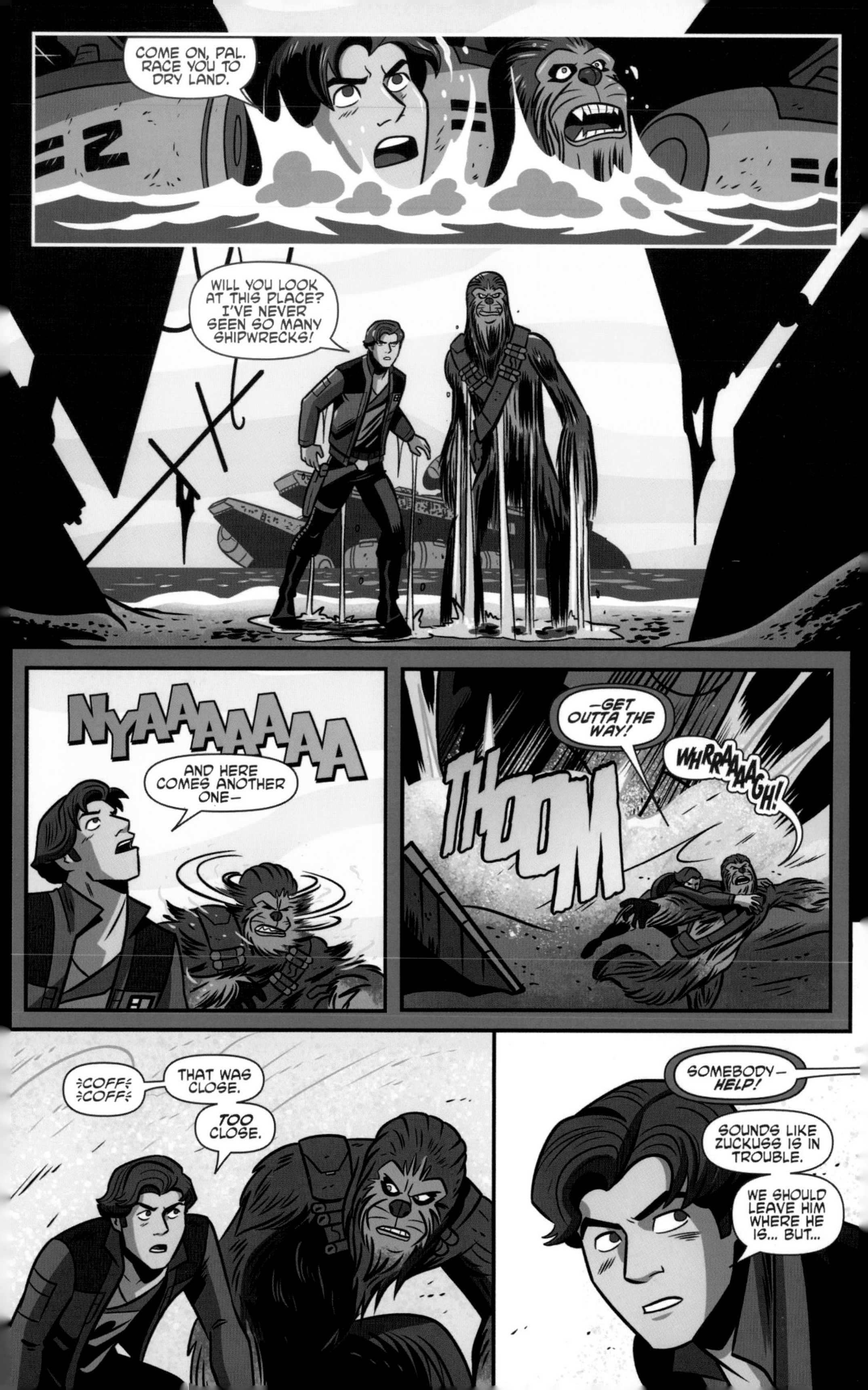
COME ON, PAL. RACE YOU TO DRY LAND.
WILL YOU LOOK AT THIS PLACE? I'VE NEVER SEEN SO MANY SHIPWRECKS!
NYAAAAAAAAA
AND HERE COMES ANOTHER ONE—
—GET OUTTA THE WAY!
THOOM
WHRRAAAAGH!
COFF *COFF*
THAT WAS CLOSE.
TOO CLOSE.
SOMEBODY— *HELP!*
SOUNDS LIKE ZUCKUSS IS IN TROUBLE.
WE SHOULD LEAVE HIM WHERE HE IS... BUT...

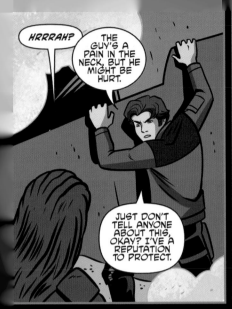

HRRRAH?

THE GUY'S A PAIN IN THE NECK, BUT HE MIGHT BE HURT.

JUST DON'T TELL ANYONE ABOUT THIS, OKAY? I'VE A REPUTATION TO PROTECT.

WHAT A MESS.

SOLO! ZUCKUSS... CAN'T MOVE... HIS LEGS... UNNNH... ARE TRAPPED.

NNNN. YOU'RE NOT KIDDING. I THOUGHT YOU'RE SUPPOSED TO HAVE SECOND SIGHT OR SOMETHING.

ZUCKUSS SAID THERE WAS SOMETHING WRONG WITH THIS PLANET, BUT 4-LOM WOULDN'T LISTEN.

AND LET ME GUESS—THE DUMB DROID DEACTIVATED AS SOON AS YOU HIT THE CLOUDS. CHEWIE CAN CHECK HIS CIRCUITS ONCE WE'VE GOT YOU OUT OF HERE.

YOU'RE GOING NOWHERE, SOLO!

KLUNK!

STUNCUFFS? SERIOUSLY? I WAS TRYING TO HELP!

HA! UNLUCKY! LOOKS LIKE NOTHING WORKS IN THIS BUCKET OF BOLTS—NOT EVEN YOUR CUFFS.

WHAT? NO! THAT'S NOT POSSIBLE.

CHING

YOU CAN'T LEAVE ZUCKUSS LIKE THIS!

YOU JUST WATCH ME. YOU HAD YOUR CHANCE, PAL—AND YOU BLEW IT!

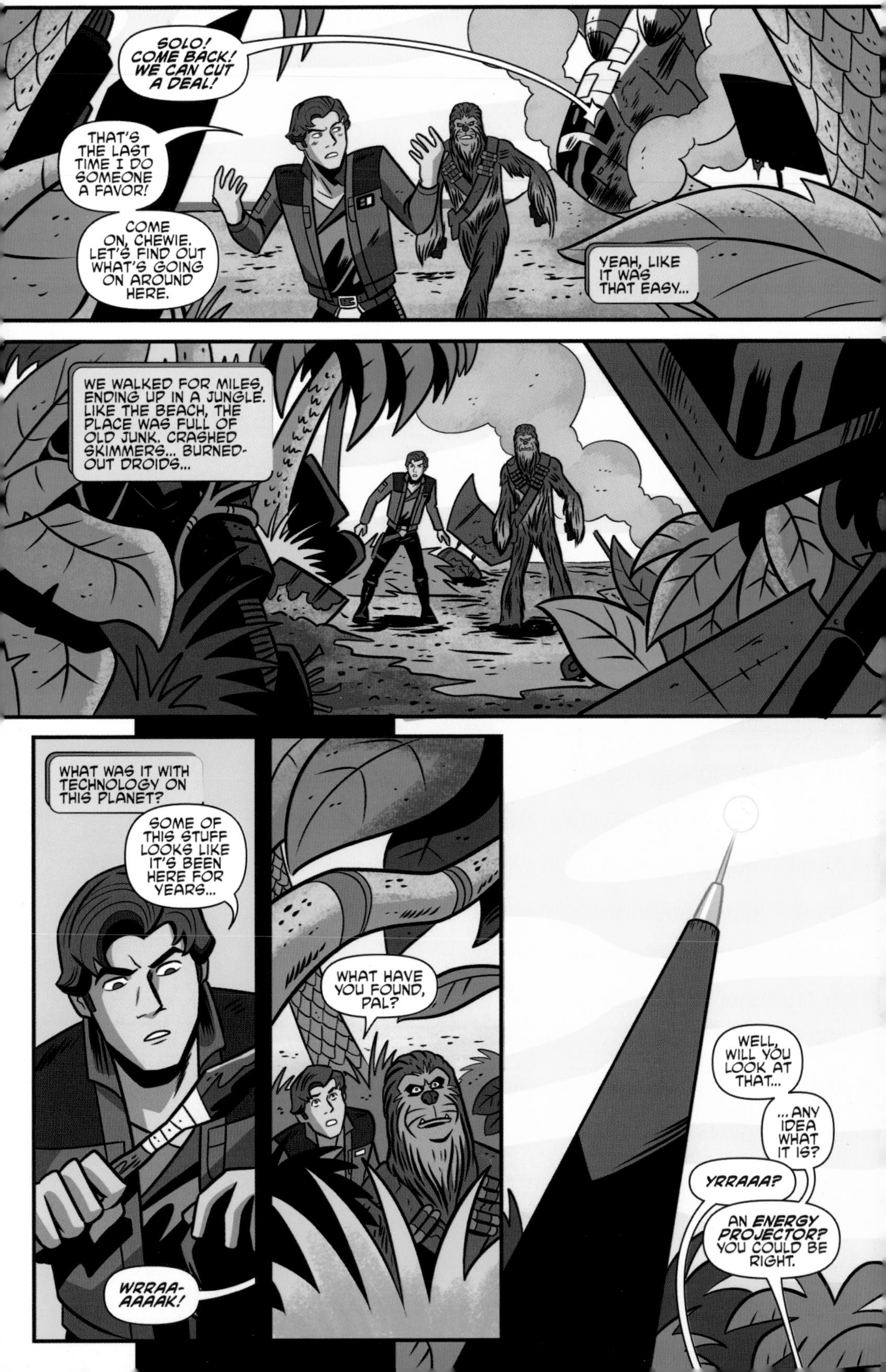
SOLO! COME BACK! WE CAN CUT A DEAL!
THAT'S THE LAST TIME I DO SOMEONE A FAVOR!
COME ON, CHEWIE. LET'S FIND OUT WHAT'S GOING ON AROUND HERE.
YEAH, LIKE IT WAS THAT EASY...
WE WALKED FOR MILES, ENDING UP IN A JUNGLE. LIKE THE BEACH, THE PLACE WAS FULL OF OLD JUNK. CRASHED SKIMMERS... BURNED-OUT DROIDS...
WHAT WAS IT WITH TECHNOLOGY ON THIS PLANET?
SOME OF THIS STUFF LOOKS LIKE IT'S BEEN HERE FOR YEARS...
WRRAA-AAAAK!
WHAT HAVE YOU FOUND, PAL?
WELL, WILL YOU LOOK AT THAT...
...ANY IDEA WHAT IT IS?
YRRAAA?
AN ENERGY PROJECTOR? YOU COULD BE RIGHT.

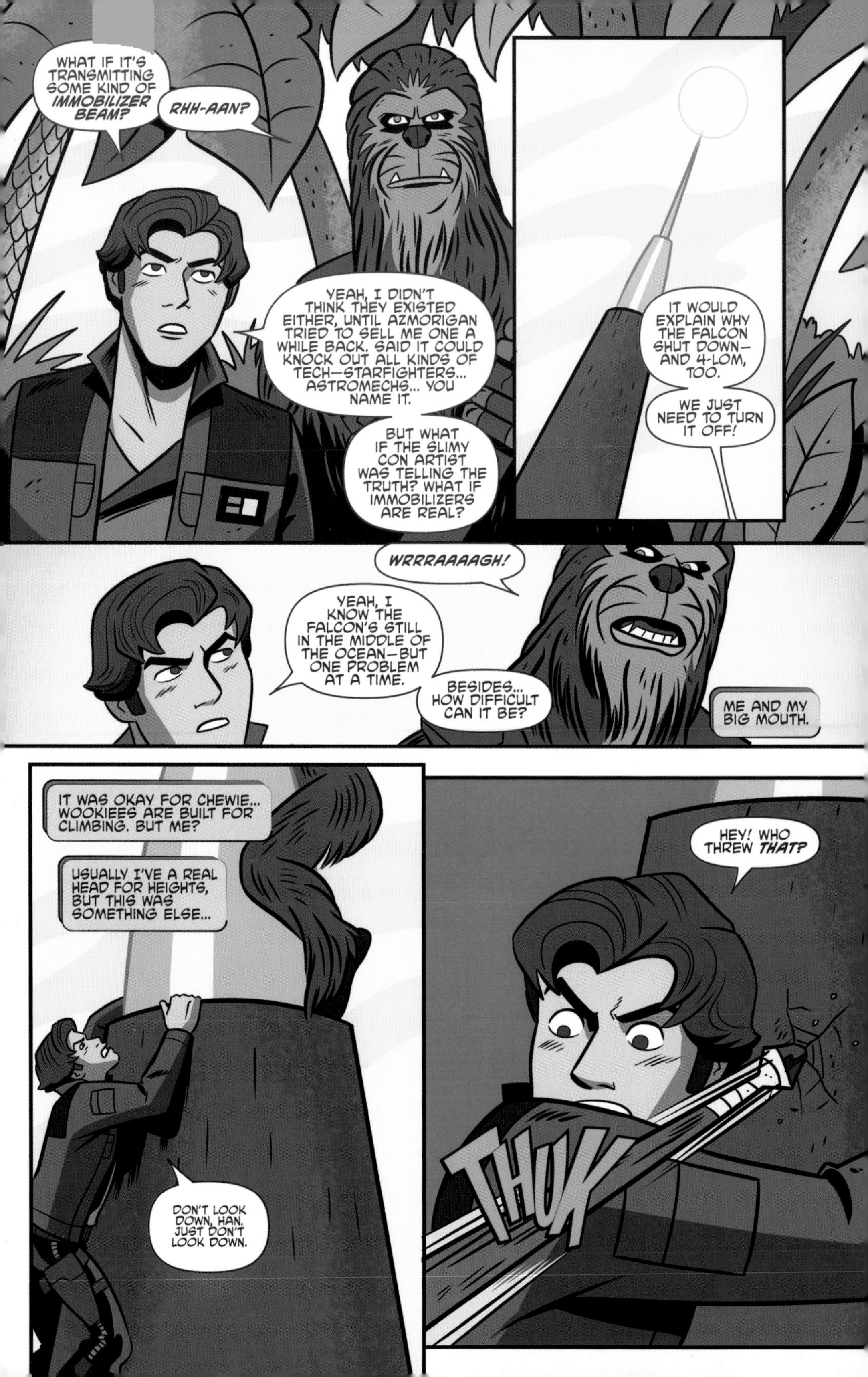
WHAT IF IT'S TRANSMITTING SOME KIND OF *IMMOBILIZER BEAM?*
RHH-AAN?
YEAH, I DIDN'T THINK THEY EXISTED EITHER, UNTIL AZMORIGAN TRIED TO SELL ME ONE A WHILE BACK. SAID IT COULD KNOCK OUT ALL KINDS OF TECH—STARFIGHTERS... ASTROMECHS... YOU NAME IT.
BUT WHAT IF THE SLIMY CON ARTIST WAS TELLING THE TRUTH? WHAT IF IMMOBILIZERS ARE REAL?
IT WOULD EXPLAIN WHY THE FALCON SHUT DOWN— AND 4-LOM, TOO.
WE JUST NEED TO TURN IT OFF!
WRRRAAAAGH!
YEAH, I KNOW THE FALCON'S STILL IN THE MIDDLE OF THE OCEAN—BUT ONE PROBLEM AT A TIME.
BESIDES... HOW DIFFICULT CAN IT BE?
ME AND MY BIG MOUTH.
IT WAS OKAY FOR CHEWIE... WOOKIEES ARE BUILT FOR CLIMBING. BUT ME?
USUALLY I'VE A REAL HEAD FOR HEIGHTS, BUT THIS WAS SOMETHING ELSE...
DON'T LOOK DOWN, HAN. JUST DON'T LOOK DOWN.
HEY! WHO THREW *THAT?*
THUK

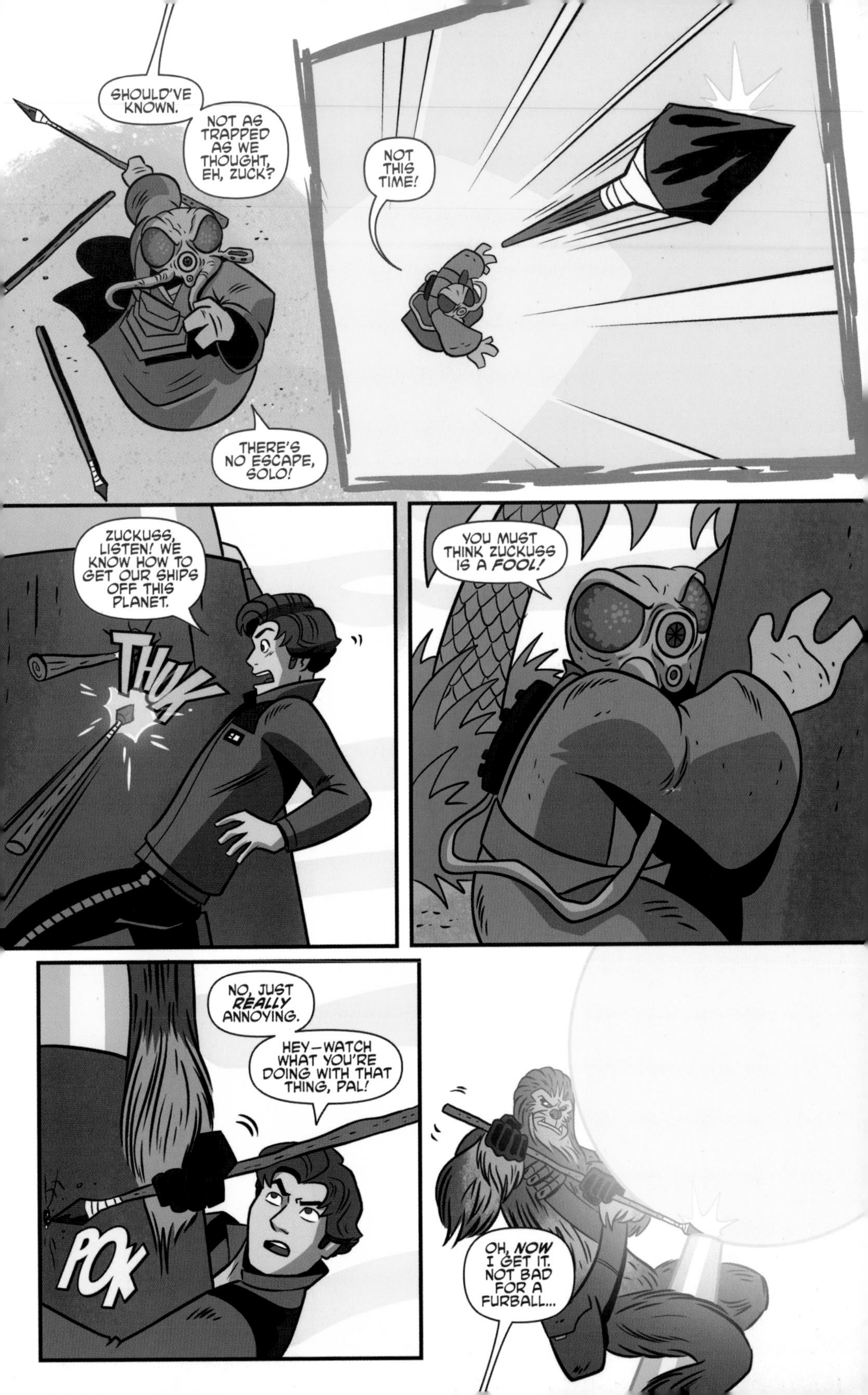
SHOULD'VE KNOWN.
NOT AS TRAPPED AS WE THOUGHT, EH, ZUCK?
NOT THIS TIME!
THERE'S NO ESCAPE, SOLO!
ZUCKUSS, LISTEN! WE KNOW HOW TO GET OUR SHIPS OFF THIS PLANET.
THUK
YOU MUST THINK ZUCKUSS IS A FOOL!
NO, JUST REALLY ANNOYING.
HEY—WATCH WHAT YOU'RE DOING WITH THAT THING, PAL!
POK
OH, NOW I GET IT. NOT BAD FOR A FURBALL...

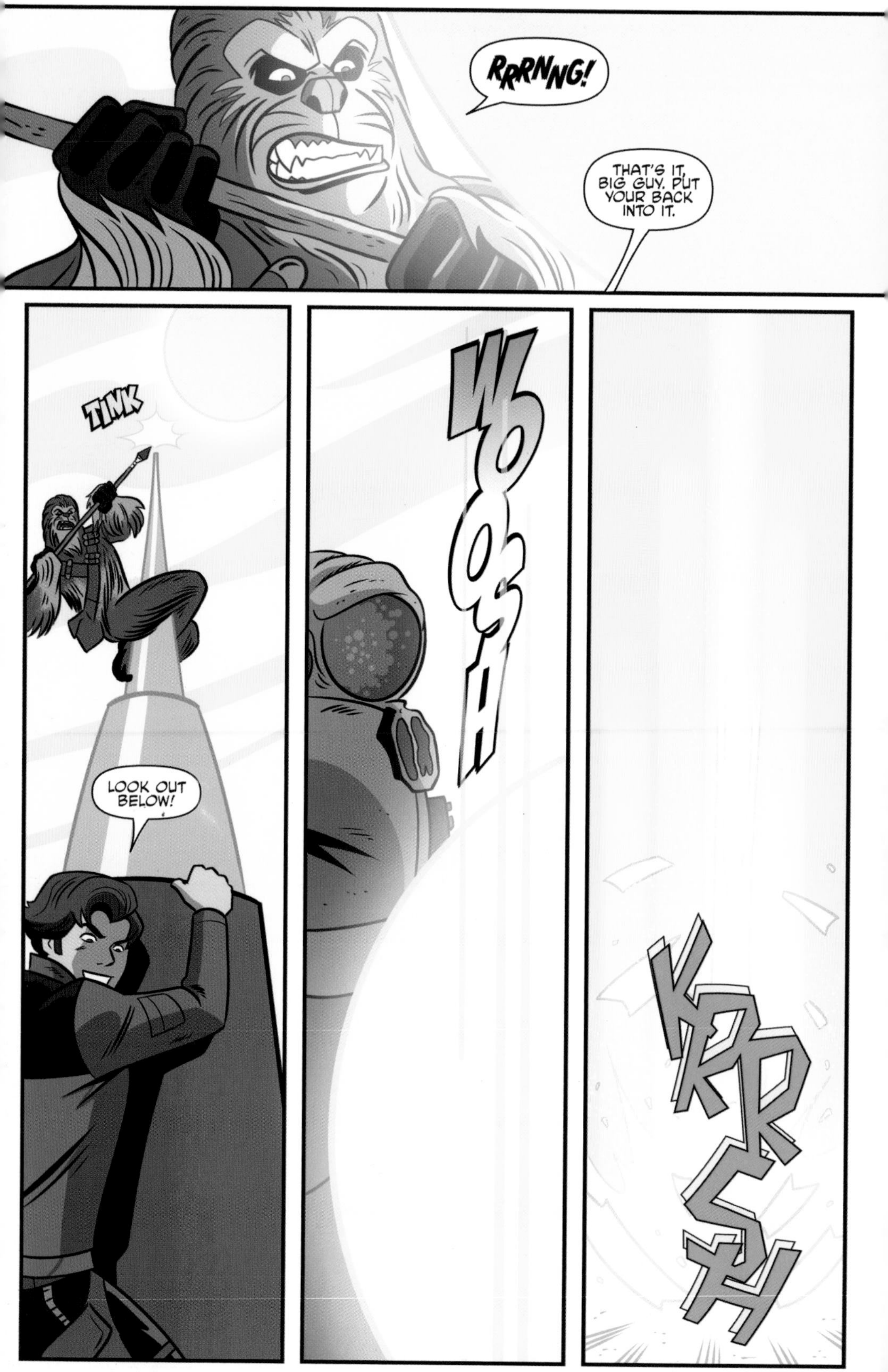
RRRNNG!
THAT'S IT, BIG GUY. PUT YOUR BACK INTO IT.
TINK
LOOK OUT BELOW!
WOOOSH
KRRRSH

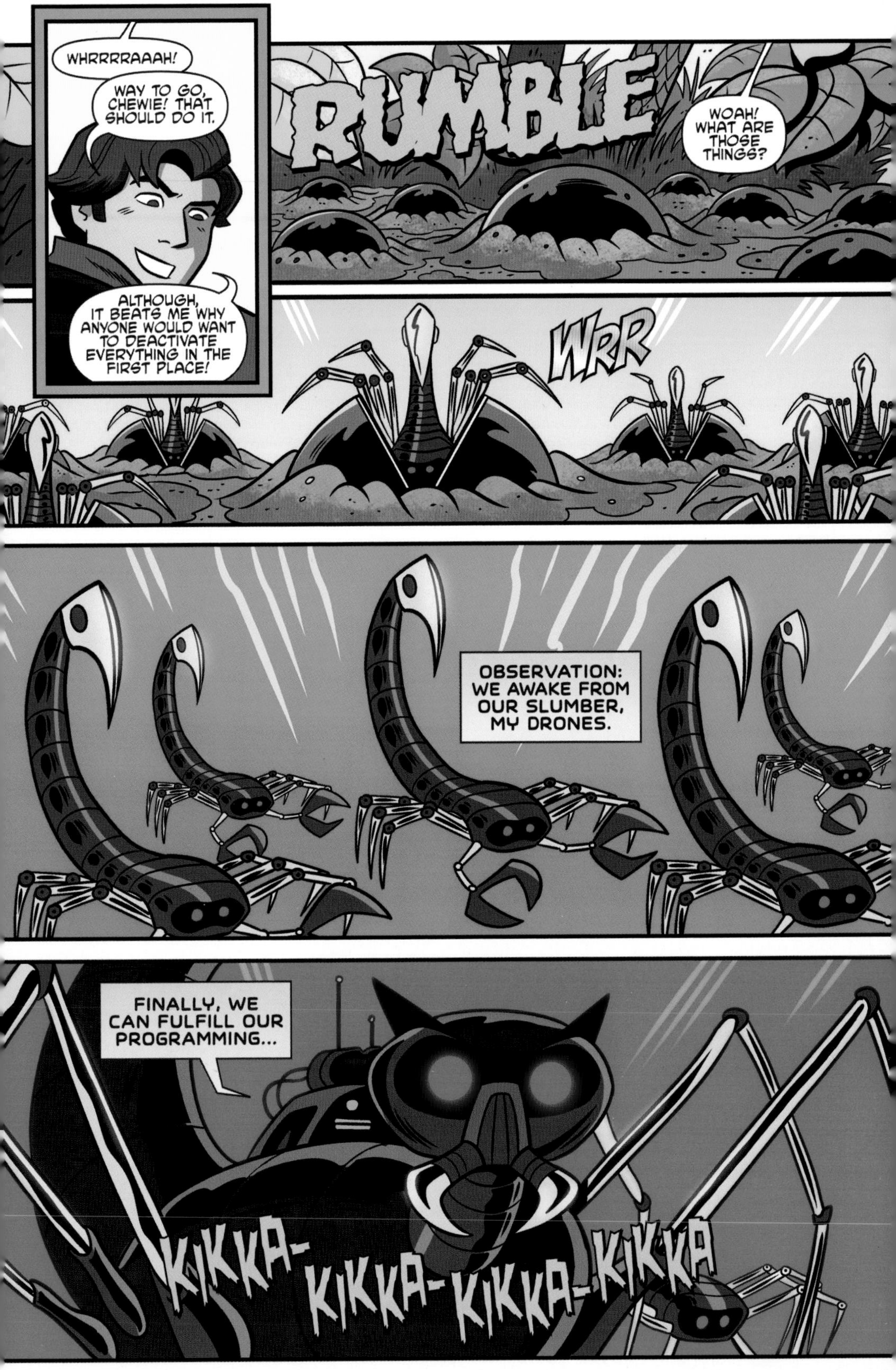
WHRRRRAAAH!
WAY TO GO, CHEWIE! THAT SHOULD DO IT.
ALTHOUGH, IT BEATS ME WHY ANYONE WOULD WANT TO DEACTIVATE EVERYTHING IN THE FIRST PLACE!
RUMBLE
WOAH! WHAT ARE THOSE THINGS?
WRR
OBSERVATION: WE AWAKE FROM OUR SLUMBER, MY DRONES.
FINALLY, WE CAN FULFILL OUR PROGRAMMING...
KIKKA-KIKKA-KIKKA-KIKKA

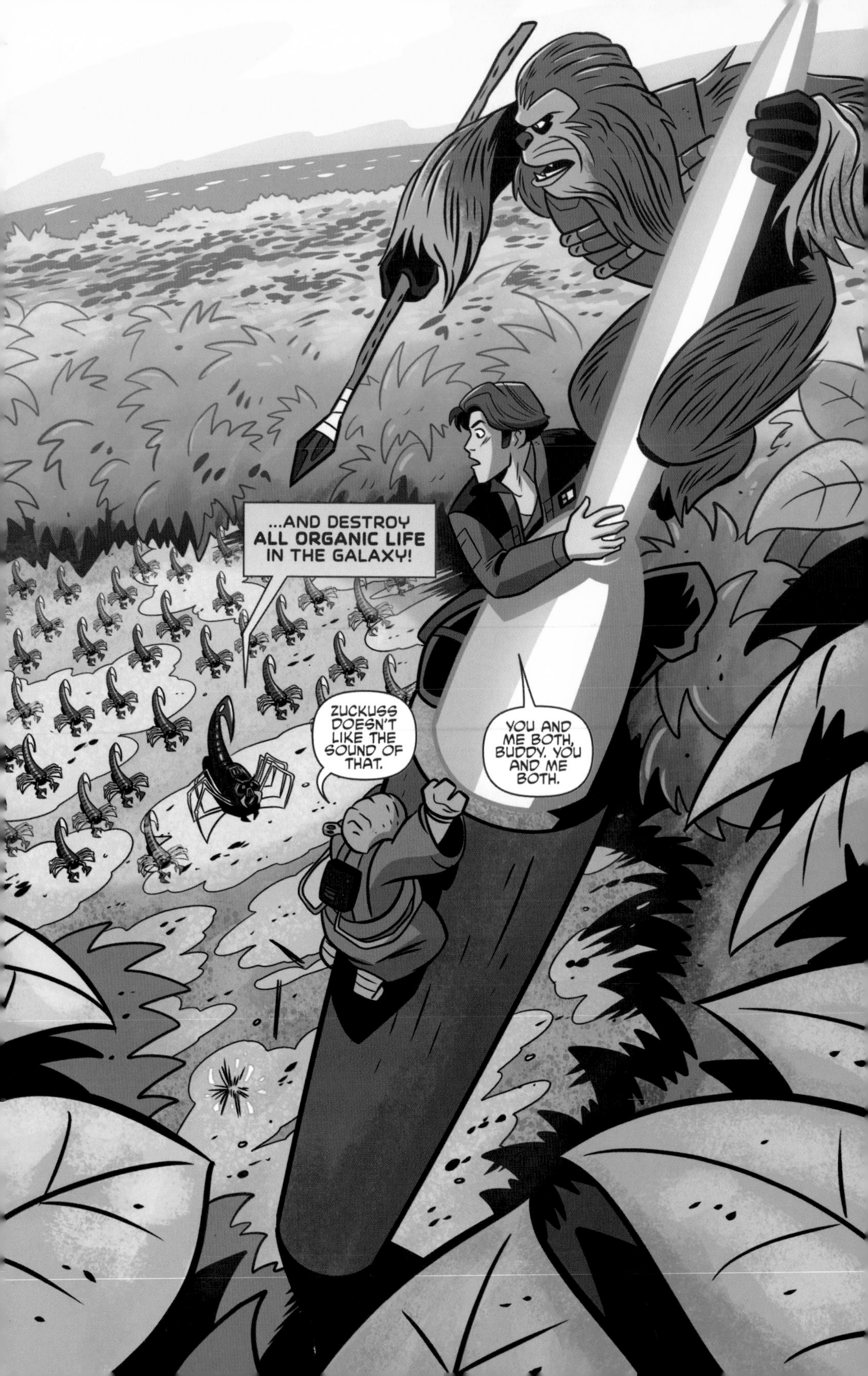
...AND DESTROY ALL ORGANIC LIFE IN THE GALAXY!
ZUCKUSS DOESN'T LIKE THE SOUND OF THAT.
YOU AND ME BOTH, BUDDY. YOU AND ME BOTH.

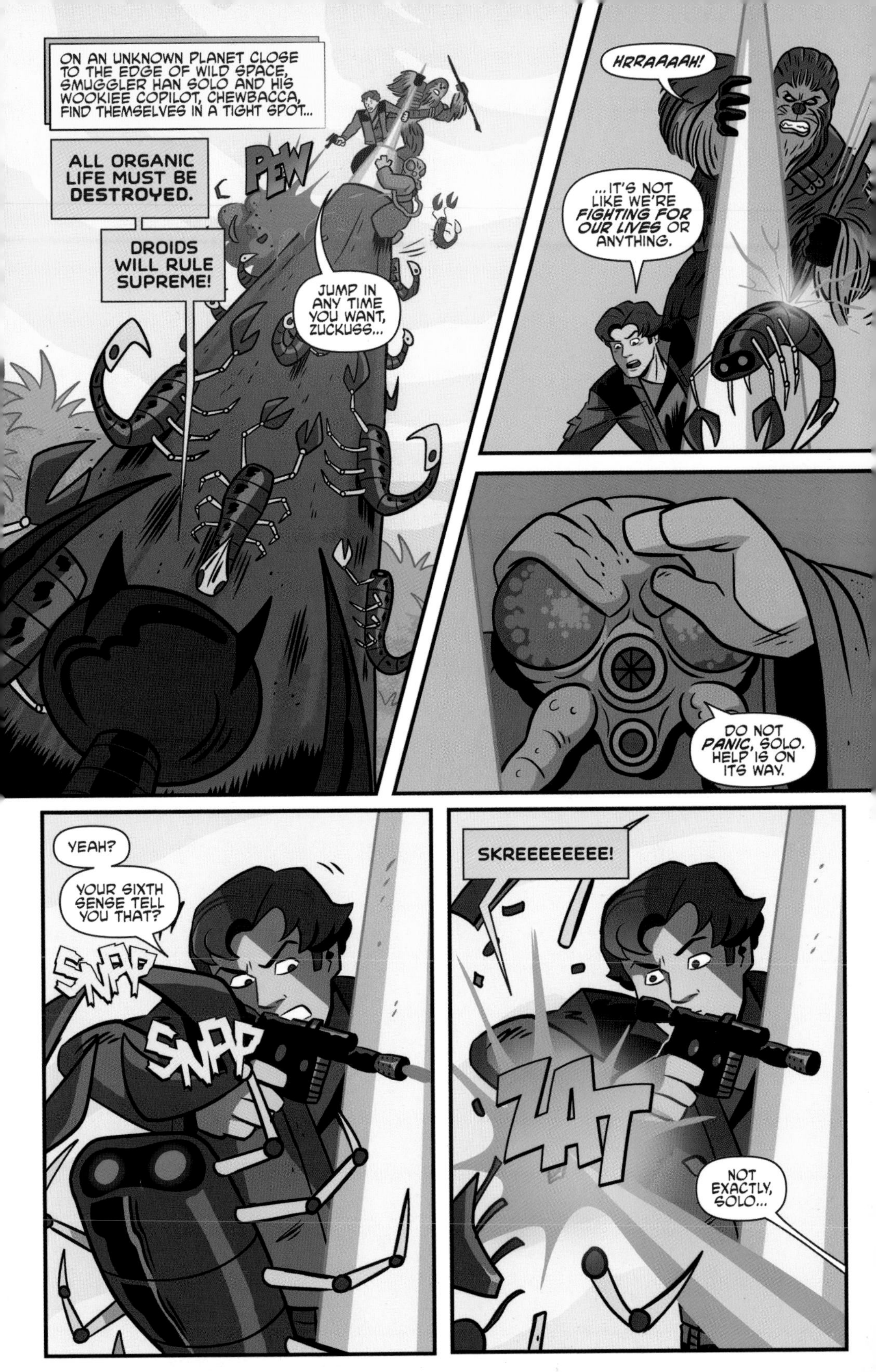
ON AN UNKNOWN PLANET CLOSE TO THE EDGE OF WILD SPACE, SMUGGLER HAN SOLO AND HIS WOOKIEE COPILOT, CHEWBACCA, FIND THEMSELVES IN A TIGHT SPOT...
ALL ORGANIC LIFE MUST BE DESTROYED.
PEW
DROIDS WILL RULE SUPREME!
JUMP IN ANY TIME YOU WANT, ZUCKUSS...
HRRAAAAH!
...IT'S NOT LIKE WE'RE FIGHTING FOR OUR LIVES OR ANYTHING.
DO NOT PANIC, SOLO. HELP IS ON ITS WAY.
YEAH?
YOUR SIXTH SENSE TELL YOU THAT?
SNAP
SNAP
SKREEEEEEEE!
ZAT
NOT EXACTLY, SOLO...

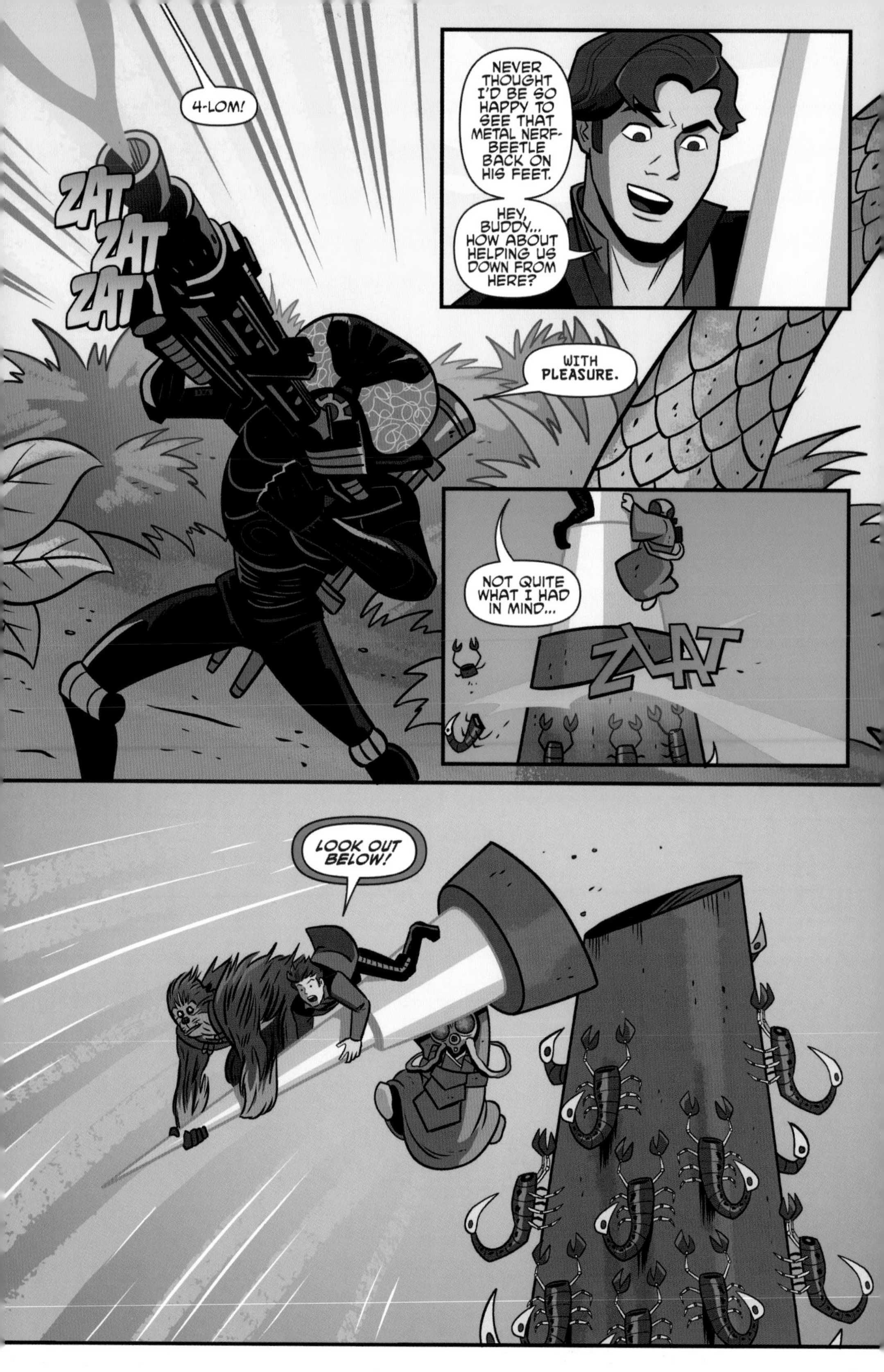
4-LOM!
ZAT ZAT ZAT
NEVER THOUGHT I'D BE SO HAPPY TO SEE THAT METAL NERF-BEETLE BACK ON HIS FEET.
HEY, BUDDY... HOW ABOUT HELPING US DOWN FROM HERE?
WITH PLEASURE.
NOT QUITE WHAT I HAD IN MIND...
ZZAT
LOOK OUT BELOW!

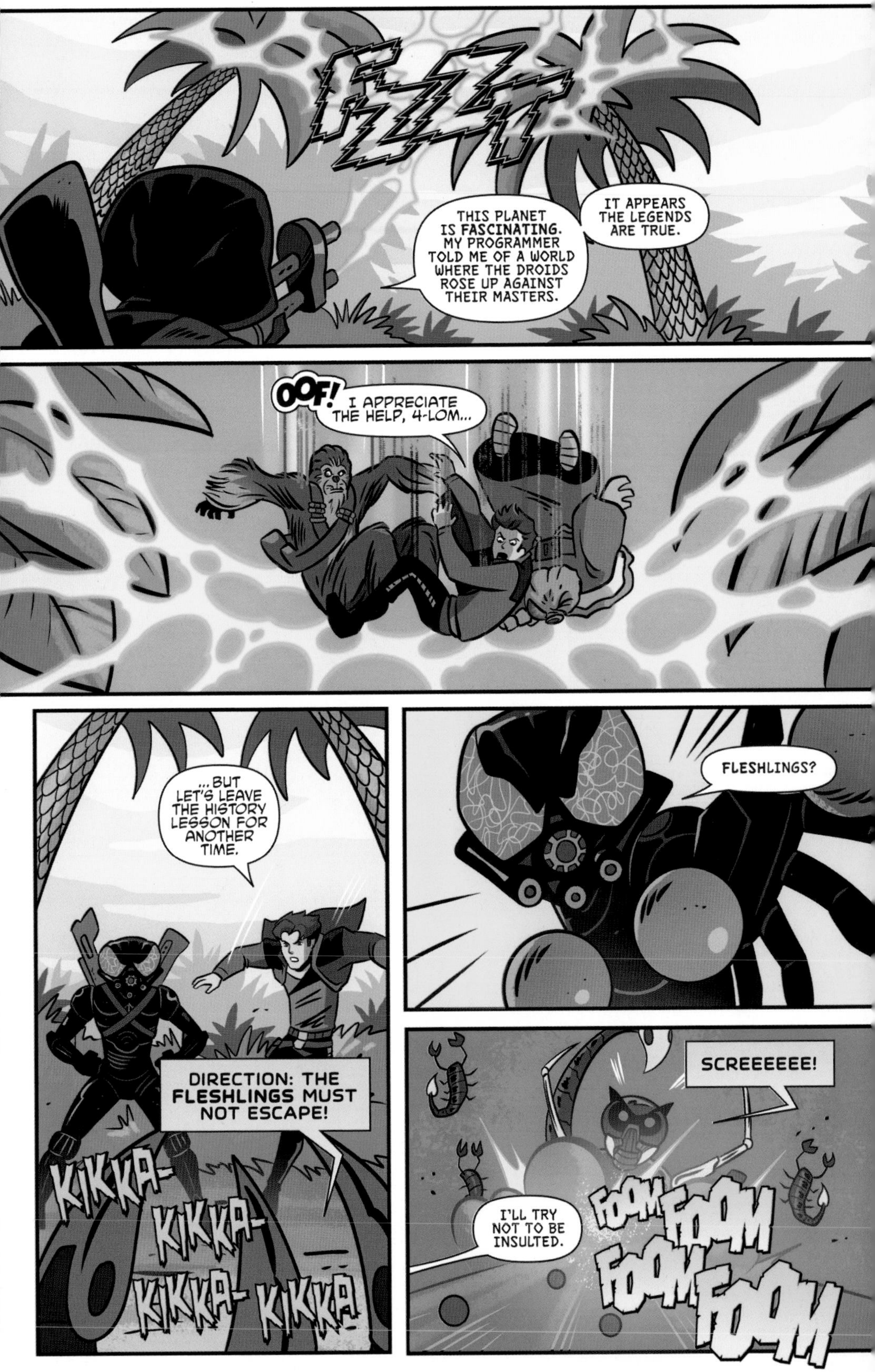
GZZZT
THIS PLANET IS FASCINATING. MY PROGRAMMER TOLD ME OF A WORLD WHERE THE DROIDS ROSE UP AGAINST THEIR MASTERS.
IT APPEARS THE LEGENDS ARE TRUE.
OOF!
I APPRECIATE THE HELP, 4-LOM...
...BUT LET'S LEAVE THE HISTORY LESSON FOR ANOTHER TIME.
DIRECTION: THE FLESHLINGS MUST NOT ESCAPE!
KIKKA- KIKKA- KIKKA- KIKKA
FLESHLINGS?
SCREEEEEE!
I'LL TRY NOT TO BE INSULTED.
FOOM FOOM FOOM FOOM

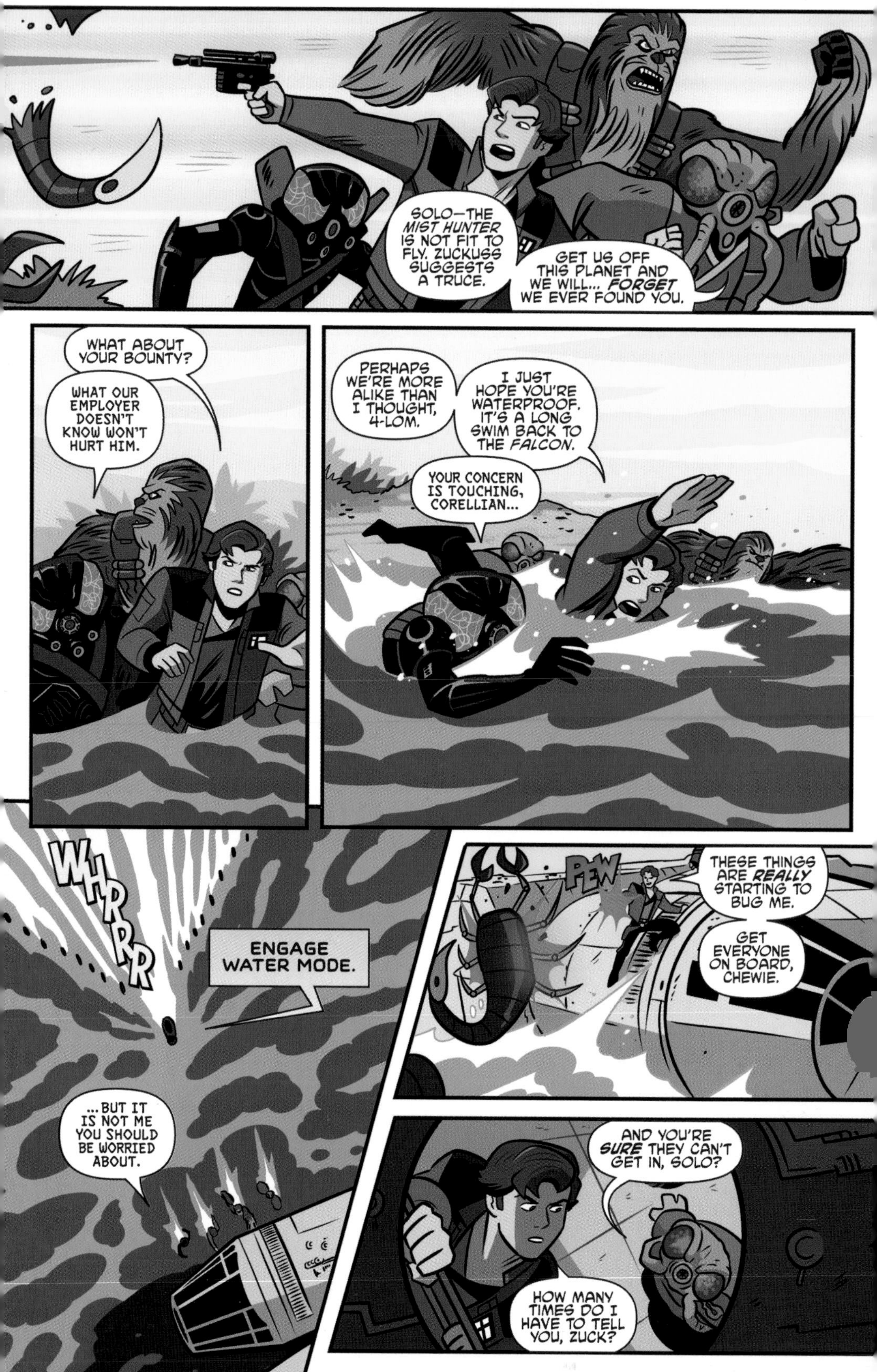
SOLO—THE MIST HUNTER IS NOT FIT TO FLY. ZUCKUSS SUGGESTS A TRUCE.
GET US OFF THIS PLANET AND WE WILL... FORGET WE EVER FOUND YOU.
WHAT ABOUT YOUR BOUNTY?
WHAT OUR EMPLOYER DOESN'T KNOW WON'T HURT HIM.
PERHAPS WE'RE MORE ALIKE THAN I THOUGHT, 4-LOM.
I JUST HOPE YOU'RE WATERPROOF. IT'S A LONG SWIM BACK TO THE FALCON.
YOUR CONCERN IS TOUCHING, CORELLIAN...
WHRRR
ENGAGE WATER MODE.
...BUT IT IS NOT ME YOU SHOULD BE WORRIED ABOUT.
PEW
THESE THINGS ARE REALLY STARTING TO BUG ME.
GET EVERYONE ON BOARD, CHEWIE.
AND YOU'RE SURE THEY CAN'T GET IN, SOLO?
HOW MANY TIMES DO I HAVE TO TELL YOU, ZUCK?

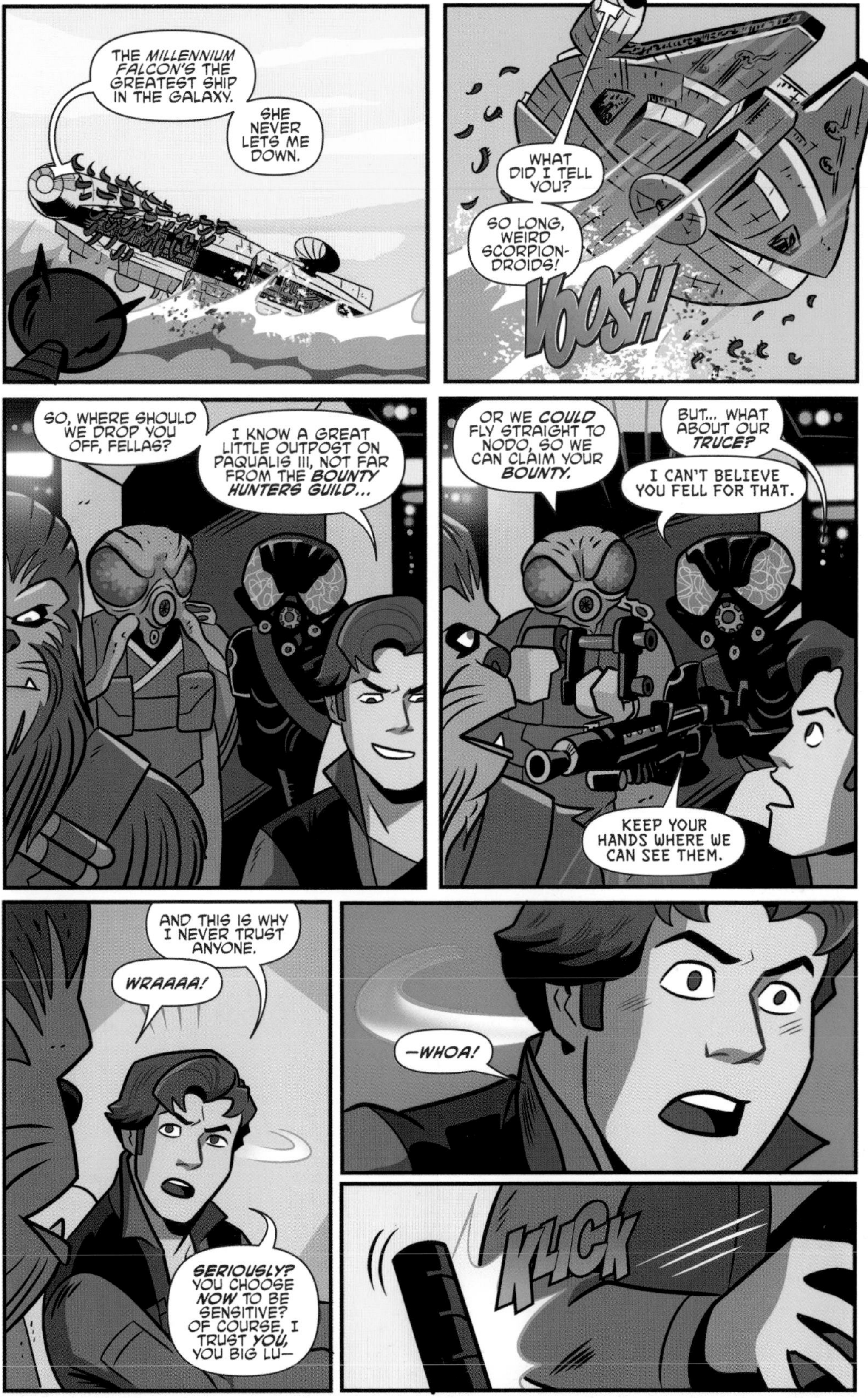

THE MILLENNIUM FALCON'S THE GREATEST SHIP IN THE GALAXY.
SHE NEVER LETS ME DOWN.
WHAT DID I TELL YOU?
SO LONG, WEIRD SCORPION-DROIDS!
VOOSH
SO, WHERE SHOULD WE DROP YOU OFF, FELLAS?
I KNOW A GREAT LITTLE OUTPOST ON PAQUALIS III, NOT FAR FROM THE BOUNTY HUNTERS GUILD...
OR WE COULD FLY STRAIGHT TO NODO, SO WE CAN CLAIM YOUR BOUNTY.
BUT... WHAT ABOUT OUR TRUCE?
I CAN'T BELIEVE YOU FELL FOR THAT.
KEEP YOUR HANDS WHERE WE CAN SEE THEM.
AND THIS IS WHY I NEVER TRUST ANYONE.
WRAAAA!
SERIOUSLY? YOU CHOOSE NOW TO BE SENSITIVE? OF COURSE, I TRUST YOU, YOU BIG LU—
—WHOA!
KLICK

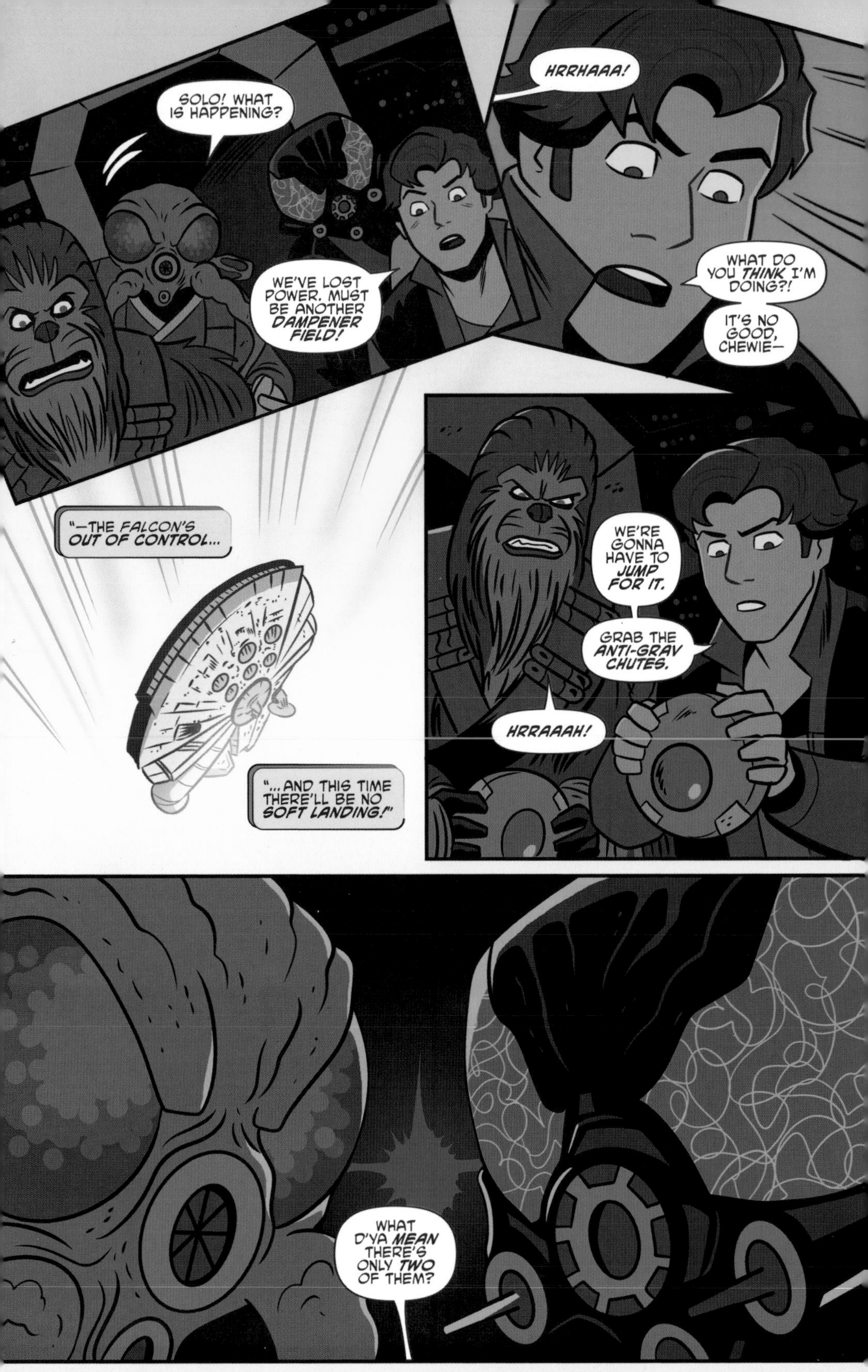
SOLO! WHAT IS HAPPENING?
WE'VE LOST POWER. MUST BE ANOTHER *DAMPENER FIELD!*
HRRHAAA!
WHAT DO YOU *THINK* I'M DOING?!
IT'S NO GOOD, CHEWIE—
"—THE *FALCON'S* **OUT OF CONTROL...**
"...AND THIS TIME THERE'LL BE NO *SOFT LANDING!"*
WE'RE GONNA HAVE TO *JUMP FOR IT.*
GRAB THE *ANTI-GRAV CHUTES.*
HRRAAAH!
WHAT D'YA *MEAN* THERE'S ONLY *TWO* OF THEM?

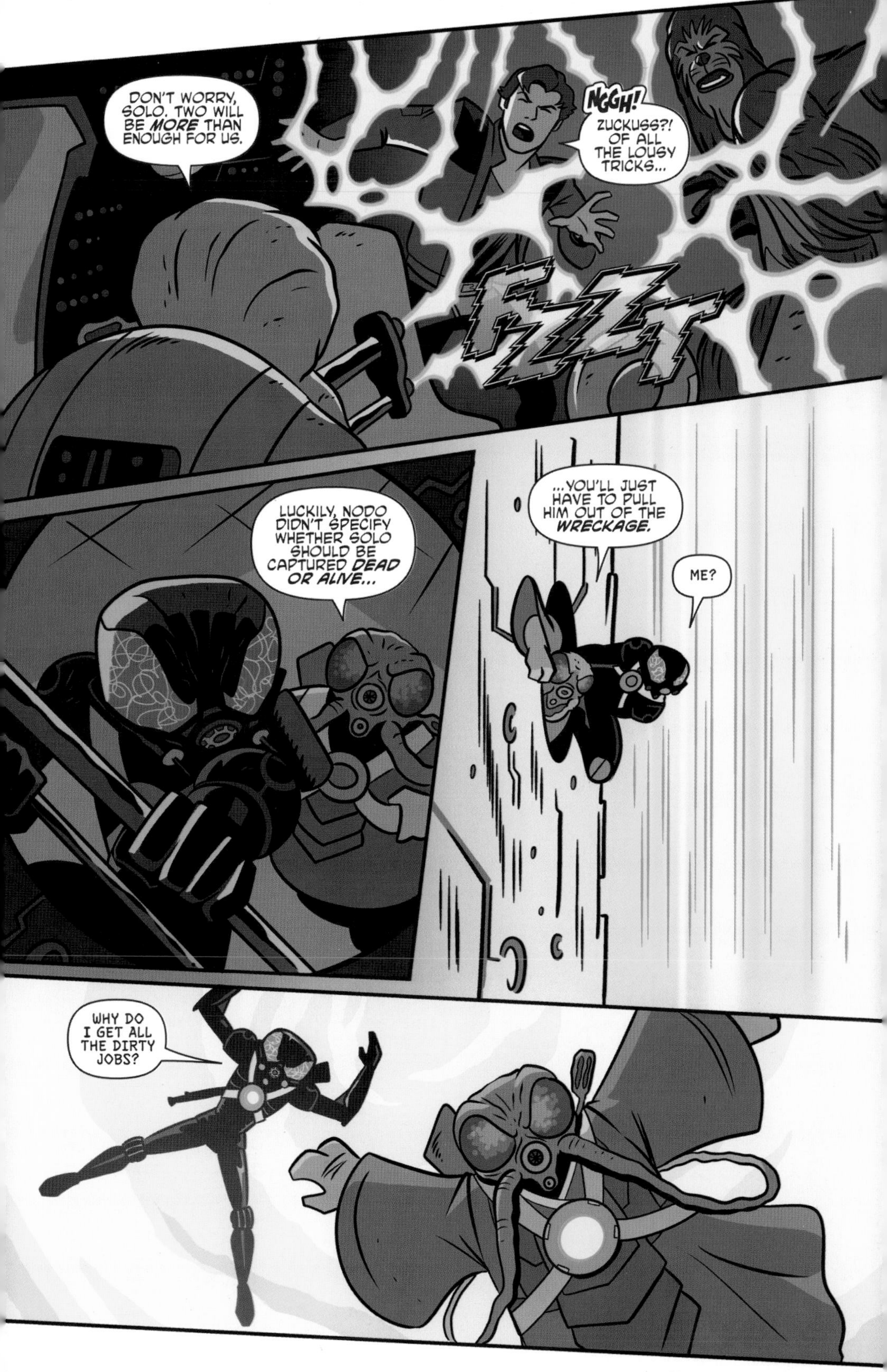
DON'T WORRY, SOLO. TWO WILL BE MORE THAN ENOUGH FOR US.
NGGH!
ZUCKUSS?! OF ALL THE LOUSY TRICKS...
FZZZT
LUCKILY, NODO DIDN'T SPECIFY WHETHER SOLO SHOULD BE CAPTURED DEAD OR ALIVE...
...YOU'LL JUST HAVE TO PULL HIM OUT OF THE WRECKAGE.
ME?
WHY DO I GET ALL THE DIRTY JOBS?

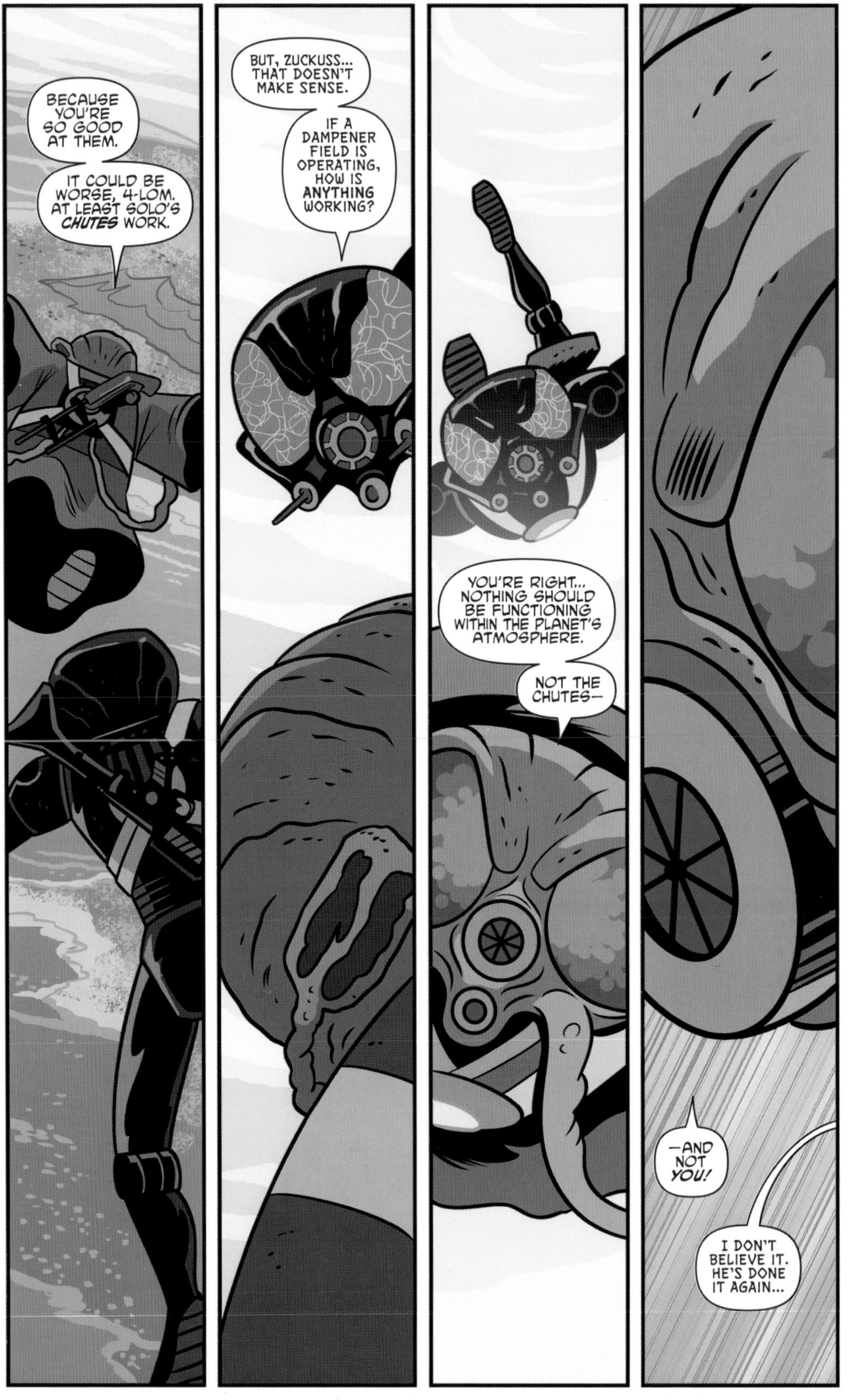
BECAUSE YOU'RE SO GOOD AT THEM.
IT COULD BE WORSE, 4-LOM. AT LEAST SOLO'S CHUTES WORK.
BUT, ZUCKUSS... THAT DOESN'T MAKE SENSE.
IF A DAMPENER FIELD IS OPERATING, HOW IS ANYTHING WORKING?
YOU'RE RIGHT... NOTHING SHOULD BE FUNCTIONING WITHIN THE PLANET'S ATMOSPHERE.
NOT THE CHUTES—
—AND NOT YOU!
I DON'T BELIEVE IT. HE'S DONE IT AGAIN...

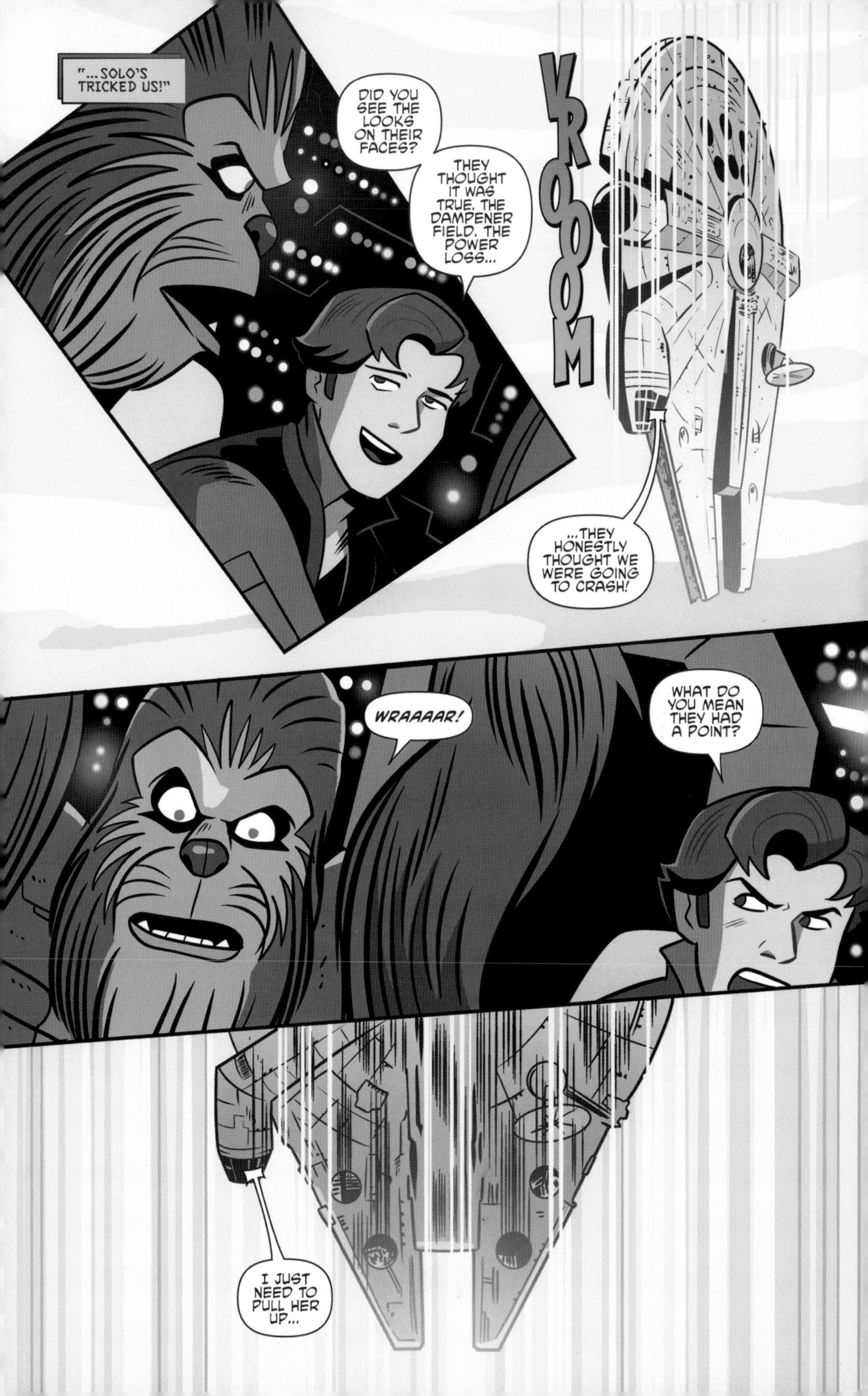
"...SOLO'S TRICKED US!"
DID YOU SEE THE LOOKS ON THEIR FACES?
THEY THOUGHT IT WAS TRUE. THE DAMPENER FIELD. THE POWER LOSS...
VROOOOM
...THEY HONESTLY THOUGHT WE WERE GOING TO CRASH!
WRAAAAR!
WHAT DO YOU MEAN THEY HAD A POINT?
I JUST NEED TO PULL HER UP...

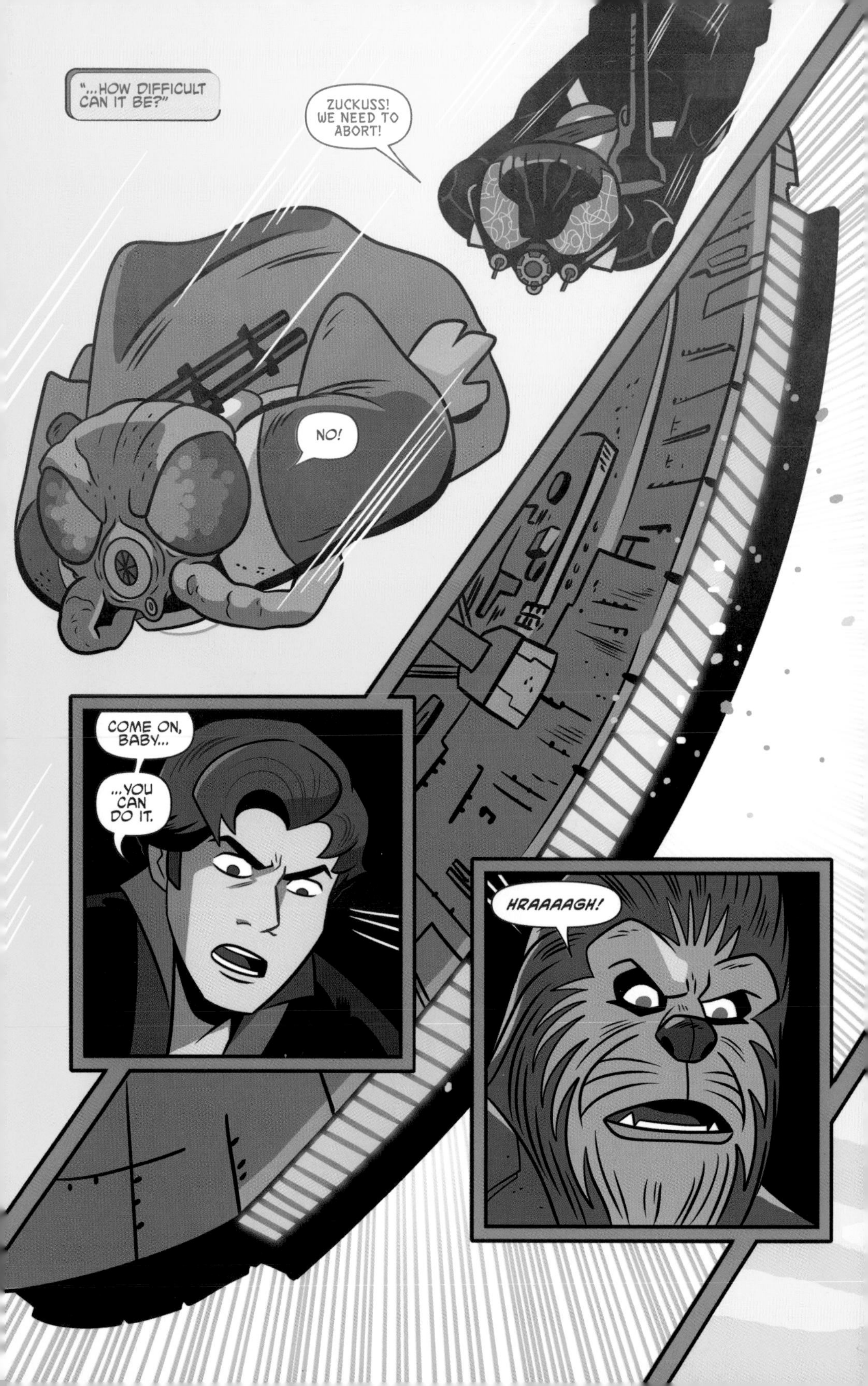
"...HOW DIFFICULT CAN IT BE?"
ZUCKUSS! WE NEED TO ABORT!
NO!
COME ON, BABY...
...YOU CAN DO IT.
HRAAAAGH!

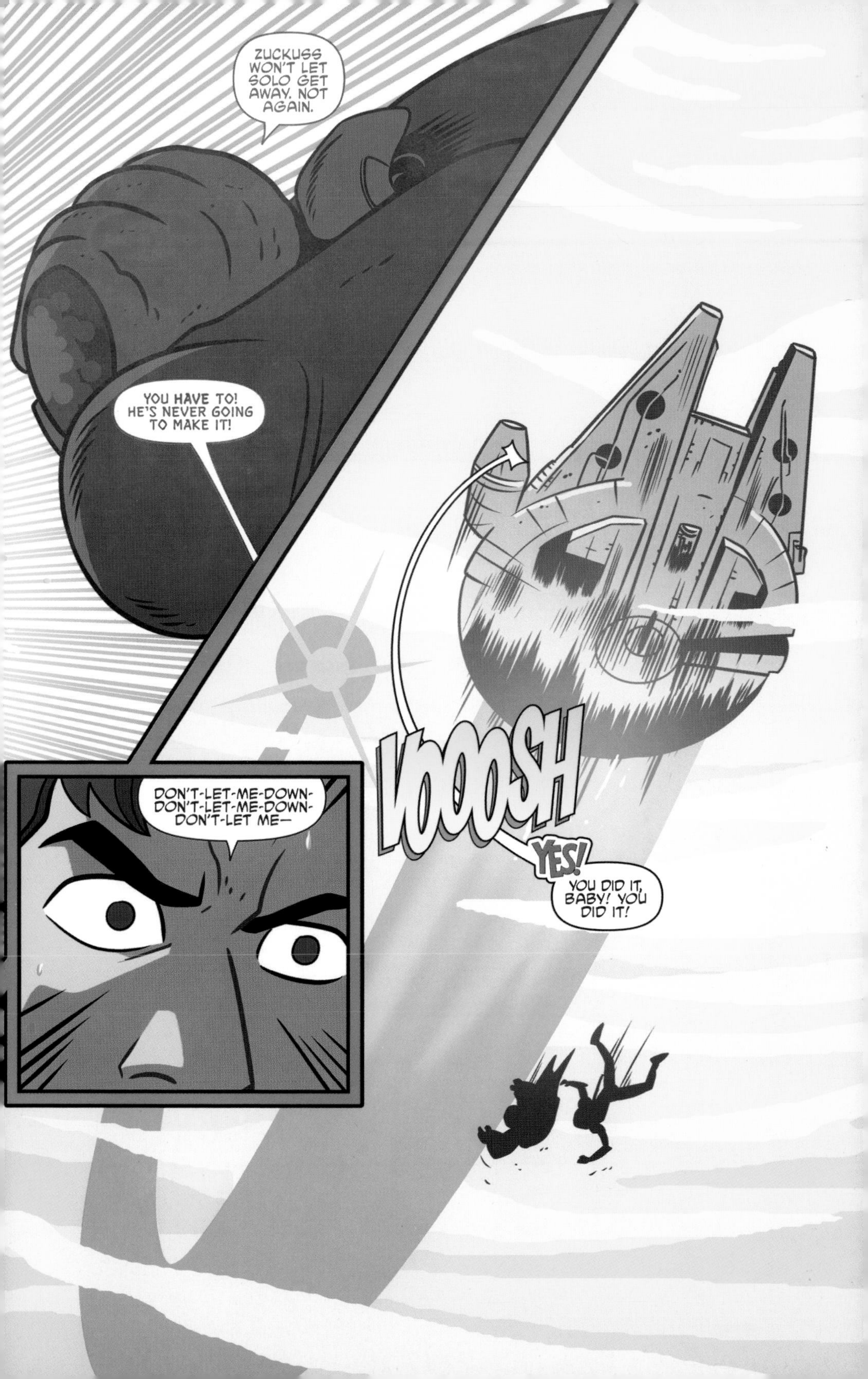
ZUCKUSS WON'T LET SOLO GET AWAY. NOT AGAIN.
YOU HAVE TO! HE'S NEVER GOING TO MAKE IT!
DON'T-LET-ME-DOWN-DON'T-LET-ME-DOWN-DON'T-LET ME—
VOOOSH
YES!
YOU DID IT, BABY! YOU DID IT!

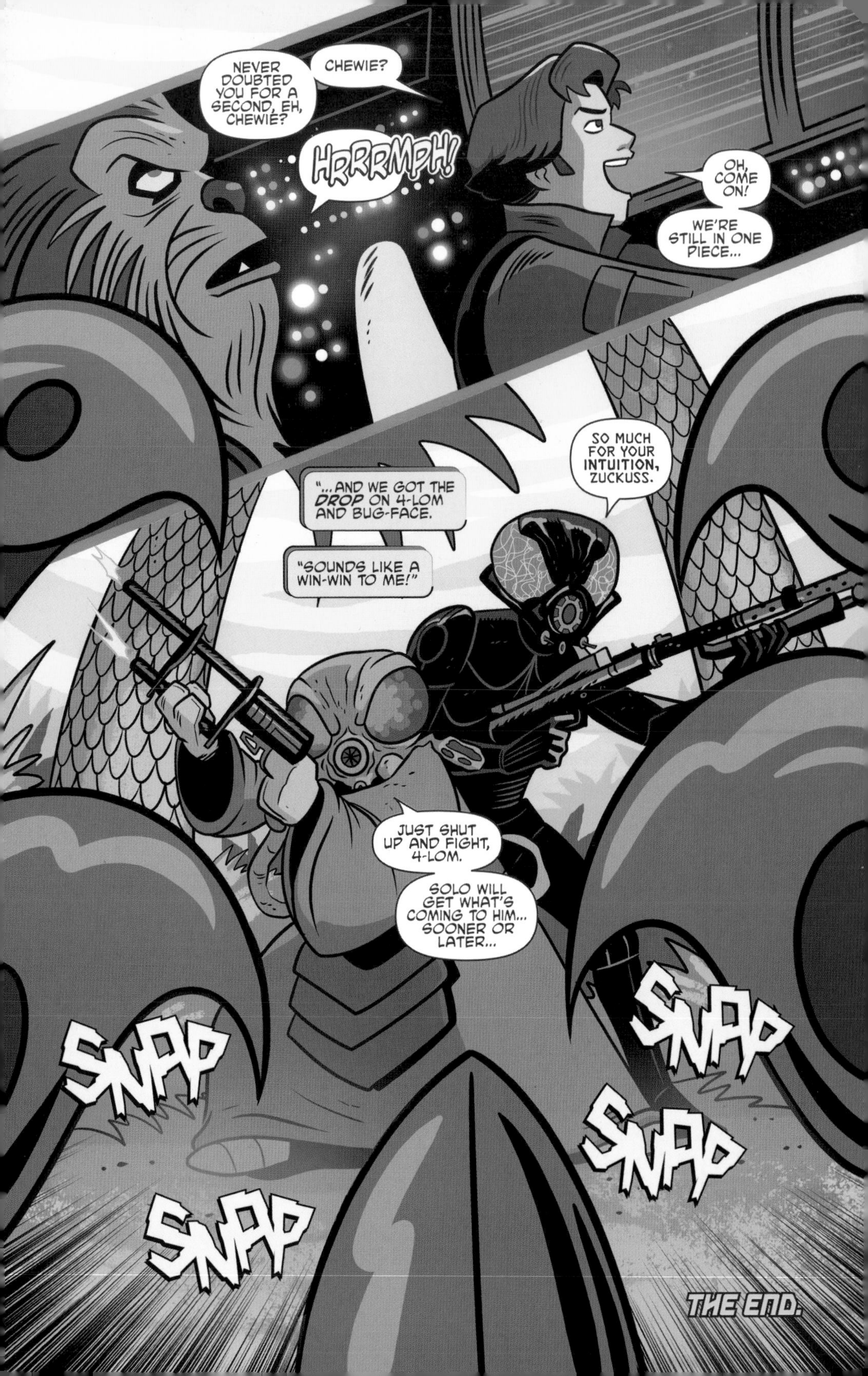
NEVER DOUBTED YOU FOR A SECOND, EH, CHEWIE?
CHEWIE?
HRRRMPH!
OH, COME ON!
WE'RE STILL IN ONE PIECE...
"...AND WE GOT THE *DROP* ON 4-LOM AND BUG-FACE.
"SOUNDS LIKE A WIN-WIN TO ME!"
SO MUCH FOR YOUR **INTUITION**, ZUCKUSS.
JUST SHUT UP AND FIGHT, 4-LOM.
SOLO WILL GET WHAT'S COMING TO HIM... SOONER OR LATER...
SNAP
SNAP
SNAP
SNAP
THE END.

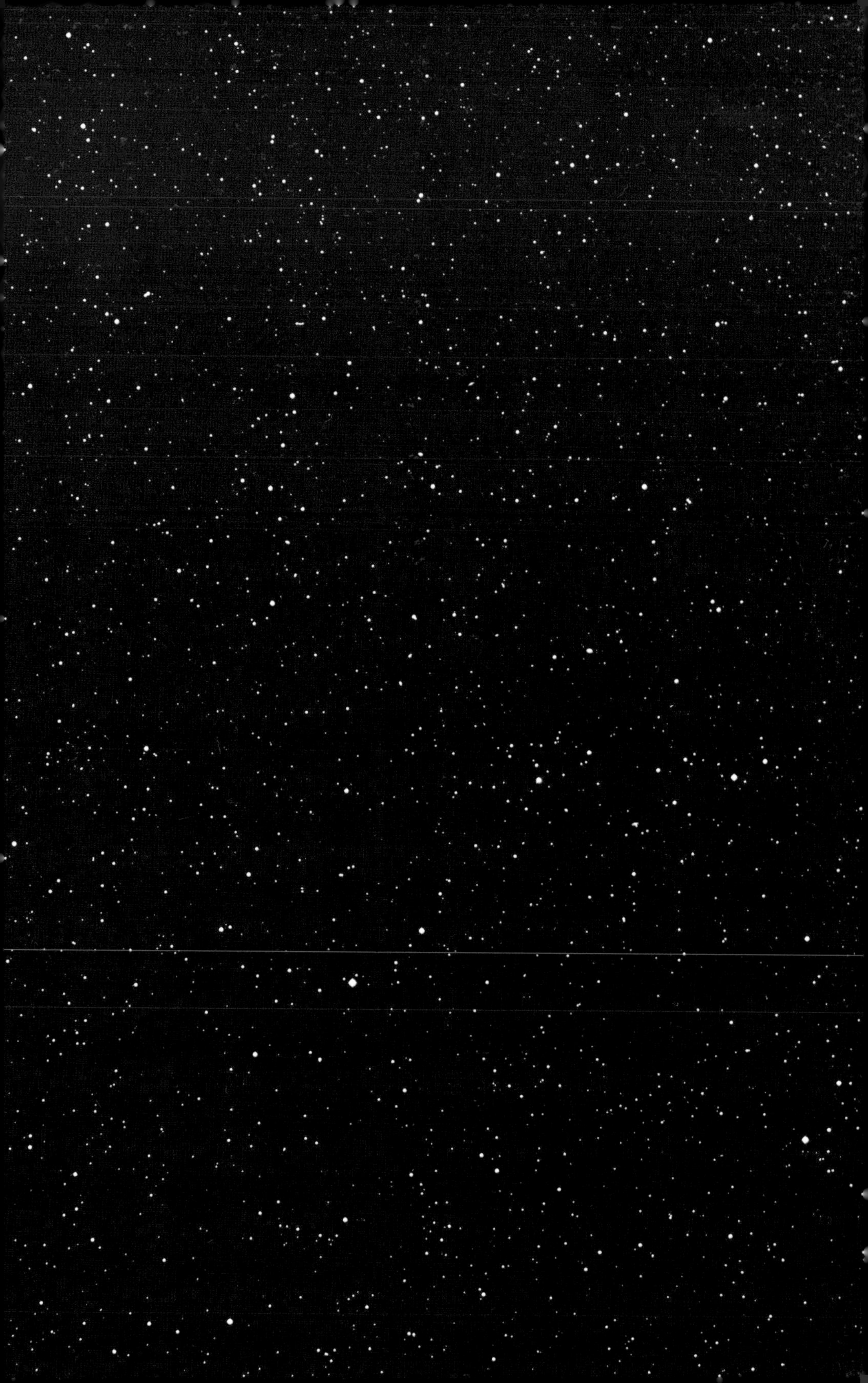

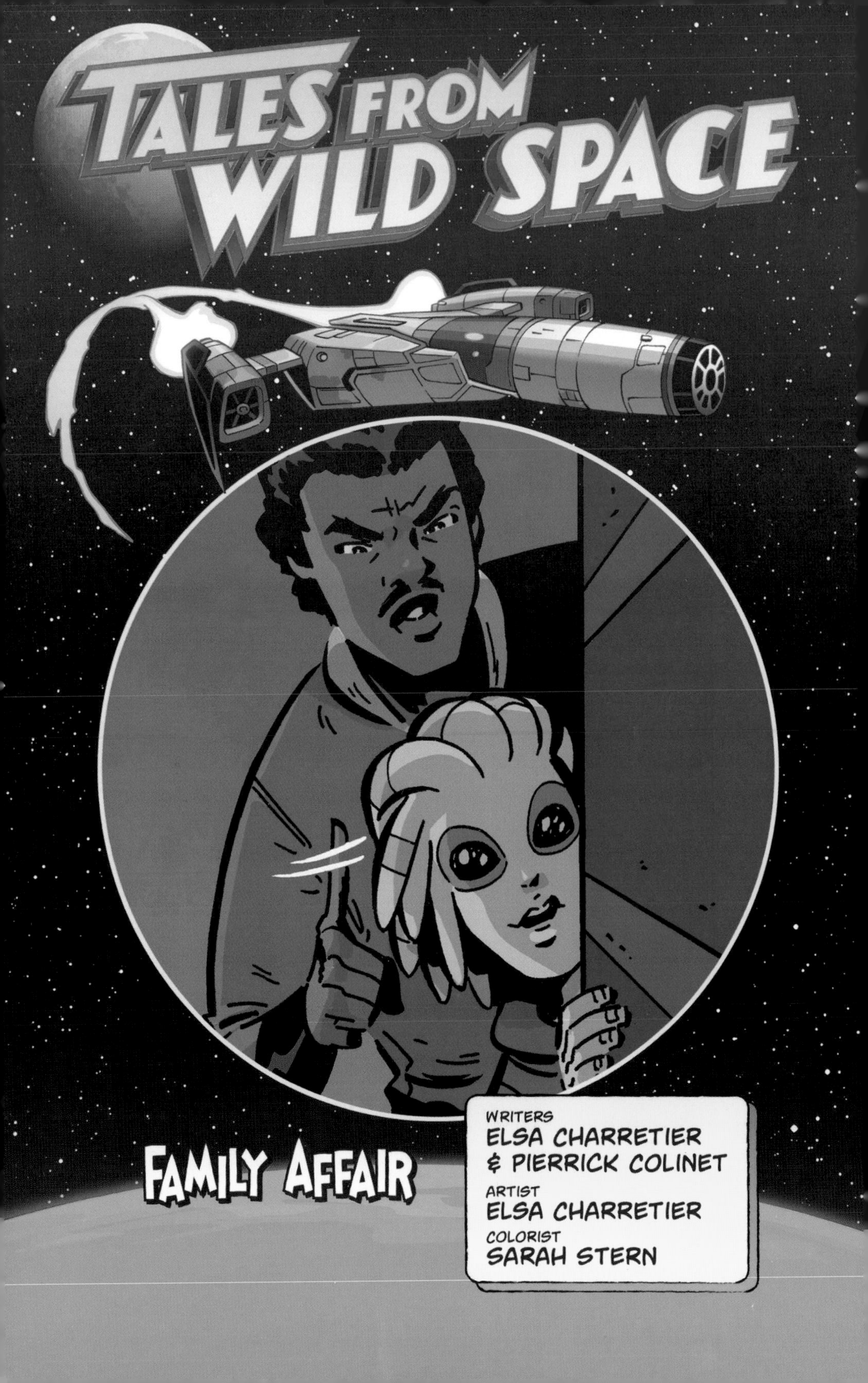

TALES FROM WILD SPACE
FAMILY AFFAIR
WRITERS
ELSA CHARRETIER
& PIERRICK COLINET
ARTIST
ELSA CHARRETIER
COLORIST
SARAH STERN

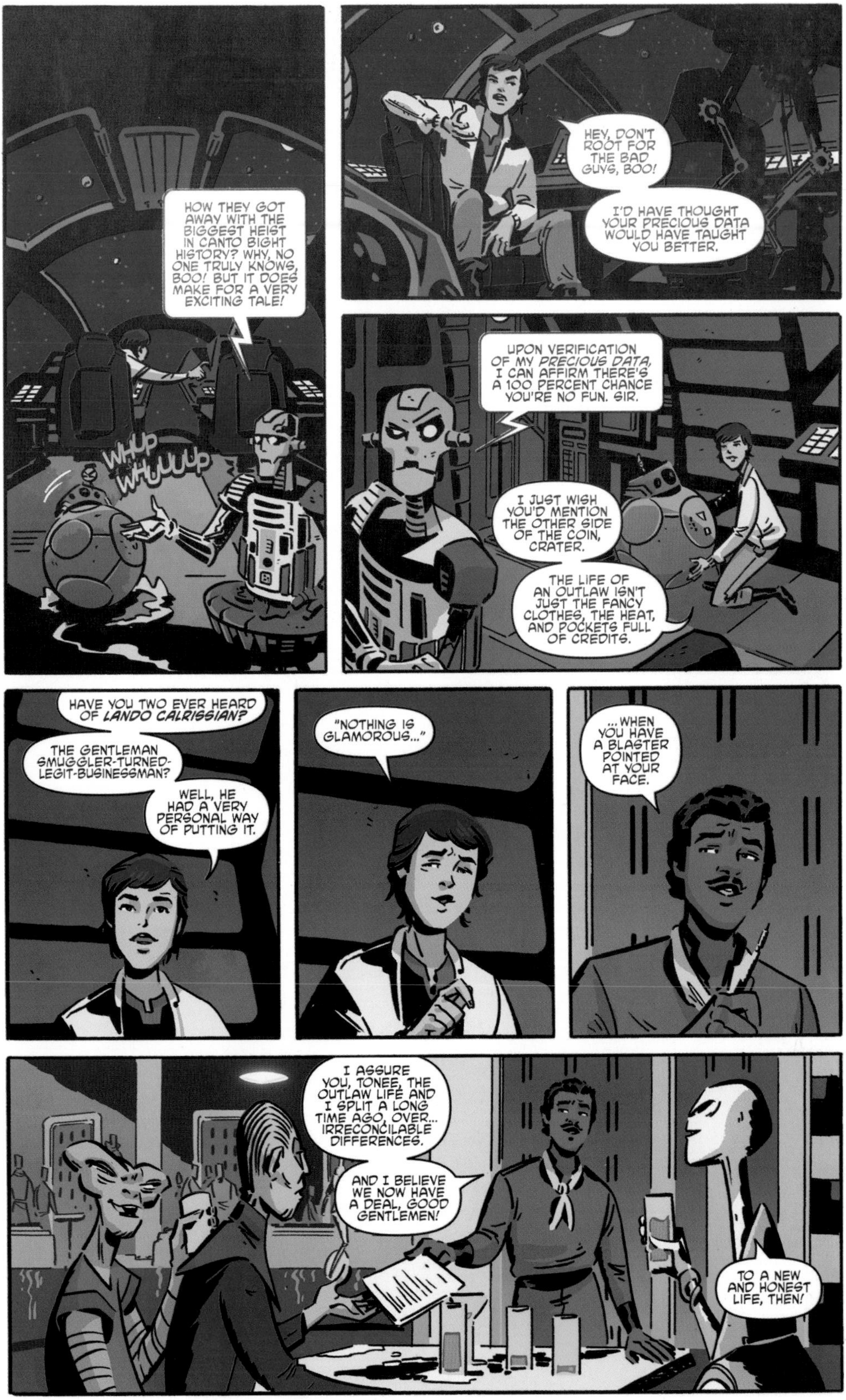
HOW THEY GOT AWAY WITH THE BIGGEST HEIST IN CANTO BIGHT HISTORY? WHY, NO ONE TRULY KNOWS, BOO! BUT IT DOES MAKE FOR A VERY EXCITING TALE!
WHUP WHUUUUP
HEY, DON'T ROOT FOR THE BAD GUYS, BOO!
I'D HAVE THOUGHT YOUR PRECIOUS DATA WOULD HAVE TAUGHT YOU BETTER.
UPON VERIFICATION OF MY *PRECIOUS DATA,* I CAN AFFIRM THERE'S A 100 PERCENT CHANCE YOU'RE NO FUN. SIR.
I JUST WISH YOU'D MENTION THE OTHER SIDE OF THE COIN, CRATER.
THE LIFE OF AN OUTLAW ISN'T JUST THE FANCY CLOTHES, THE HEAT, AND POCKETS FULL OF CREDITS.
HAVE YOU TWO EVER HEARD OF *LANDO CALRISSIAN?*
THE GENTLEMAN SMUGGLER-TURNED-LEGIT-BUSINESSMAN?
WELL, HE HAD A VERY PERSONAL WAY OF PUTTING IT.
"NOTHING IS GLAMOROUS..."
...WHEN YOU HAVE A BLASTER POINTED AT YOUR FACE.
I ASSURE YOU, TONEE, THE OUTLAW LIFE AND I SPLIT A LONG TIME AGO, OVER... IRRECONCILABLE DIFFERENCES.
AND I BELIEVE WE NOW HAVE A DEAL, GOOD GENTLEMEN!
TO A NEW AND HONEST LIFE, THEN!

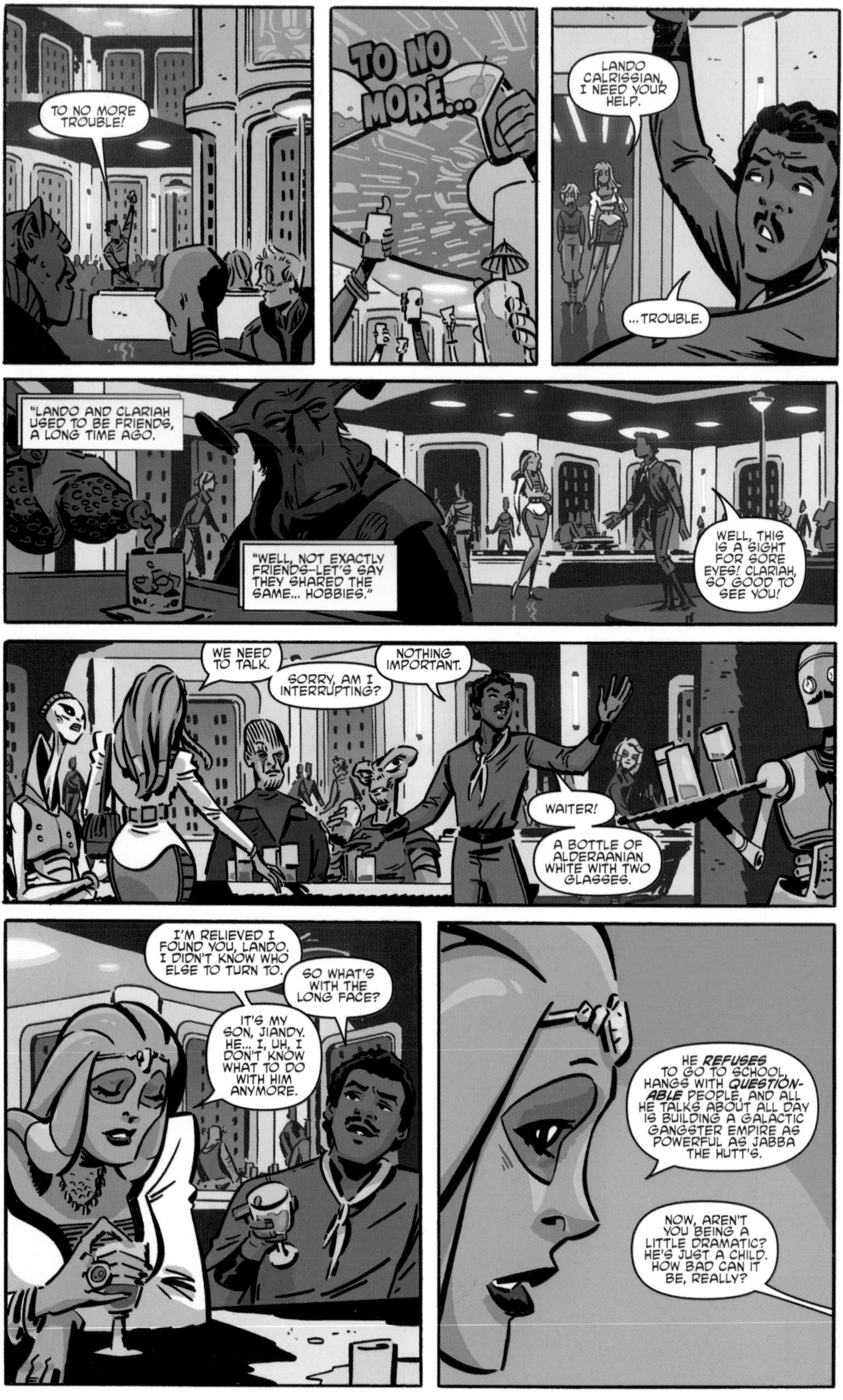
TO NO MORE TROUBLE!
TO NO MORE...
LANDO CALRISSIAN, I NEED YOUR HELP.
...TROUBLE.
"LANDO AND CLARIAH USED TO BE FRIENDS, A LONG TIME AGO.
"WELL, NOT EXACTLY FRIENDS–LET'S SAY THEY SHARED THE SAME... HOBBIES."
WELL, THIS IS A SIGHT FOR SORE EYES! CLARIAH, SO GOOD TO SEE YOU!
WE NEED TO TALK.
SORRY, AM I INTERRUPTING?
NOTHING IMPORTANT.
WAITER!
A BOTTLE OF ALDERAANIAN WHITE WITH TWO GLASSES.
I'M RELIEVED I FOUND YOU, LANDO. I DIDN'T KNOW WHO ELSE TO TURN TO.
SO WHAT'S WITH THE LONG FACE?
IT'S MY SON, JIANDY. HE... I, UH, I DON'T KNOW WHAT TO DO WITH HIM ANYMORE.
HE *REFUSES* TO GO TO SCHOOL, HANGS WITH *QUESTIONABLE* PEOPLE, AND ALL HE TALKS ABOUT ALL DAY IS BUILDING A GALACTIC GANGSTER EMPIRE AS POWERFUL AS JABBA THE HUTT'S.
NOW, AREN'T YOU BEING A LITTLE DRAMATIC? HE'S JUST A CHILD. HOW BAD CAN IT BE, REALLY?

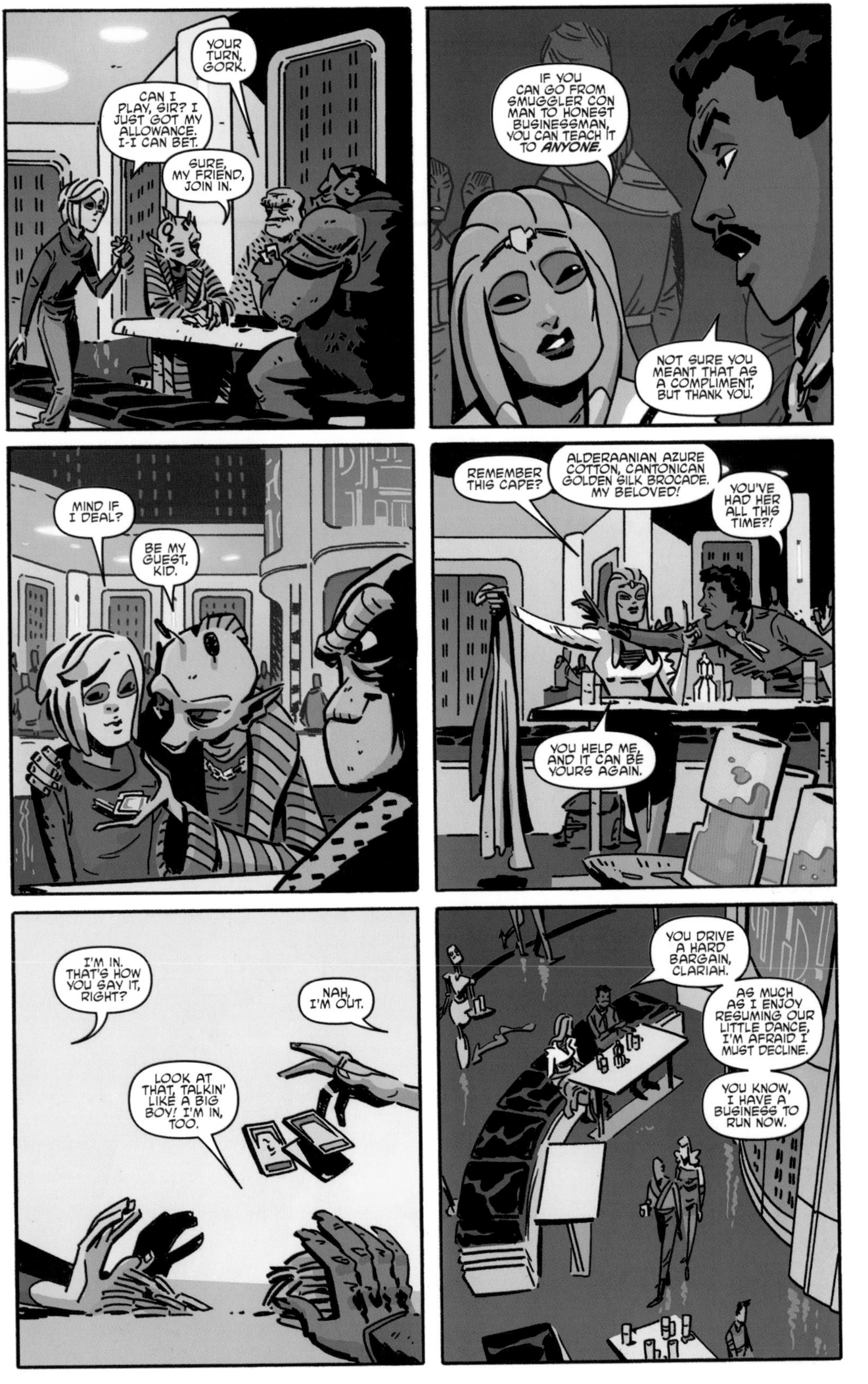

YOUR TURN, GORK.
CAN I PLAY, SIR? I JUST GOT MY ALLOWANCE. I-I CAN BET.
SURE, MY FRIEND, JOIN IN.
IF YOU CAN GO FROM SMUGGLER CON MAN TO HONEST BUSINESSMAN, YOU CAN TEACH IT TO ANYONE.
NOT SURE YOU MEANT THAT AS A COMPLIMENT, BUT THANK YOU.
MIND IF I DEAL?
BE MY GUEST, KID.
REMEMBER THIS CAPE?
ALDERAANIAN AZURE COTTON, CANTONICAN GOLDEN SILK BROCADE. MY BELOVED!
YOU'VE HAD HER ALL THIS TIME?!
YOU HELP ME, AND IT CAN BE YOURS AGAIN.
I'M IN. THAT'S HOW YOU SAY IT, RIGHT?
NAH, I'M OUT.
LOOK AT THAT, TALKIN' LIKE A BIG BOY! I'M IN, TOO.
YOU DRIVE A HARD BARGAIN, CLARIAH.
AS MUCH AS I ENJOY RESUMING OUR LITTLE DANCE, I'M AFRAID I MUST DECLINE.
YOU KNOW, I HAVE A BUSINESS TO RUN NOW.

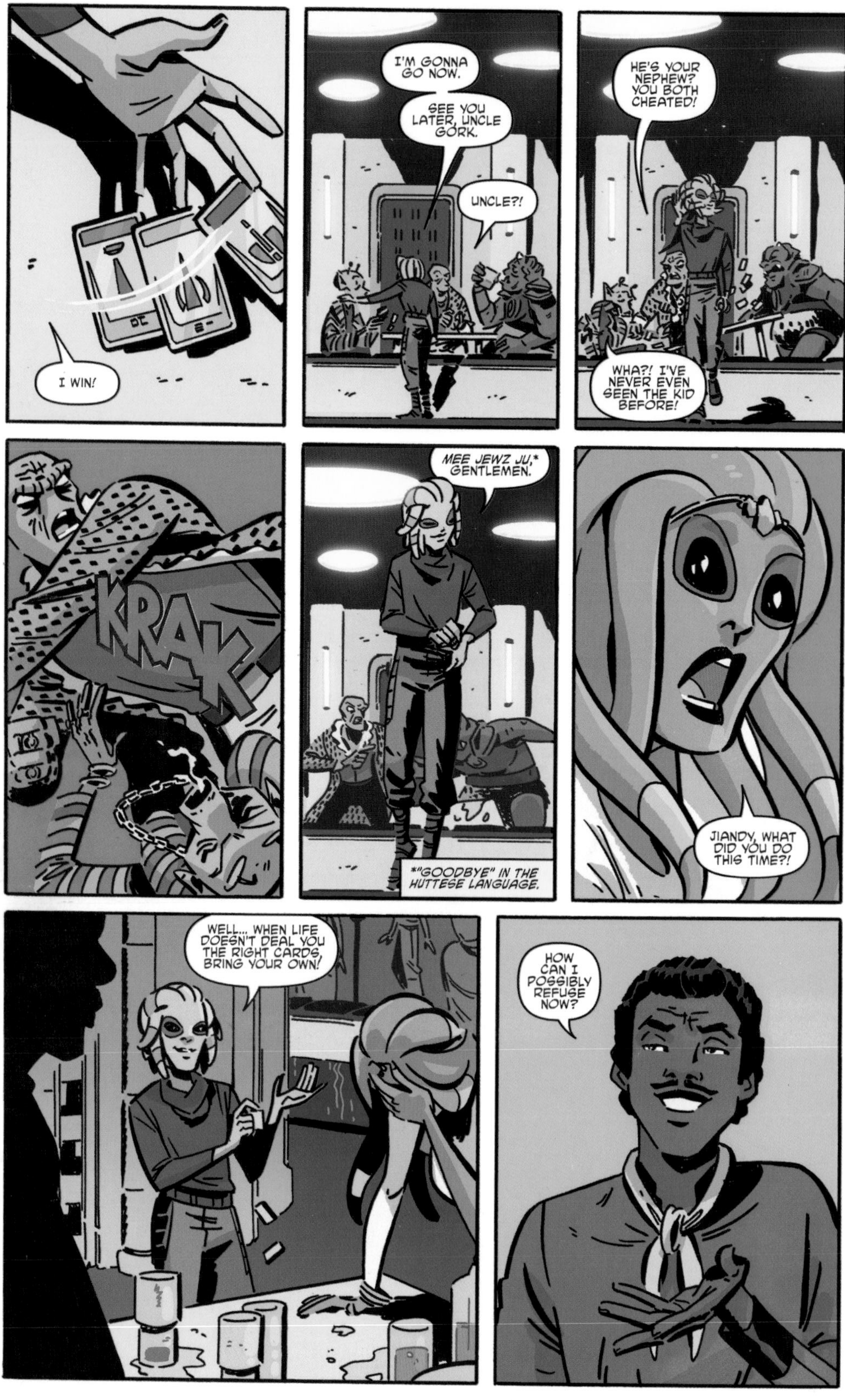
I WIN!
I'M GONNA GO NOW.
SEE YOU LATER, UNCLE GORK.
UNCLE?!
HE'S YOUR NEPHEW? YOU BOTH CHEATED!
WHA?! I'VE NEVER EVEN SEEN THE KID BEFORE!
KRAK
MEE JEWZ JU,* GENTLEMEN.
*"GOODBYE" IN THE HUTTESE LANGUAGE.
JIANDY, WHAT DID YOU DO THIS TIME?!
WELL... WHEN LIFE DOESN'T DEAL YOU THE RIGHT CARDS, BRING YOUR OWN!
HOW CAN I POSSIBLY REFUSE NOW?

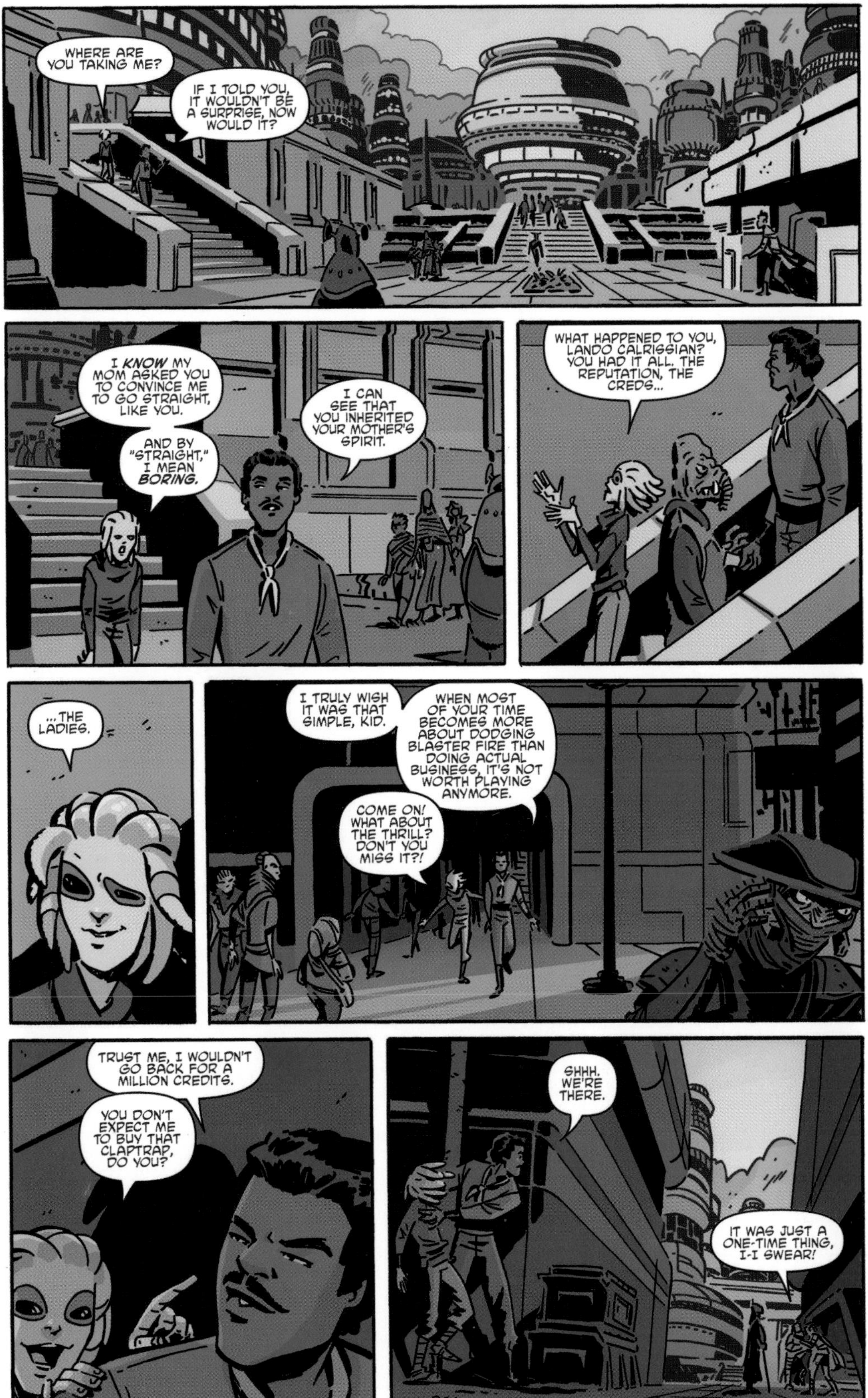
WHERE ARE YOU TAKING ME?
IF I TOLD YOU, IT WOULDN'T BE A SURPRISE, NOW WOULD IT?
I KNOW MY MOM ASKED YOU TO CONVINCE ME TO GO STRAIGHT, LIKE YOU.
AND BY "STRAIGHT," I MEAN BORING.
I CAN SEE THAT YOU INHERITED YOUR MOTHER'S SPIRIT.
WHAT HAPPENED TO YOU, LANDO CALRISSIAN? YOU HAD IT ALL. THE REPUTATION, THE CREDS...
...THE LADIES.
I TRULY WISH IT WAS THAT SIMPLE, KID.
WHEN MOST OF YOUR TIME BECOMES MORE ABOUT DODGING BLASTER FIRE THAN DOING ACTUAL BUSINESS, IT'S NOT WORTH PLAYING ANYMORE.
COME ON! WHAT ABOUT THE THRILL? DON'T YOU MISS IT?!
TRUST ME, I WOULDN'T GO BACK FOR A MILLION CREDITS.
YOU DON'T EXPECT ME TO BUY THAT CLAPTRAP, DO YOU?
SHHH. WE'RE THERE.
IT WAS JUST A ONE-TIME THING, I-I SWEAR!

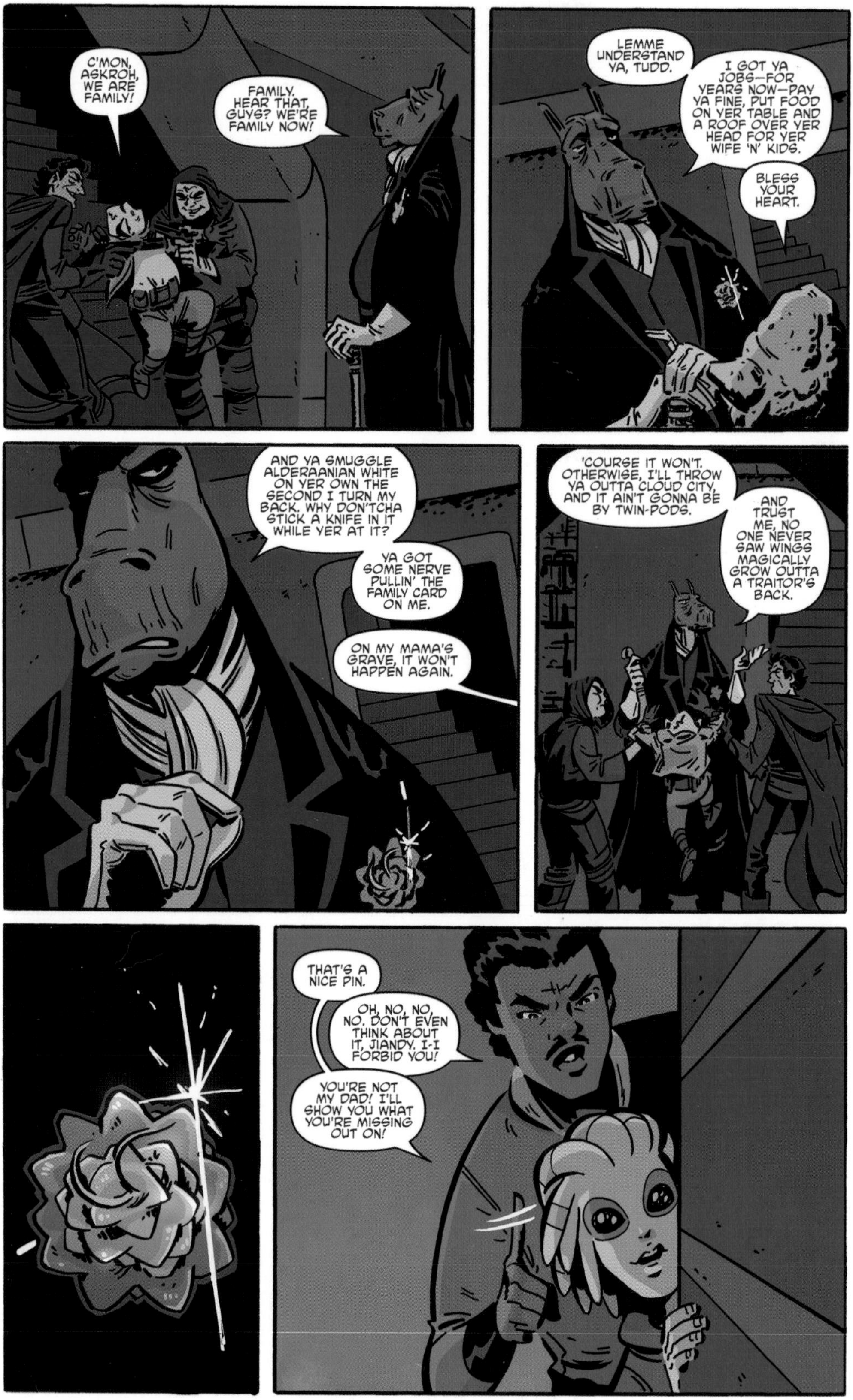
C'MON, ASKROH, WE ARE FAMILY!
FAMILY. HEAR THAT, GUYS? WE'RE FAMILY NOW!
LEMME UNDERSTAND YA, TUDD.
I GOT YA JOBS—FOR YEARS NOW—PAY YA FINE, PUT FOOD ON YER TABLE AND A ROOF OVER YER HEAD FOR YER WIFE 'N' KIDS.
BLESS YOUR HEART.
AND YA SMUGGLE ALDERAANIAN WHITE ON YER OWN THE SECOND I TURN MY BACK. WHY DON'TCHA STICK A KNIFE IN IT WHILE YER AT IT?
YA GOT SOME NERVE PULLIN' THE FAMILY CARD ON ME.
ON MY MAMA'S GRAVE, IT WON'T HAPPEN AGAIN.
'COURSE IT WON'T. OTHERWISE, I'LL THROW YA OUTTA CLOUD CITY, AND IT AIN'T GONNA BE BY TWIN-PODS.
AND TRUST ME, NO ONE NEVER SAW WINGS MAGICALLY GROW OUTTA A TRAITOR'S BACK.
THAT'S A NICE PIN.
OH, NO, NO, NO. DON'T EVEN THINK ABOUT IT, JIANDY. I-I FORBID YOU!
YOU'RE NOT MY DAD! I'LL SHOW YOU WHAT YOU'RE MISSING OUT ON!

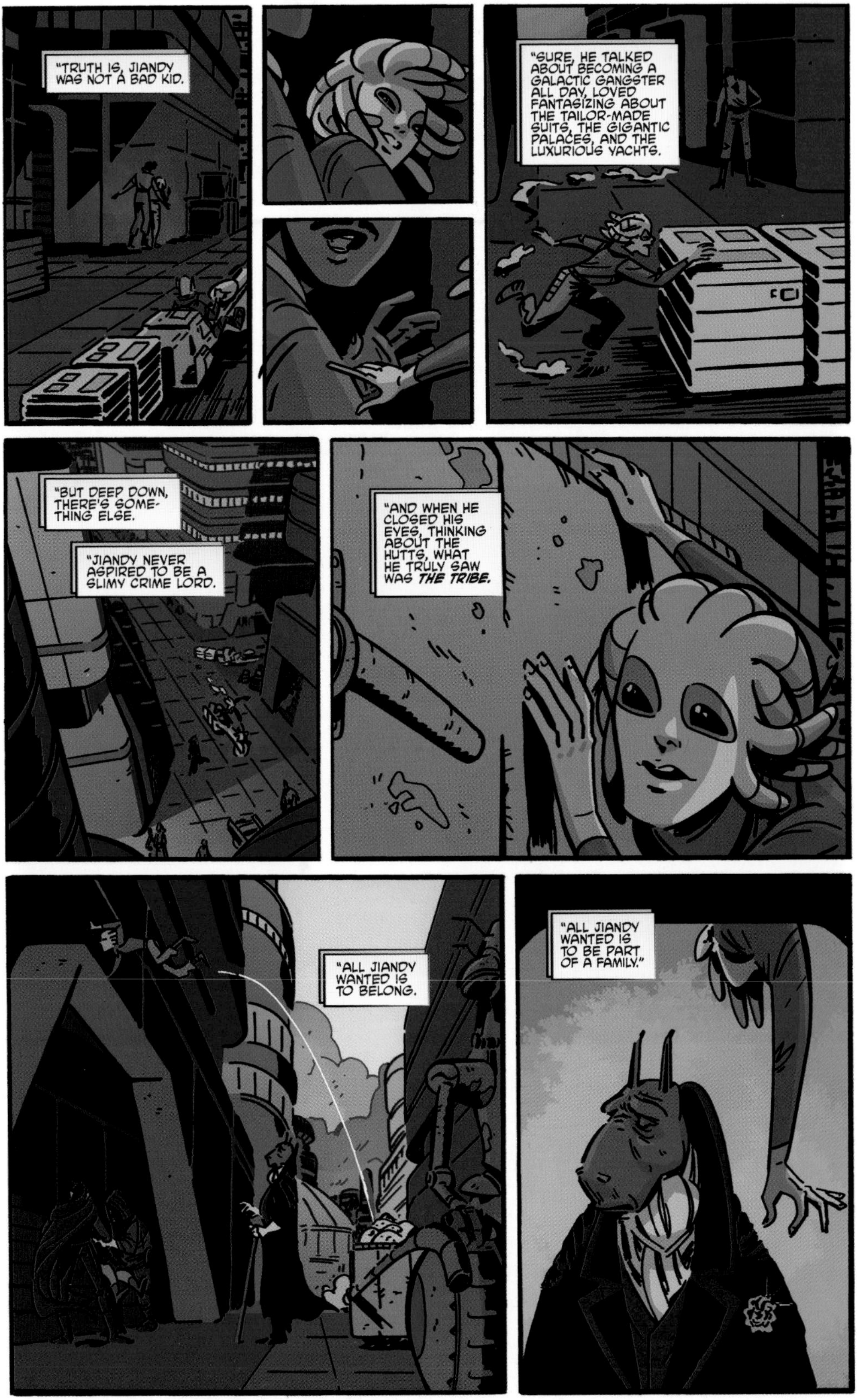
"TRUTH IS, JIANDY WAS NOT A BAD KID.
"SURE, HE TALKED ABOUT BECOMING A GALACTIC GANGSTER ALL DAY, LOVED FANTASIZING ABOUT THE TAILOR-MADE SUITS, THE GIGANTIC PALACES, AND THE LUXURIOUS YACHTS.
"BUT DEEP DOWN, THERE'S SOME-THING ELSE.
"JIANDY NEVER ASPIRED TO BE A SLIMY CRIME LORD.
"AND WHEN HE CLOSED HIS EYES, THINKING ABOUT THE HUTTS, WHAT HE TRULY SAW WAS THE TRIBE.
"ALL JIANDY WANTED IS TO BELONG.
"ALL JIANDY WANTED IS TO BE PART OF A FAMILY."

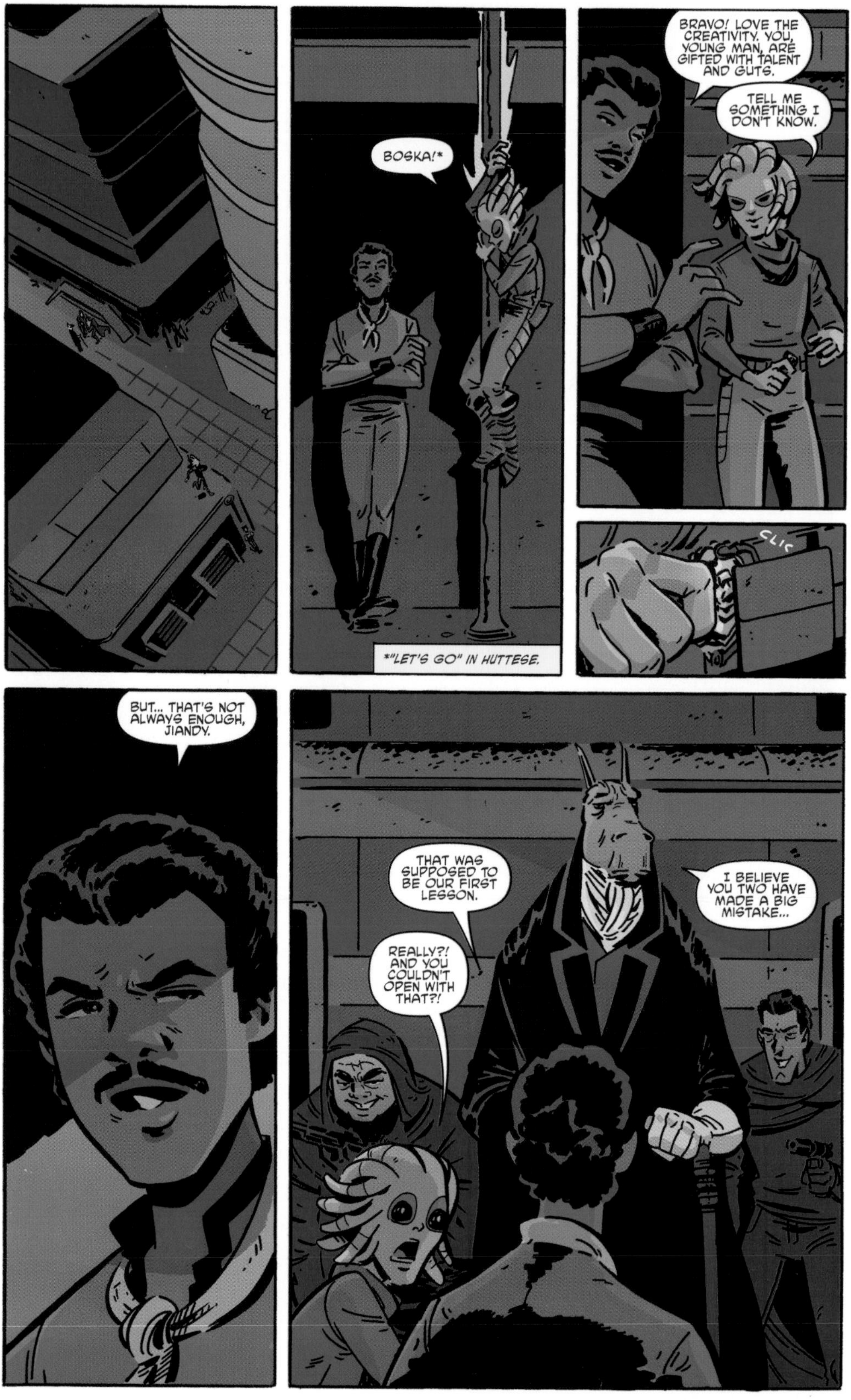
BOSKA!*
*"LET'S GO" IN HUTTESE.
BRAVO! LOVE THE CREATIVITY. YOU, YOUNG MAN, ARE GIFTED WITH TALENT AND GUTS.
TELL ME SOMETHING I DON'T KNOW.
CLIC
BUT... THAT'S NOT ALWAYS ENOUGH, JIANDY.
THAT WAS SUPPOSED TO BE OUR FIRST LESSON.
REALLY?! AND YOU COULDN'T OPEN WITH THAT?!
I BELIEVE YOU TWO HAVE MADE A BIG MISTAKE...

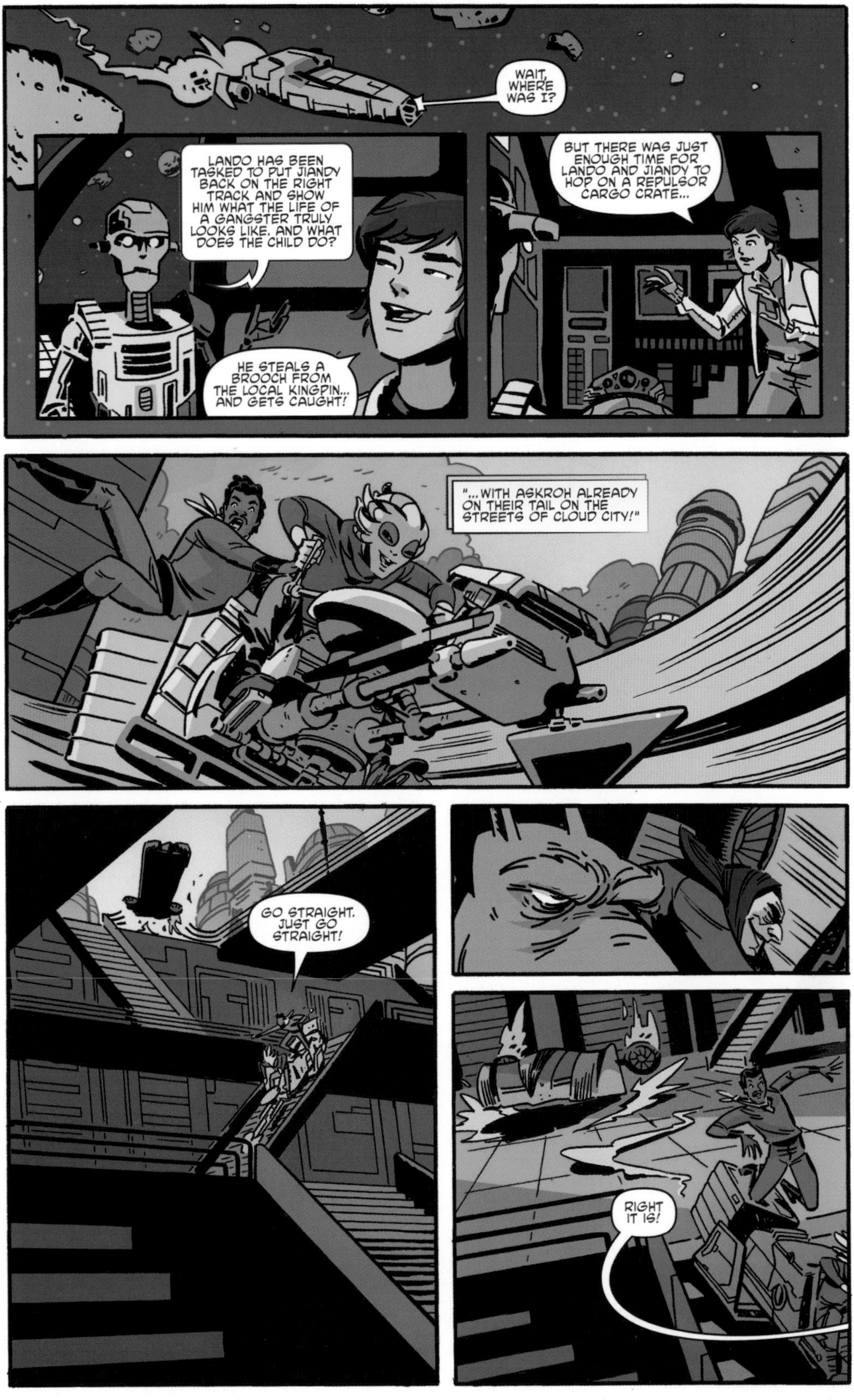
WAIT, WHERE WAS I?
LANDO HAS BEEN TASKED TO PUT JIANDY BACK ON THE RIGHT TRACK AND SHOW HIM WHAT THE LIFE OF A GANGSTER TRULY LOOKS LIKE. AND WHAT DOES THE CHILD DO?
HE STEALS A BROOCH FROM THE LOCAL KINGPIN... AND GETS CAUGHT!
BUT THERE WAS JUST ENOUGH TIME FOR LANDO AND JIANDY TO HOP ON A REPULSOR CARGO CRATE...
"...WITH ASKROH ALREADY ON THEIR TAIL ON THE STREETS OF CLOUD CITY!"
GO STRAIGHT. JUST GO STRAIGHT!
RIGHT IT IS!

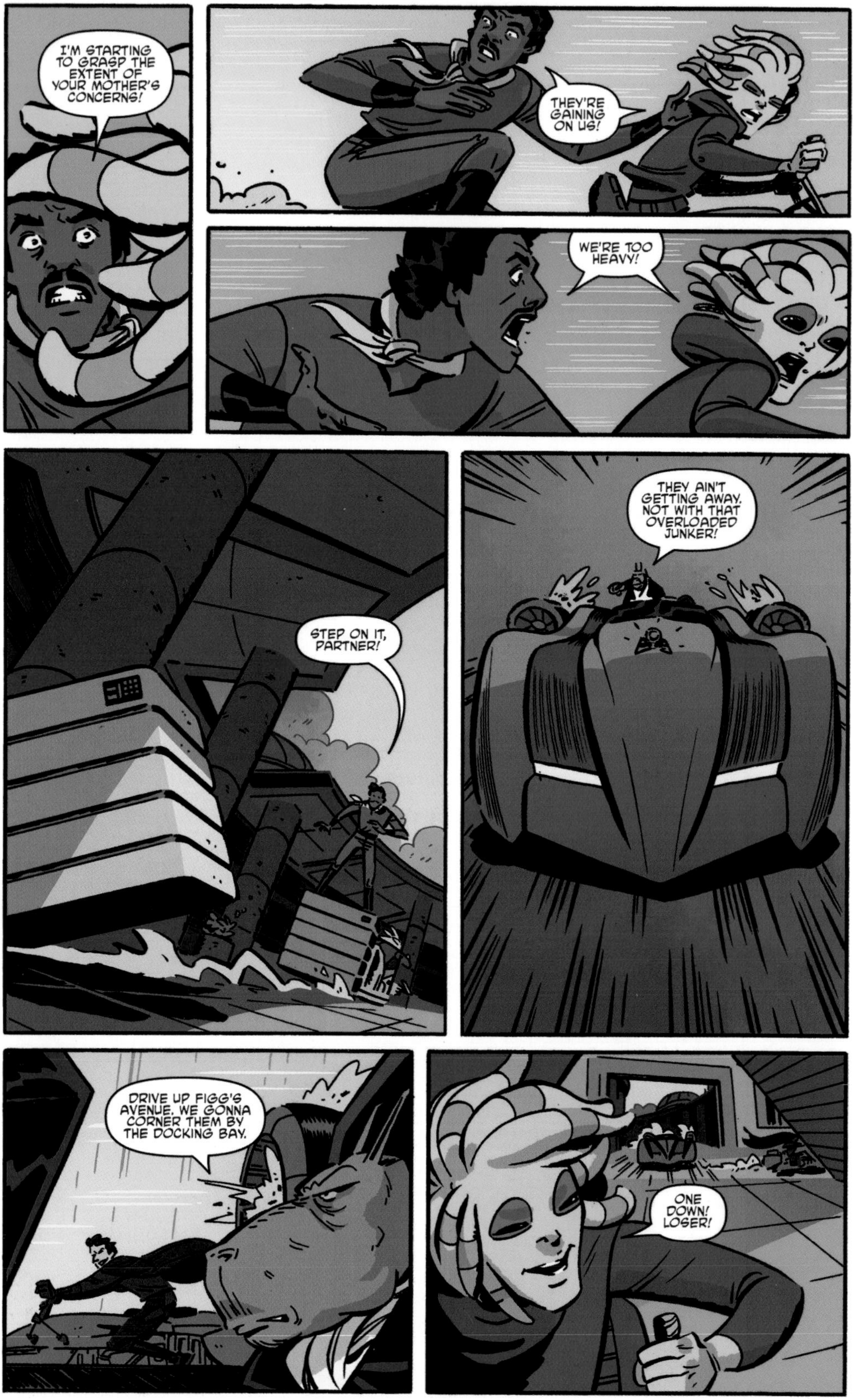
I'M STARTING TO GRASP THE EXTENT OF YOUR MOTHER'S CONCERNS!
THEY'RE GAINING ON US!
WE'RE TOO HEAVY!
STEP ON IT, PARTNER!
THEY AIN'T GETTING AWAY. NOT WITH THAT OVERLOADED JUNKER!
DRIVE UP FIGG'S AVENUE. WE GONNA CORNER THEM BY THE DOCKING BAY.
ONE DOWN! LOSER!

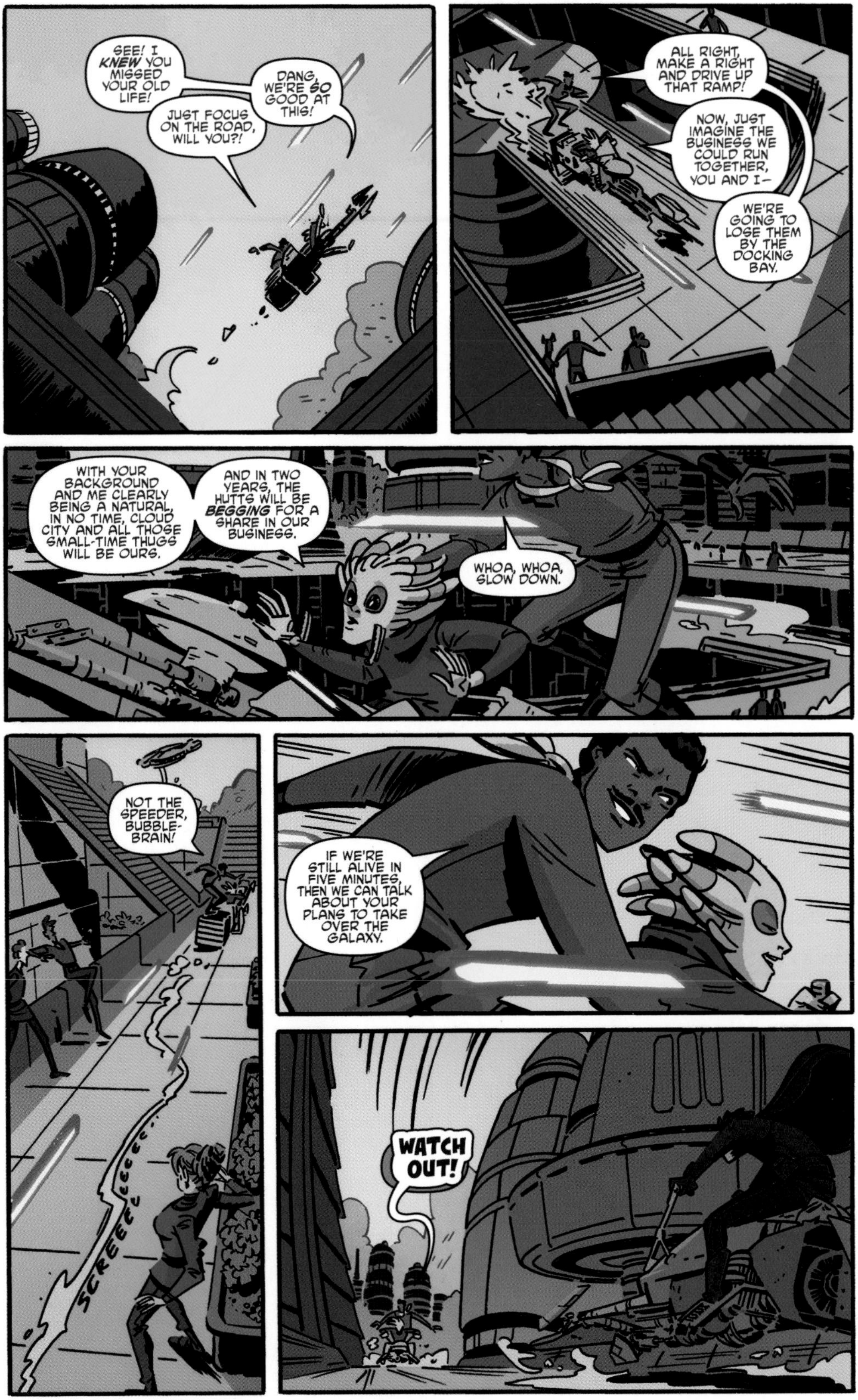

SEE! I *KNEW* YOU MISSED YOUR OLD LIFE!
DANG, WE'RE *SO* GOOD AT THIS!
JUST FOCUS ON THE ROAD, WILL YOU?!
ALL RIGHT, MAKE A RIGHT AND DRIVE UP THAT RAMP!
NOW, JUST IMAGINE THE BUSINESS WE COULD RUN TOGETHER, YOU AND I—
WE'RE GOING TO LOSE THEM BY THE DOCKING BAY.
WITH YOUR BACKGROUND AND ME CLEARLY BEING A NATURAL, IN NO TIME, CLOUD CITY AND ALL THOSE SMALL-TIME THUGS WILL BE OURS.
AND IN TWO YEARS, THE HUTTS WILL BE *BEGGING* FOR A SHARE IN OUR BUSINESS.
WHOA, WHOA, SLOW DOWN.
NOT THE SPEEDER, BUBBLE-BRAIN!
SCREEEEeeeee...
IF WE'RE STILL ALIVE IN FIVE MINUTES, THEN WE CAN TALK ABOUT YOUR PLANS TO TAKE OVER THE GALAXY.
WATCH OUT!

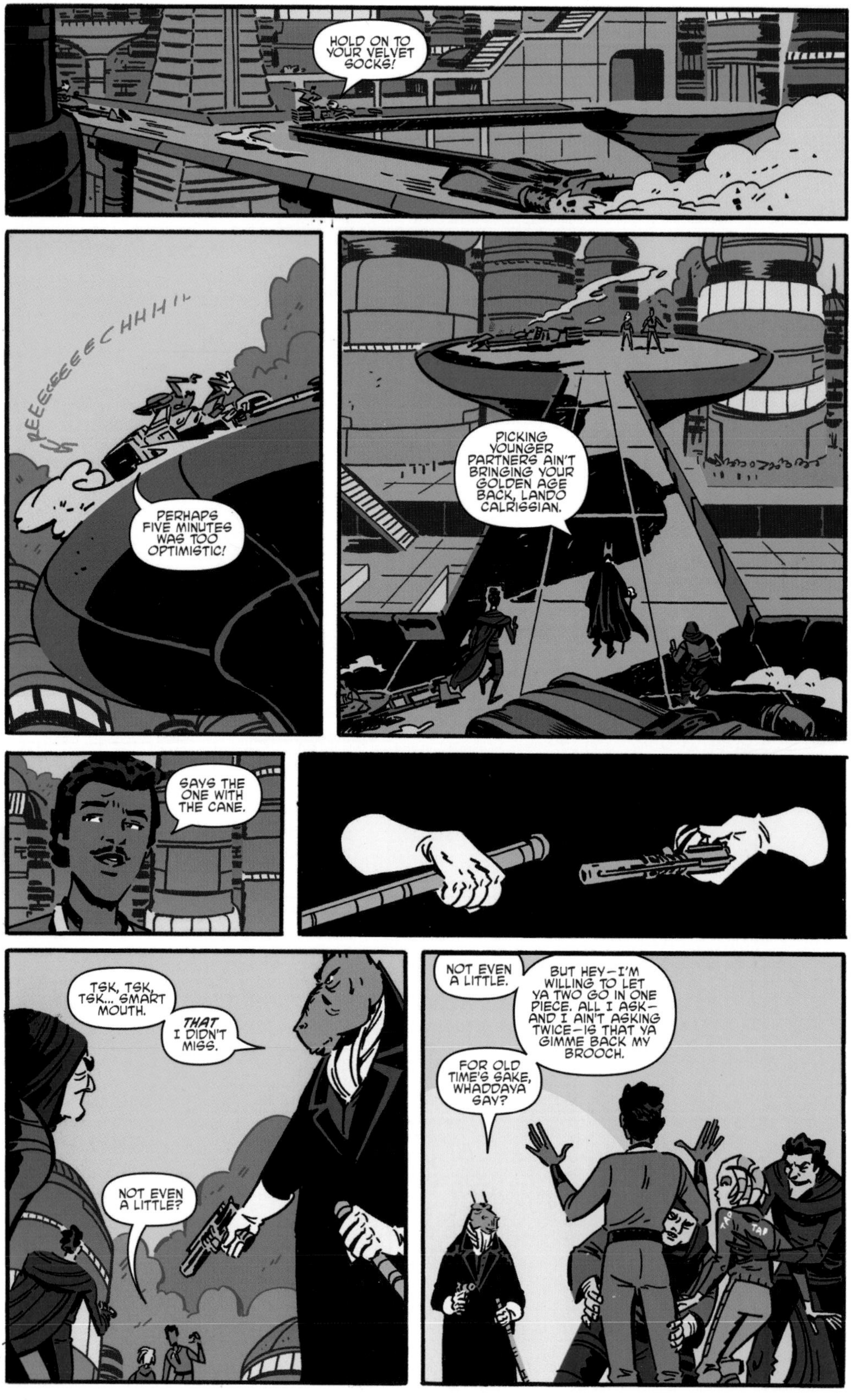
HOLD ON TO YOUR VELVET SOCKS!
KREEEEEEEECHHHH!!
PERHAPS FIVE MINUTES WAS TOO OPTIMISTIC!
PICKING YOUNGER PARTNERS AIN'T BRINGING YOUR GOLDEN AGE BACK, LANDO CALRISSIAN.
SAYS THE ONE WITH THE CANE.
TSK, TSK, TSK... SMART MOUTH.
THAT I DIDN'T MISS.
NOT EVEN A LITTLE?
NOT EVEN A LITTLE.
BUT HEY—I'M WILLING TO LET YA TWO GO IN ONE PIECE. ALL I ASK—AND I AIN'T ASKING TWICE—IS THAT YA GIMME BACK MY BROOCH.
FOR OLD TIME'S SAKE, WHADDAYA SAY?
TAP
TAP

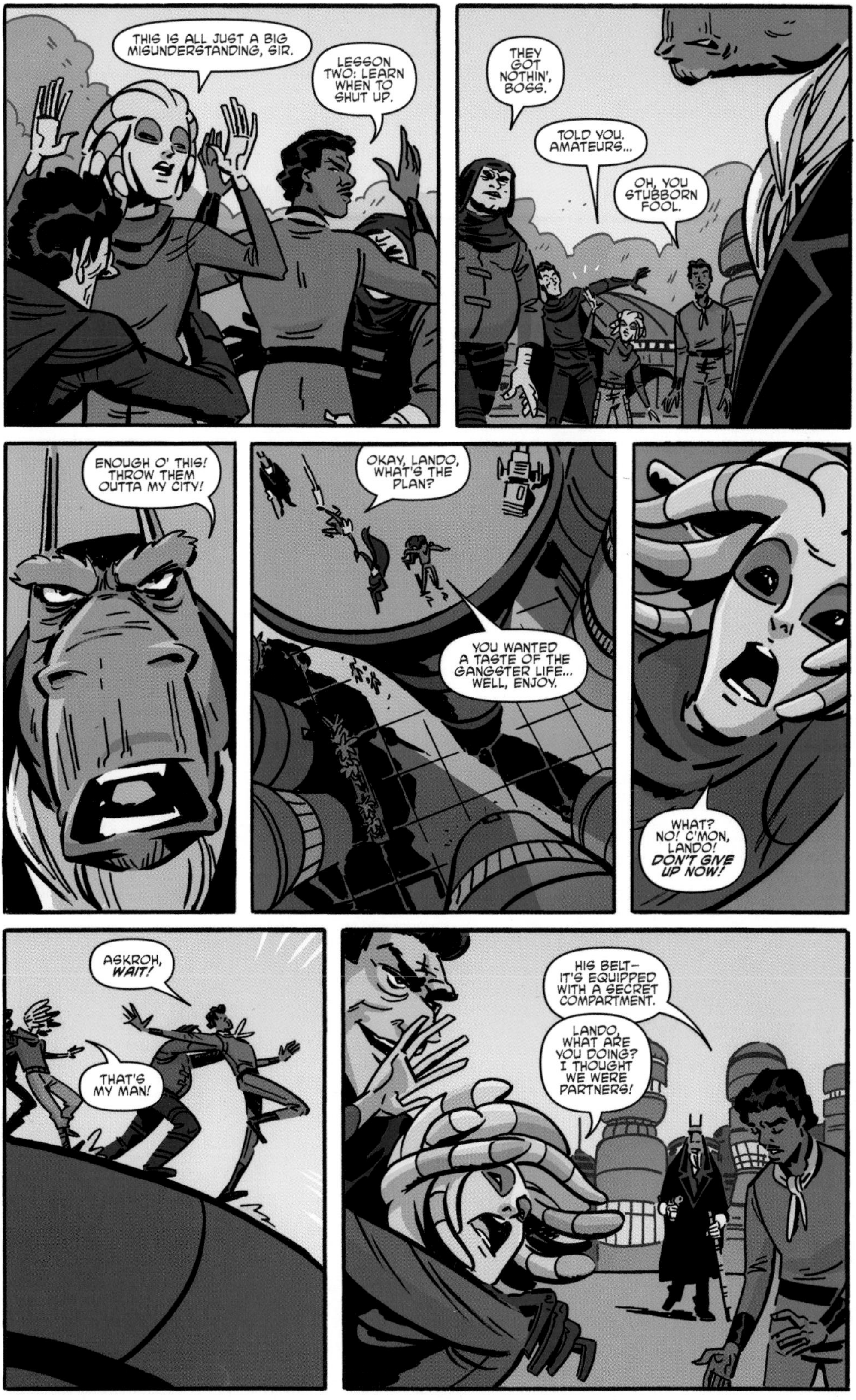
THIS IS ALL JUST A BIG MISUNDERSTANDING, SIR.
LESSON TWO: LEARN WHEN TO SHUT UP.
THEY GOT NOTHIN', BOSS.
TOLD YOU. AMATEURS...
OH, YOU STUBBORN FOOL.
ENOUGH O' THIS! THROW THEM OUTTA MY CITY!
OKAY, LANDO, WHAT'S THE PLAN?
YOU WANTED A TASTE OF THE GANGSTER LIFE... WELL, ENJOY.
WHAT? NO! C'MON, LANDO! DON'T GIVE UP NOW!
ASKROH, WAIT!
THAT'S MY MAN!
HIS BELT— IT'S EQUIPPED WITH A SECRET COMPARTMENT.
LANDO, WHAT ARE YOU DOING? I THOUGHT WE WERE PARTNERS!

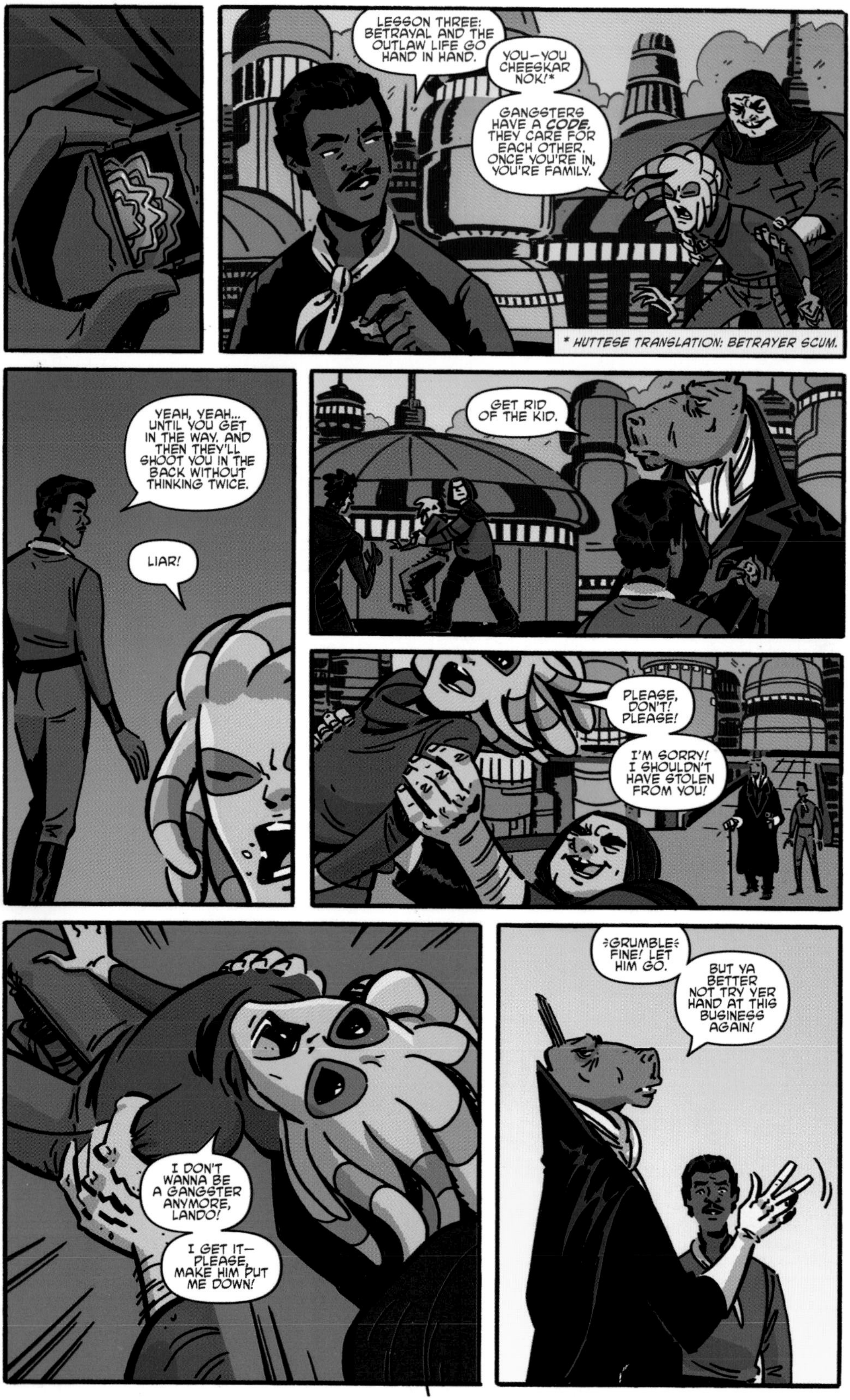
LESSON THREE: BETRAYAL AND THE OUTLAW LIFE GO HAND IN HAND.
YOU—YOU CHEESKAR NOK!*
GANGSTERS HAVE A CODE. THEY CARE FOR EACH OTHER. ONCE YOU'RE IN, YOU'RE FAMILY.
* HUTTESE TRANSLATION: BETRAYER SCUM.
YEAH, YEAH... UNTIL YOU GET IN THE WAY. AND THEN THEY'LL SHOOT YOU IN THE BACK WITHOUT THINKING TWICE.
LIAR!
GET RID OF THE KID.
PLEASE, DON'T! PLEASE!
I'M SORRY! I SHOULDN'T HAVE STOLEN FROM YOU!
I DON'T WANNA BE A GANGSTER ANYMORE, LANDO!
I GET IT— PLEASE, MAKE HIM PUT ME DOWN!
GRUMBLE FINE! LET HIM GO.
BUT YA BETTER NOT TRY YER HAND AT THIS BUSINESS AGAIN!

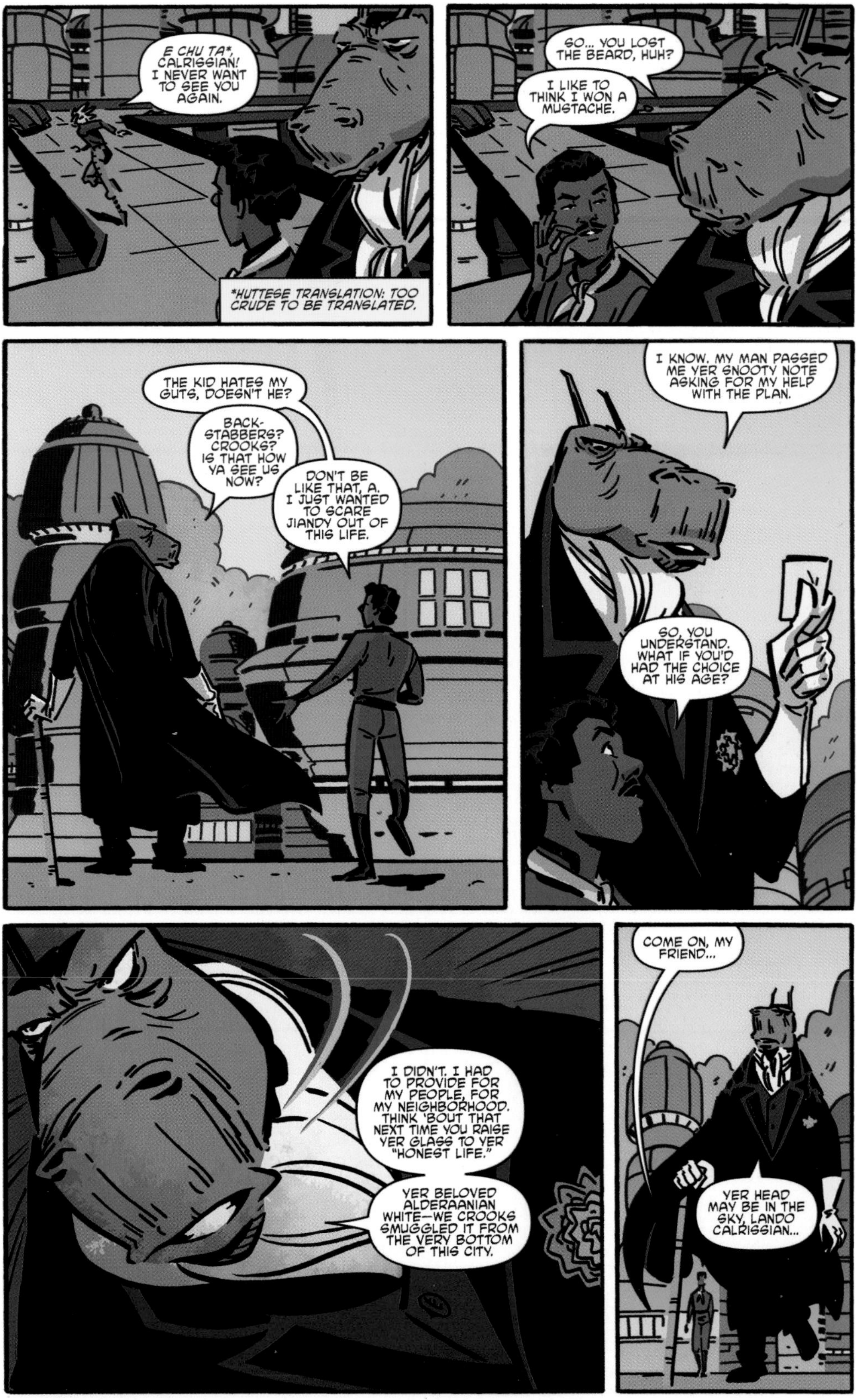
E CHU TA*, CALRISSIAN! I NEVER WANT TO SEE YOU AGAIN.
*HUTTESE TRANSLATION: TOO CRUDE TO BE TRANSLATED.
SO... YOU LOST THE BEARD, HUH?
I LIKE TO THINK I WON A MUSTACHE.
THE KID HATES MY GUTS, DOESN'T HE?
BACK-STABBERS? CROOKS? IS THAT HOW YA SEE US NOW?
DON'T BE LIKE THAT, A. I JUST WANTED TO SCARE JIANDY OUT OF THIS LIFE.
I KNOW. MY MAN PASSED ME YER SNOOTY NOTE ASKING FOR MY HELP WITH THE PLAN.
SO, YOU UNDERSTAND. WHAT IF YOU'D HAD THE CHOICE AT HIS AGE?
I DIDN'T. I HAD TO PROVIDE FOR MY PEOPLE, FOR MY NEIGHBORHOOD. THINK 'BOUT THAT NEXT TIME YOU RAISE YER GLASS TO YER "HONEST LIFE."
YER BELOVED ALDERAANIAN WHITE—WE CROOKS SMUGGLED IT FROM THE VERY BOTTOM OF THIS CITY.
COME ON, MY FRIEND...
YER HEAD MAY BE IN THE SKY, LANDO CALRISSIAN...

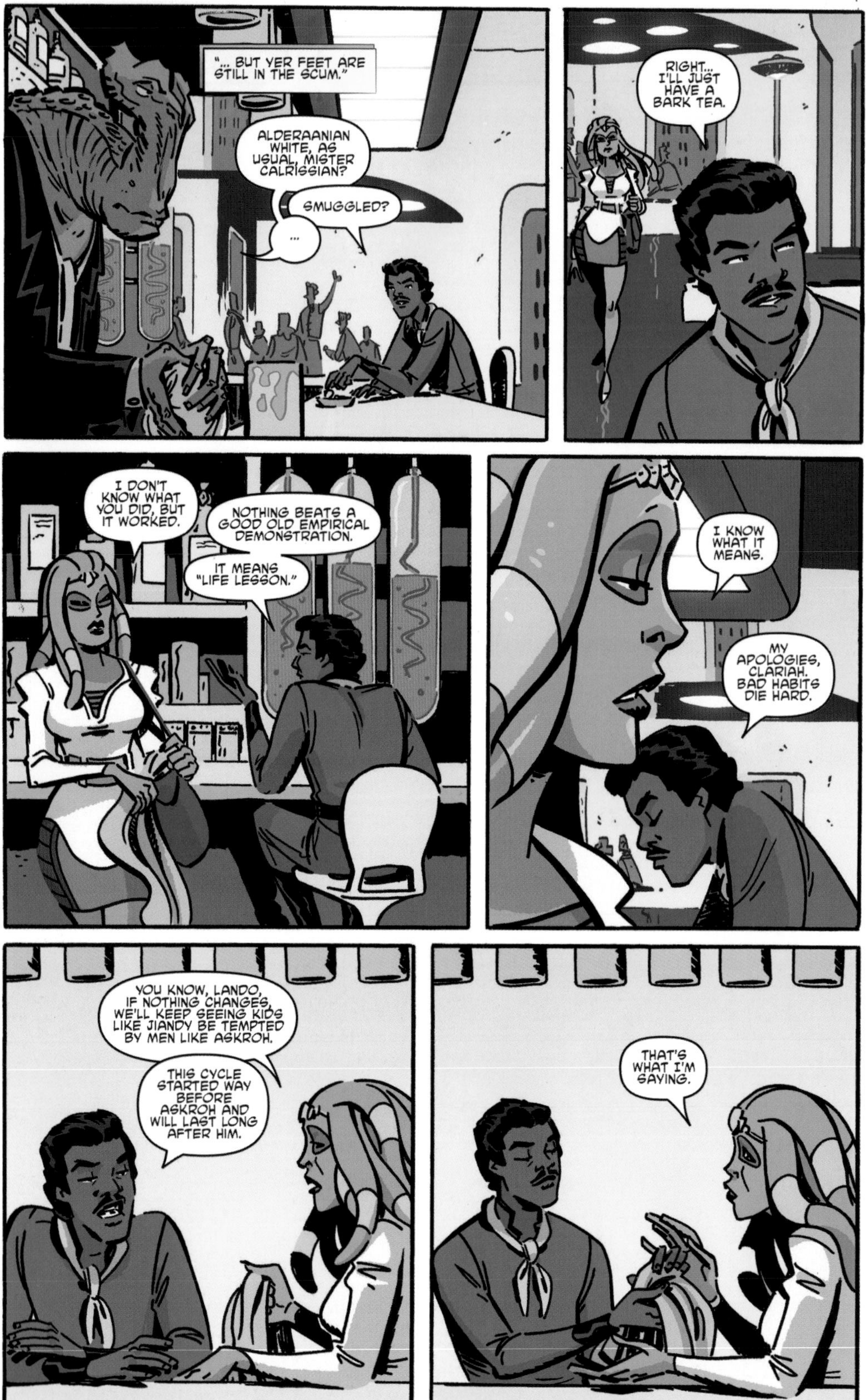
"... BUT YER FEET ARE STILL IN THE SCUM."
ALDERAANIAN WHITE, AS USUAL, MISTER CALRISSIAN?
SMUGGLED?
...
RIGHT... I'LL JUST HAVE A BARK TEA.
I DON'T KNOW WHAT YOU DID, BUT IT WORKED.
NOTHING BEATS A GOOD OLD EMPIRICAL DEMONSTRATION.
IT MEANS "LIFE LESSON."
I KNOW WHAT IT MEANS.
MY APOLOGIES, CLARIAH. BAD HABITS DIE HARD.
YOU KNOW, LANDO, IF NOTHING CHANGES, WE'LL KEEP SEEING KIDS LIKE JIANDY BE TEMPTED BY MEN LIKE ASKROH.
THIS CYCLE STARTED WAY BEFORE ASKROH AND WILL LAST LONG AFTER HIM.
THAT'S WHAT I'M SAYING.

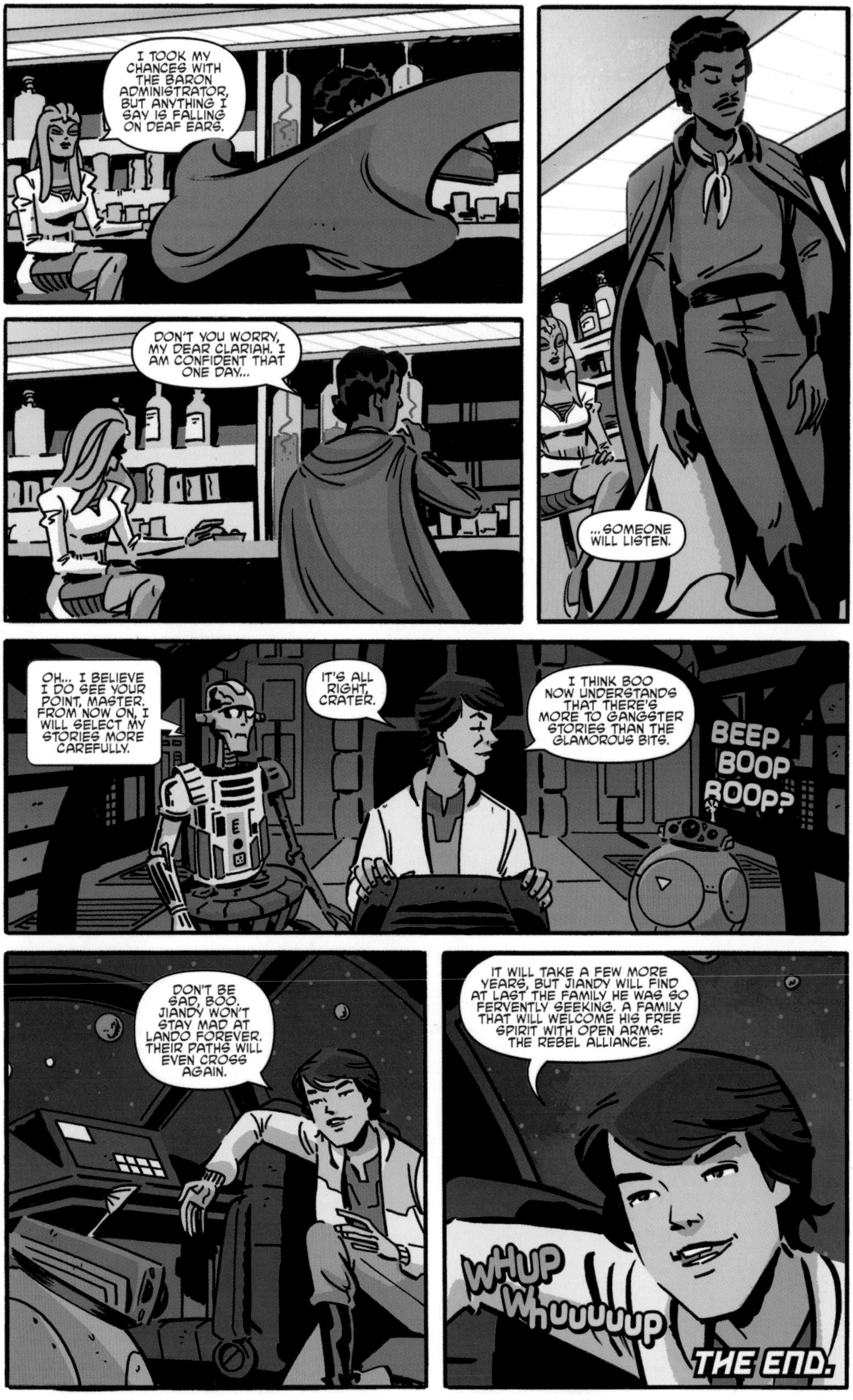

I TOOK MY CHANCES WITH THE BARON ADMINISTRATOR, BUT ANYTHING I SAY IS FALLING ON DEAF EARS.
DON'T YOU WORRY, MY DEAR CLARIAH. I AM CONFIDENT THAT ONE DAY...
...SOMEONE WILL LISTEN.
OH... I BELIEVE I DO SEE YOUR POINT, MASTER. FROM NOW ON, I WILL SELECT MY STORIES MORE CAREFULLY.
IT'S ALL RIGHT, CRATER.
I THINK BOO NOW UNDERSTANDS THAT THERE'S MORE TO GANGSTER STORIES THAN THE GLAMOROUS BITS.
BEEP BOOP BOOP?
DON'T BE SAD, BOO. JIANDY WON'T STAY MAD AT LANDO FOREVER. THEIR PATHS WILL EVEN CROSS AGAIN.
IT WILL TAKE A FEW MORE YEARS, BUT JIANDY WILL FIND AT LAST THE FAMILY HE WAS SO FERVENTLY SEEKING. A FAMILY THAT WILL WELCOME HIS FREE SPIRIT WITH OPEN ARMS: THE REBEL ALLIANCE.
WHUP
Whuuuuup
THE END.

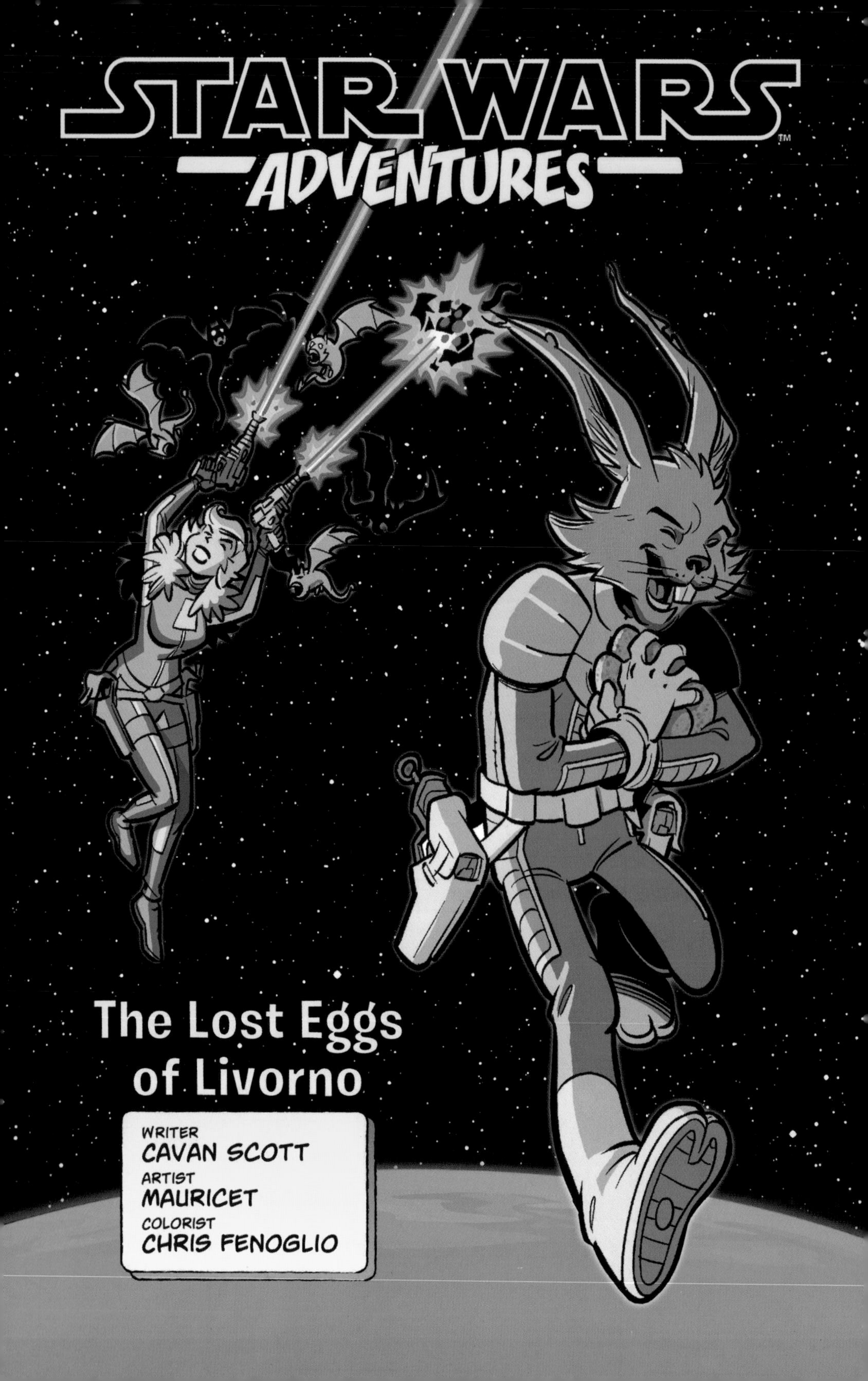
STAR WARS
ADVENTURES
The Lost Eggs of Livorno
WRITER
CAVAN SCOTT
ARTIST
MAURICET
COLORIST
CHRIS FENOGLIO

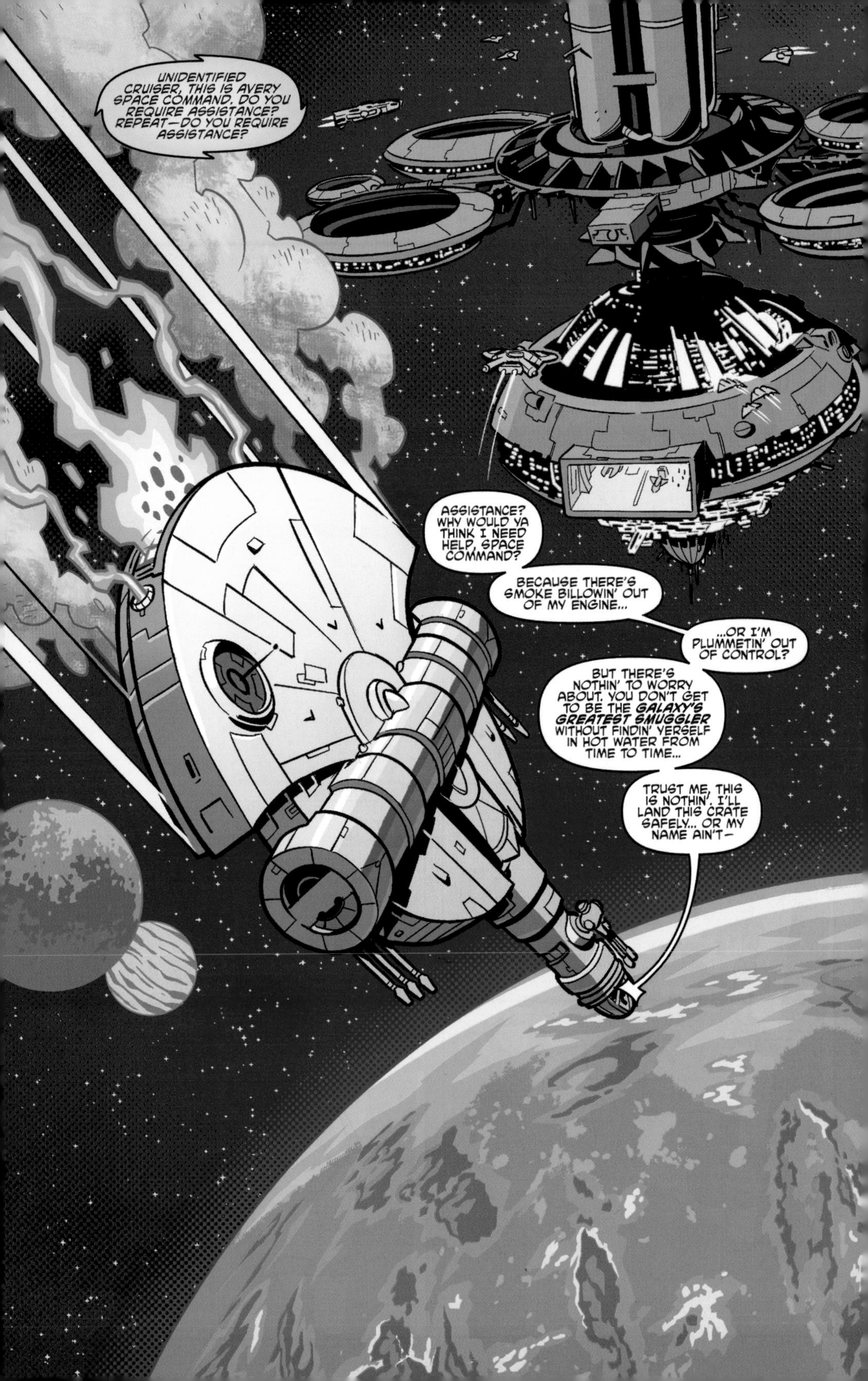
UNIDENTIFIED CRUISER, THIS IS AVERY SPACE COMMAND. DO YOU REQUIRE ASSISTANCE? REPEAT—DO YOU REQUIRE ASSISTANCE?
ASSISTANCE? WHY WOULD YA THINK I NEED HELP, SPACE COMMAND?
BECAUSE THERE'S SMOKE BILLOWIN' OUT OF MY ENGINE...
...OR I'M PLUMMETIN' OUT OF CONTROL?
BUT THERE'S NOTHIN' TO WORRY ABOUT. YOU DON'T GET TO BE THE GALAXY'S GREATEST SMUGGLER WITHOUT FINDIN' YERSELF IN HOT WATER FROM TIME TO TIME...
TRUST ME, THIS IS NOTHIN'. I'LL LAND THIS CRATE SAFELY... OR MY NAME AIN'T—

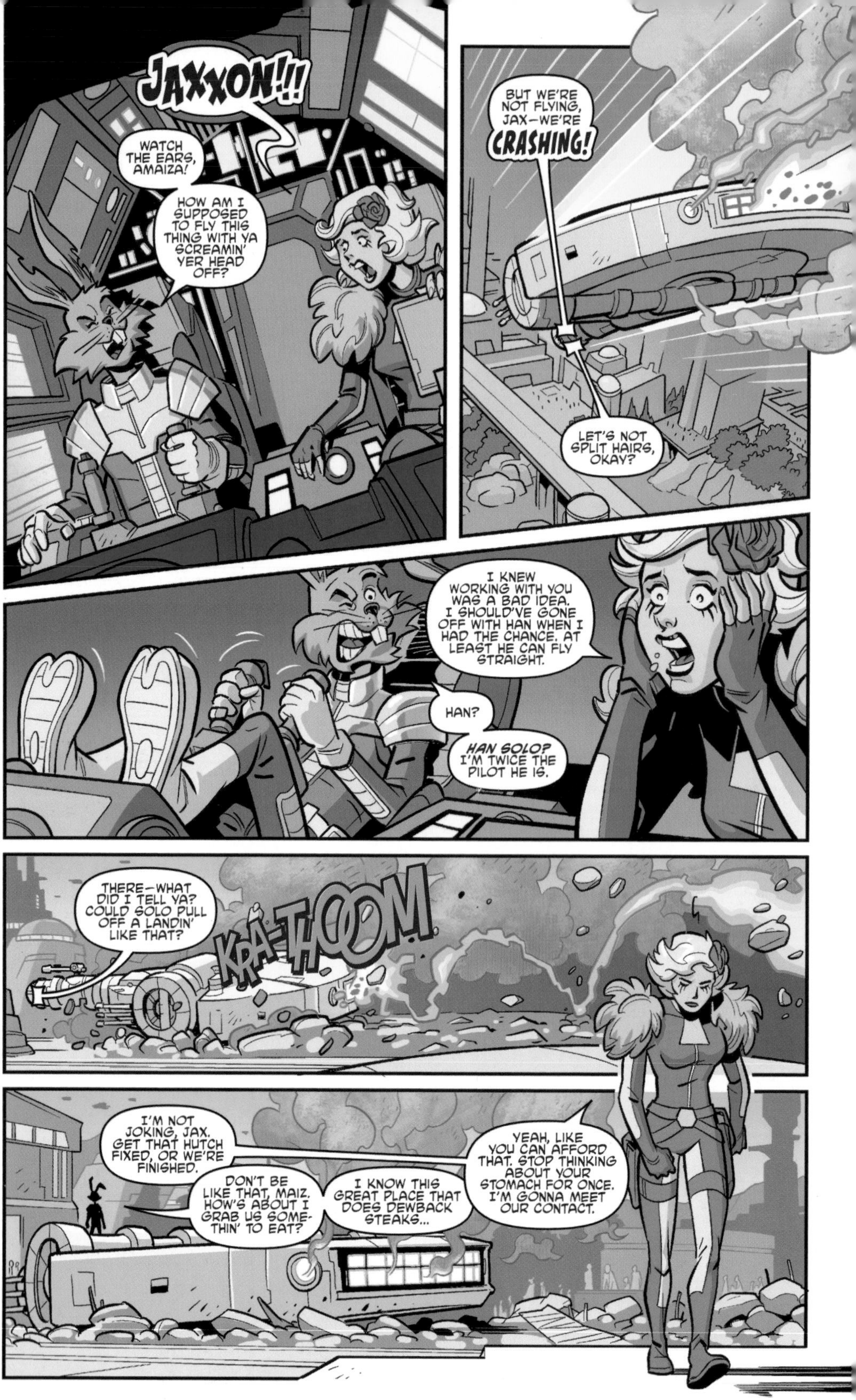
JAXXON!!!
WATCH THE EARS, AMAIZA!
HOW AM I SUPPOSED TO FLY THIS THING WITH YA SCREAMIN' YER HEAD OFF?
BUT WE'RE NOT FLYING, JAX—WE'RE CRASHING!
LET'S NOT SPLIT HAIRS, OKAY?
I KNEW WORKING WITH YOU WAS A BAD IDEA. I SHOULD'VE GONE OFF WITH HAN WHEN I HAD THE CHANCE. AT LEAST HE CAN FLY STRAIGHT.
HAN?
HAN SOLO? I'M TWICE THE PILOT HE IS.
THERE—WHAT DID I TELL YA? COULD SOLO PULL OFF A LANDIN' LIKE THAT?
KRA-THOOM!
I'M NOT JOKING, JAX. GET THAT HUTCH FIXED, OR WE'RE FINISHED.
DON'T BE LIKE THAT, MAIZ. HOW'S ABOUT I GRAB US SOME-THIN' TO EAT?
I KNOW THIS GREAT PLACE THAT DOES DEWBACK STEAKS...
YEAH, LIKE YOU CAN AFFORD THAT. STOP THINKING ABOUT YOUR STOMACH FOR ONCE. I'M GONNA MEET OUR CONTACT.

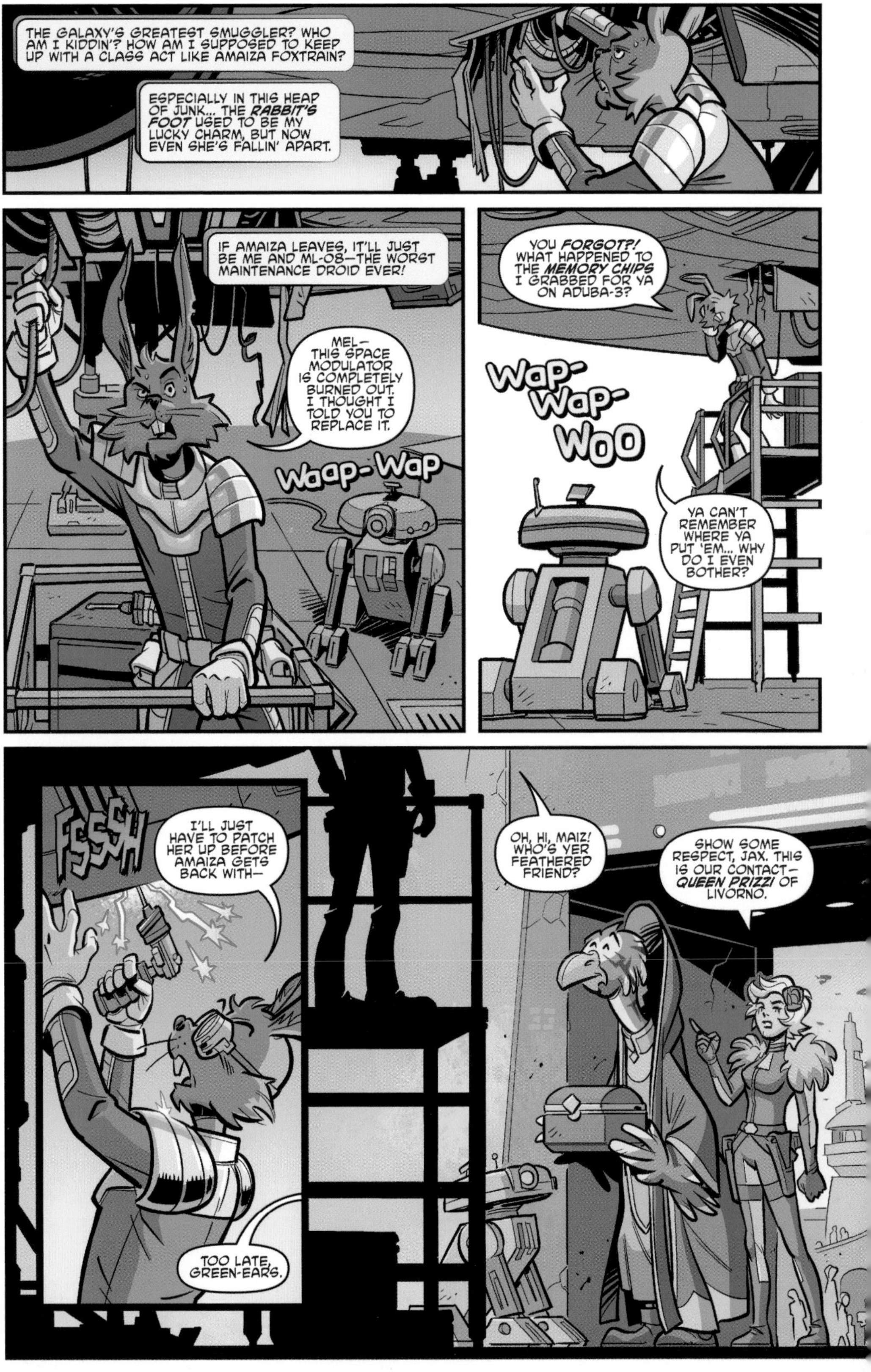
THE GALAXY'S GREATEST SMUGGLER? WHO AM I KIDDIN'? HOW AM I SUPPOSED TO KEEP UP WITH A CLASS ACT LIKE AMAIZA FOXTRAIN?
ESPECIALLY IN THIS HEAP OF JUNK... THE RABBIT'S FOOT USED TO BE MY LUCKY CHARM, BUT NOW EVEN SHE'S FALLIN' APART.
IF AMAIZA LEAVES, IT'LL JUST BE ME AND ML-08—THE WORST MAINTENANCE DROID EVER!
MEL— THIS SPACE MODULATOR IS COMPLETELY BURNED OUT. I THOUGHT I TOLD YOU TO REPLACE IT.
Waap-Wap
YOU FORGOT?! WHAT HAPPENED TO THE MEMORY CHIPS I GRABBED FOR YA ON ADUBA-3?
Wap-Wap-Woo
YA CAN'T REMEMBER WHERE YA PUT 'EM... WHY DO I EVEN BOTHER?
FSSSH
I'LL JUST HAVE TO PATCH HER UP BEFORE AMAIZA GETS BACK WITH—
TOO LATE, GREEN-EARS.
OH, HI, MAIZ! WHO'S YER FEATHERED FRIEND?
SHOW SOME RESPECT, JAX. THIS IS OUR CONTACT—QUEEN PRIZZI OF LIVORNO.

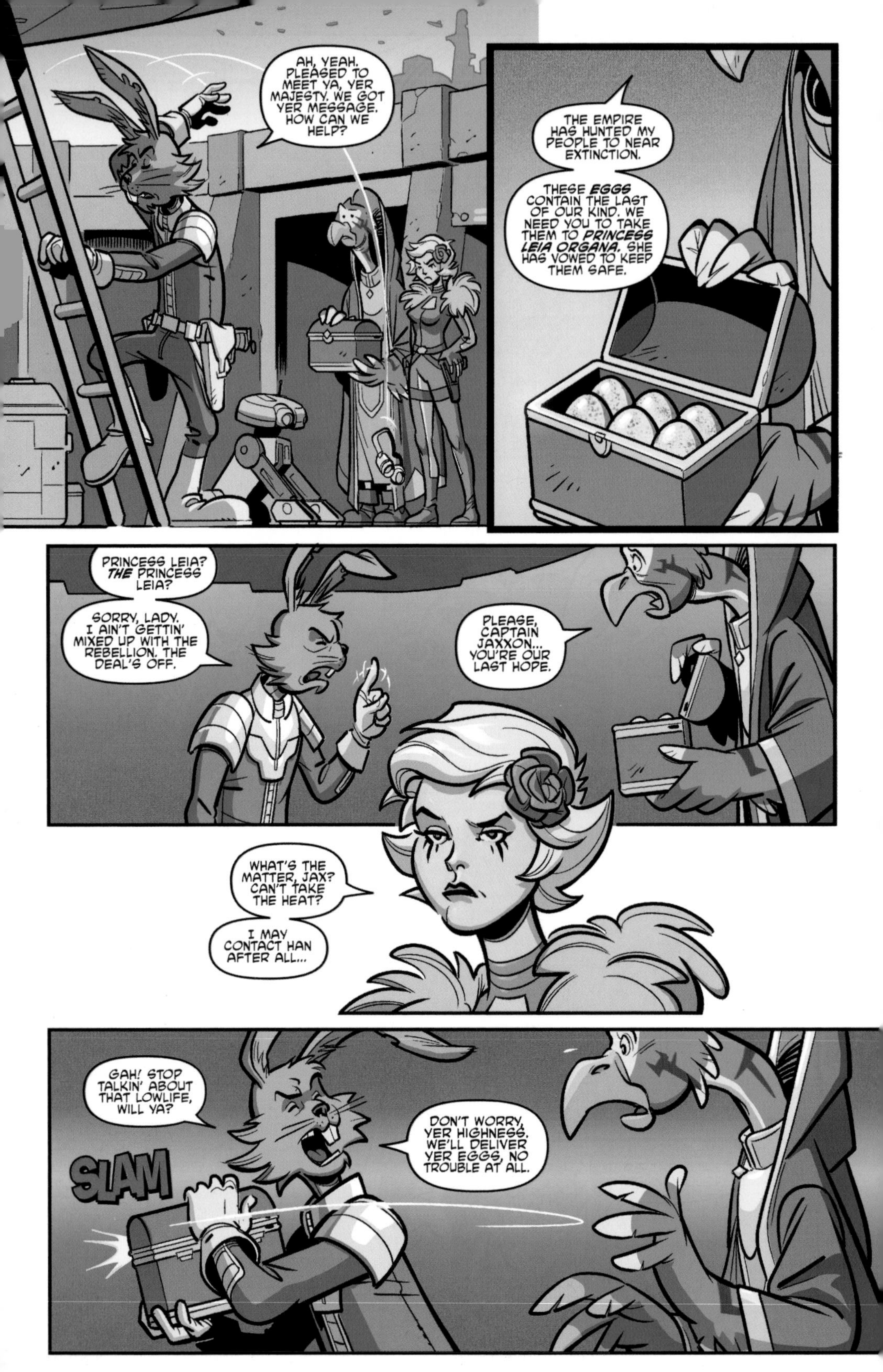
AH, YEAH. PLEASED TO MEET YA, YER MAJESTY. WE GOT YER MESSAGE. HOW CAN WE HELP?
THE EMPIRE HAS HUNTED MY PEOPLE TO NEAR EXTINCTION.
THESE EGGS CONTAIN THE LAST OF OUR KIND. WE NEED YOU TO TAKE THEM TO PRINCESS LEIA ORGANA. SHE HAS VOWED TO KEEP THEM SAFE.
PRINCESS LEIA? THE PRINCESS LEIA?
SORRY, LADY. I AIN'T GETTIN' MIXED UP WITH THE REBELLION. THE DEAL'S OFF.
PLEASE, CAPTAIN JAXXON... YOU'RE OUR LAST HOPE.
WHAT'S THE MATTER, JAX? CAN'T TAKE THE HEAT?
I MAY CONTACT HAN AFTER ALL...
GAH! STOP TALKIN' ABOUT THAT LOWLIFE, WILL YA?
SLAM
DON'T WORRY, YER HIGHNESS. WE'LL DELIVER YER EGGS, NO TROUBLE AT ALL.

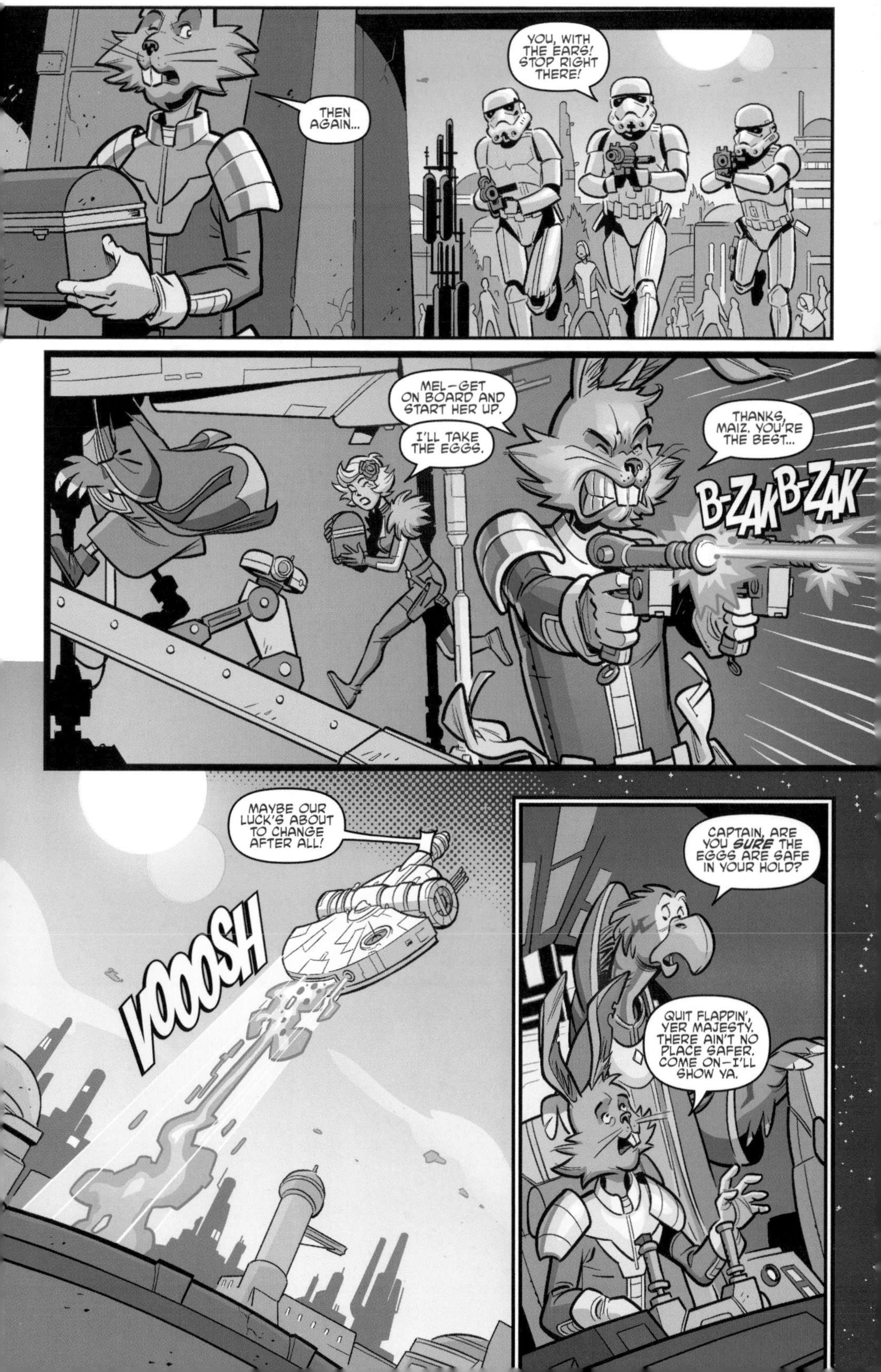
THEN AGAIN...
YOU, WITH THE EARS! STOP RIGHT THERE!
MEL—GET ON BOARD AND START HER UP.
I'LL TAKE THE EGGS.
THANKS, MAIZ. YOU'RE THE BEST...
B-ZAK B-ZAK
MAYBE OUR LUCK'S ABOUT TO CHANGE AFTER ALL!
VOOOSH
CAPTAIN, ARE YOU SURE THE EGGS ARE SAFE IN YOUR HOLD?
QUIT FLAPPIN', YER MAJESTY. THERE AIN'T NO PLACE SAFER. COME ON—I'LL SHOW YA.

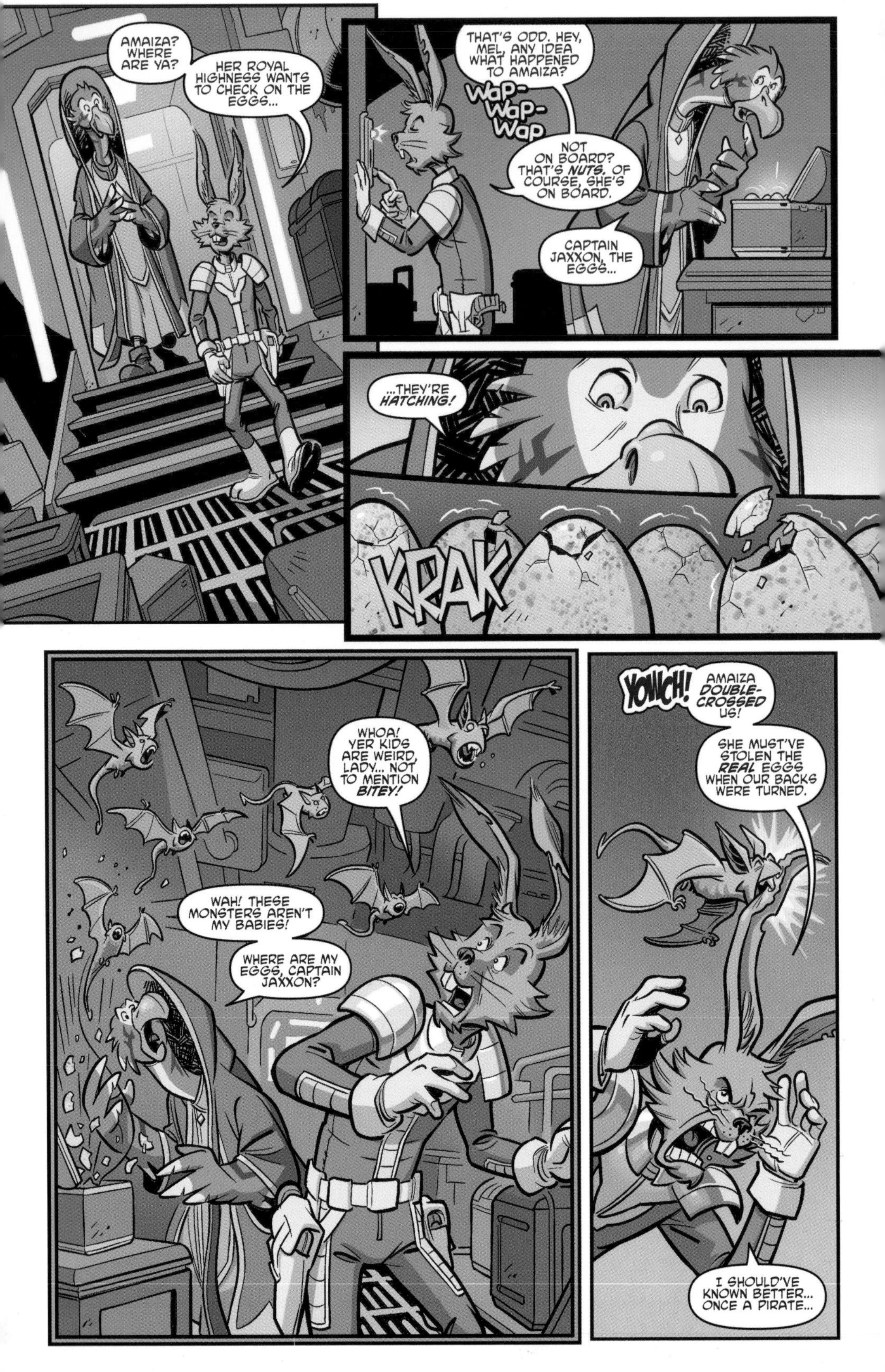
AMAIZA? WHERE ARE YA?
HER ROYAL HIGHNESS WANTS TO CHECK ON THE EGGS...
THAT'S ODD. HEY, MEL, ANY IDEA WHAT HAPPENED TO AMAIZA?
WAP-WAP-WAP
NOT ON BOARD? THAT'S NUTS, OF COURSE, SHE'S ON BOARD.
CAPTAIN JAXXON, THE EGGS...
...THEY'RE HATCHING!
KRAK
WHOA! YER KIDS ARE WEIRD, LADY... NOT TO MENTION BITEY!
WAH! THESE MONSTERS AREN'T MY BABIES!
WHERE ARE MY EGGS, CAPTAIN JAXXON?
YOWCH!
AMAIZA DOUBLE-CROSSED US!
SHE MUST'VE STOLEN THE REAL EGGS WHEN OUR BACKS WERE TURNED.
I SHOULD'VE KNOWN BETTER... ONCE A PIRATE...

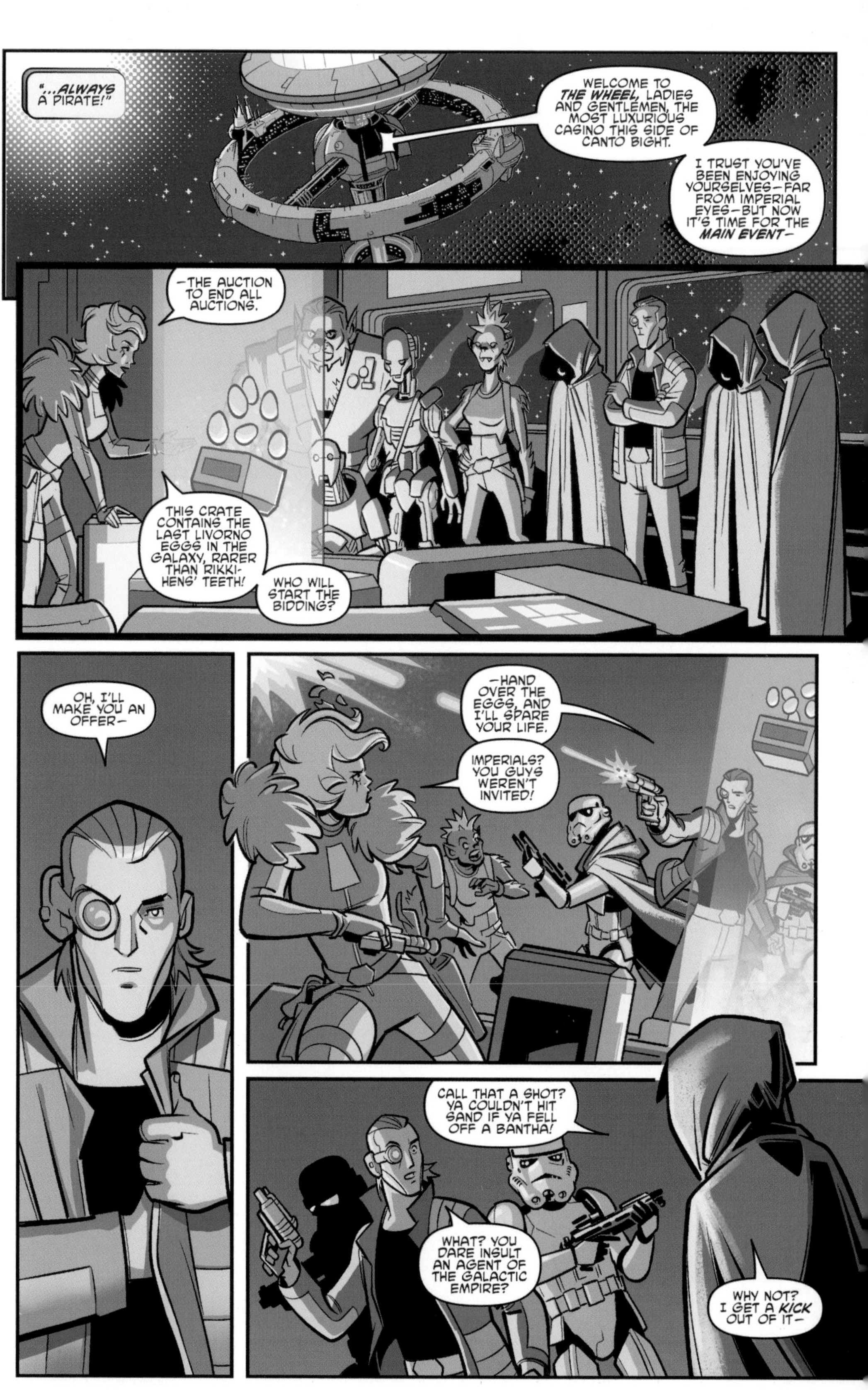
"...ALWAYS A PIRATE!"
WELCOME TO THE WHEEL, LADIES AND GENTLEMEN, THE MOST LUXURIOUS CASINO THIS SIDE OF CANTO BIGHT.
I TRUST YOU'VE BEEN ENJOYING YOURSELVES—FAR FROM IMPERIAL EYES—BUT NOW IT'S TIME FOR THE MAIN EVENT—
—THE AUCTION TO END ALL AUCTIONS.
THIS CRATE CONTAINS THE LAST LIVORNO EGGS IN THE GALAXY, RARER THAN RIKKI-HENS' TEETH!
WHO WILL START THE BIDDING?
OH, I'LL MAKE YOU AN OFFER—
—HAND OVER THE EGGS, AND I'LL SPARE YOUR LIFE.
IMPERIALS? YOU GUYS WEREN'T INVITED!
CALL THAT A SHOT? YA COULDN'T HIT SAND IF YA FELL OFF A BANTHA!
WHAT? YOU DARE INSULT AN AGENT OF THE GALACTIC EMPIRE?
WHY NOT? I GET A KICK OUT OF IT—

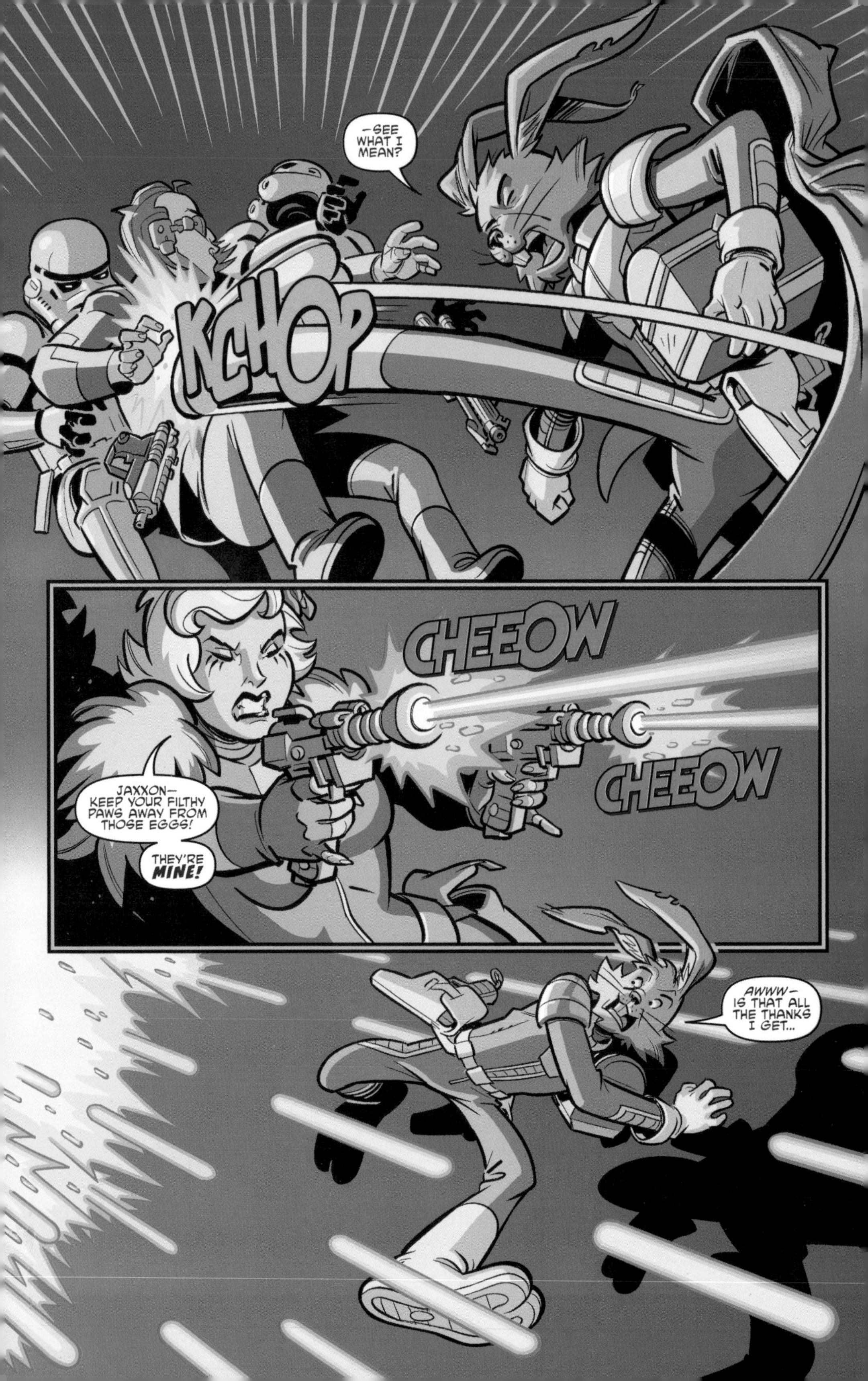

—SEE WHAT I MEAN?
KCHOP
CHEEOW
CHEEOW
JAXXON— KEEP YOUR FILTHY PAWS AWAY FROM THOSE EGGS!
THEY'RE **MINE!**
AWWW— IS THAT ALL THE THANKS I GET...

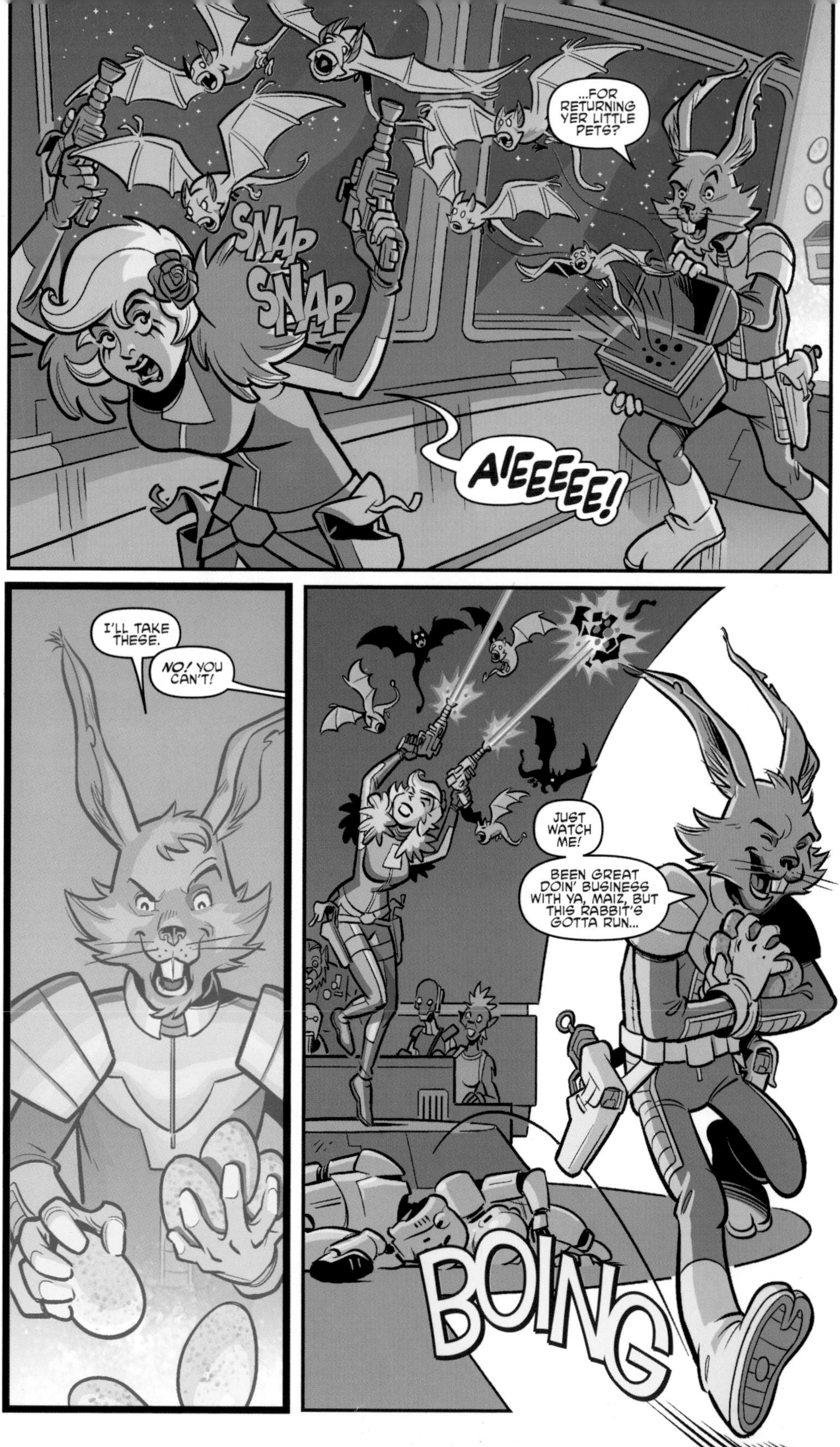
...FOR RETURNING YER LITTLE PETS?
SNAP
SNAP
SNAP
AIEEEEEE!
I'LL TAKE THESE.
NO! YOU CAN'T!
JUST WATCH ME!
BEEN GREAT DOIN' BUSINESS WITH YA, MAIZ, BUT THIS RABBIT'S GOTTA RUN...
BOING

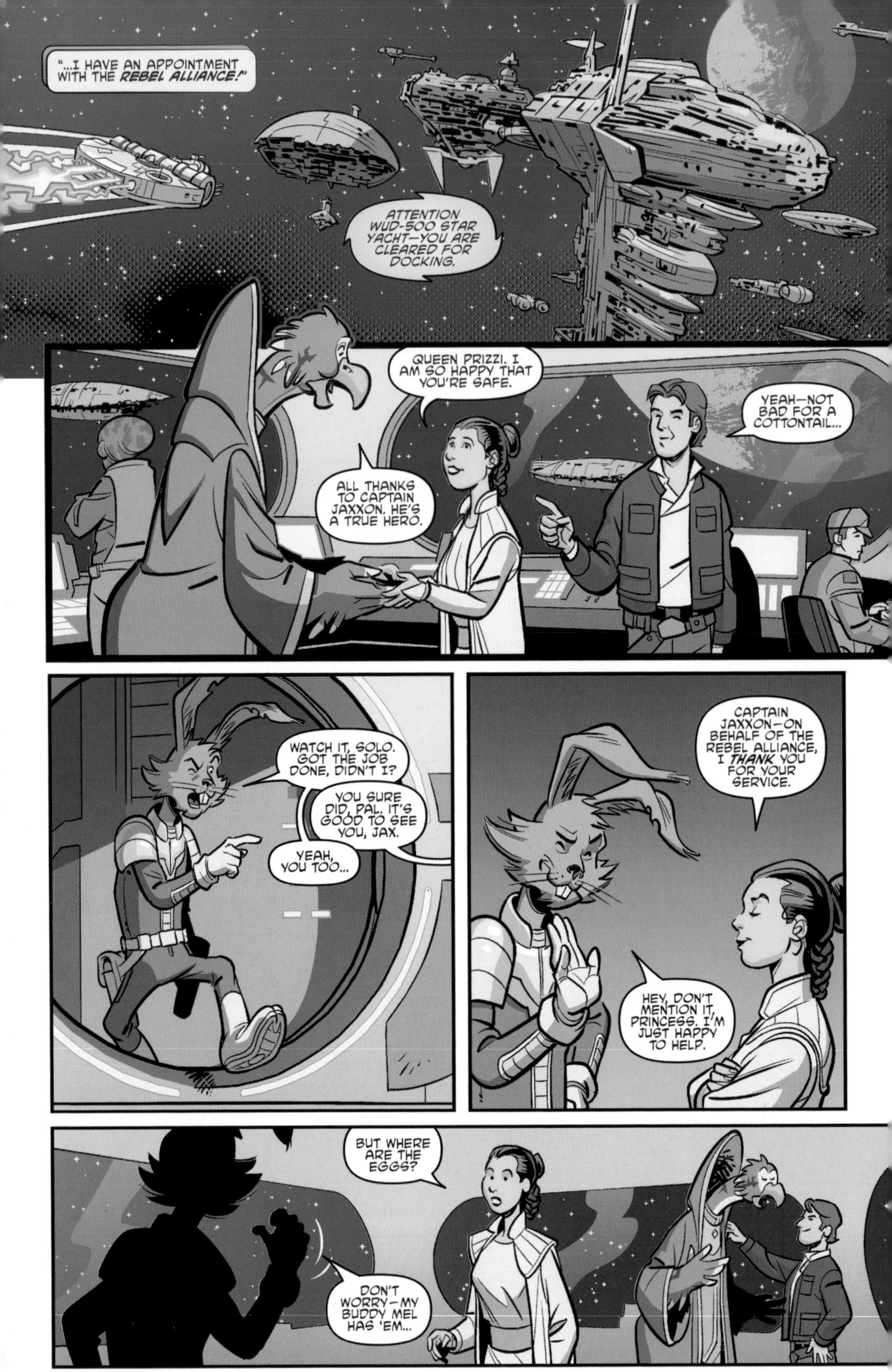
"...I HAVE AN APPOINTMENT WITH THE *REBEL ALLIANCE!*"
ATTENTION WUD-500 STAR YACHT—YOU ARE CLEARED FOR DOCKING.
QUEEN PRIZZI. I AM SO HAPPY THAT YOU'RE SAFE.
ALL THANKS TO CAPTAIN JAXXON. HE'S A TRUE HERO.
YEAH—NOT BAD FOR A COTTONTAIL...
WATCH IT, SOLO. GOT THE JOB DONE, DIDN'T I?
YOU SURE DID, PAL. IT'S GOOD TO SEE YOU, JAX.
YEAH, YOU TOO...
CAPTAIN JAXXON—ON BEHALF OF THE REBEL ALLIANCE, I *THANK* YOU FOR YOUR SERVICE.
HEY, DON'T MENTION IT, PRINCESS. I'M JUST HAPPY TO HELP.
BUT WHERE ARE THE EGGS?
DON'T WORRY—MY BUDDY MEL HAS 'EM...

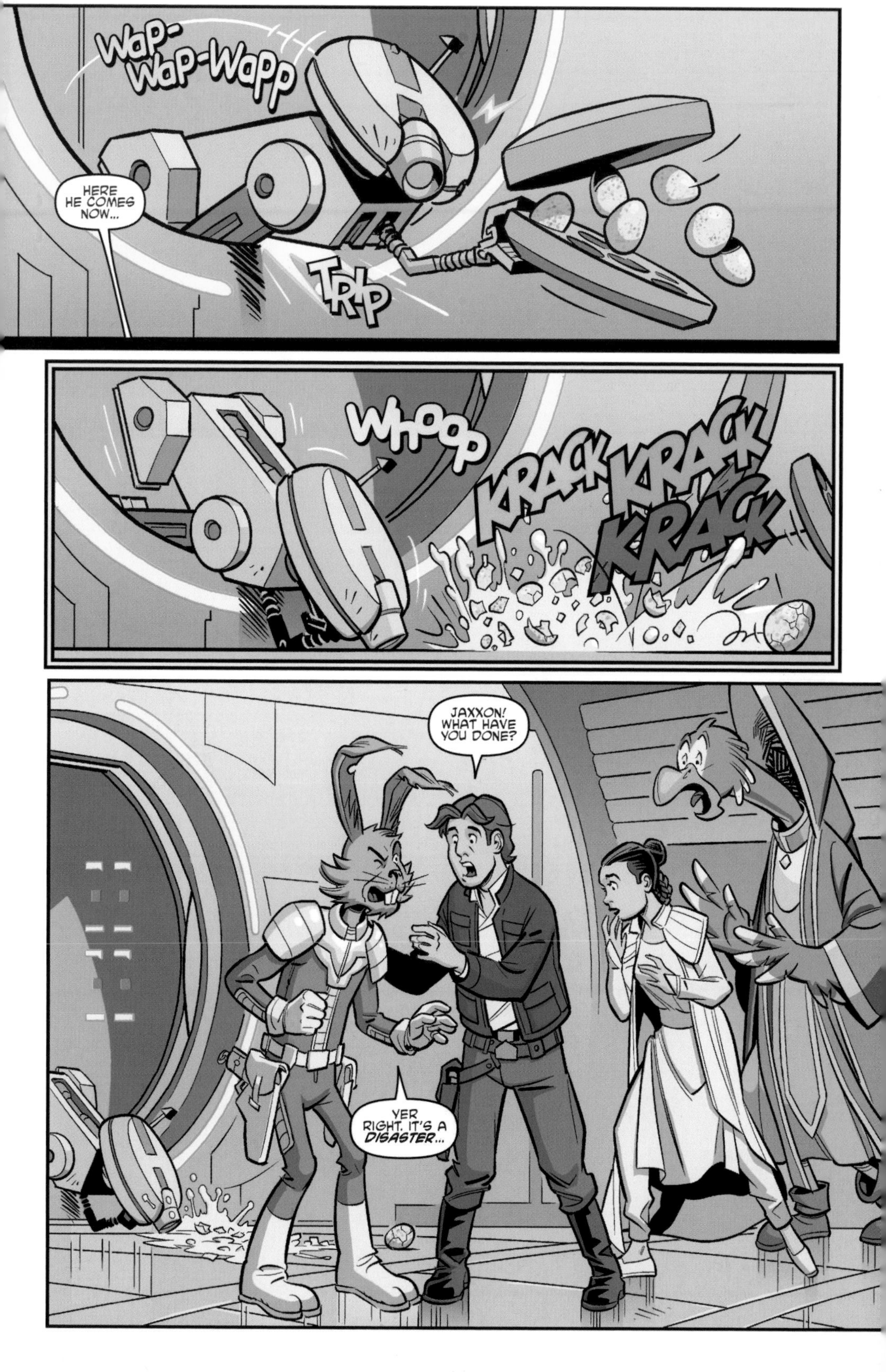
Wap-Wap-Wapp
HERE HE COMES NOW...
TRIP
WHOOP
KRACK KRACK KRACK
JAXXON! WHAT HAVE YOU DONE?
YER RIGHT. IT'S A *DISASTER*...

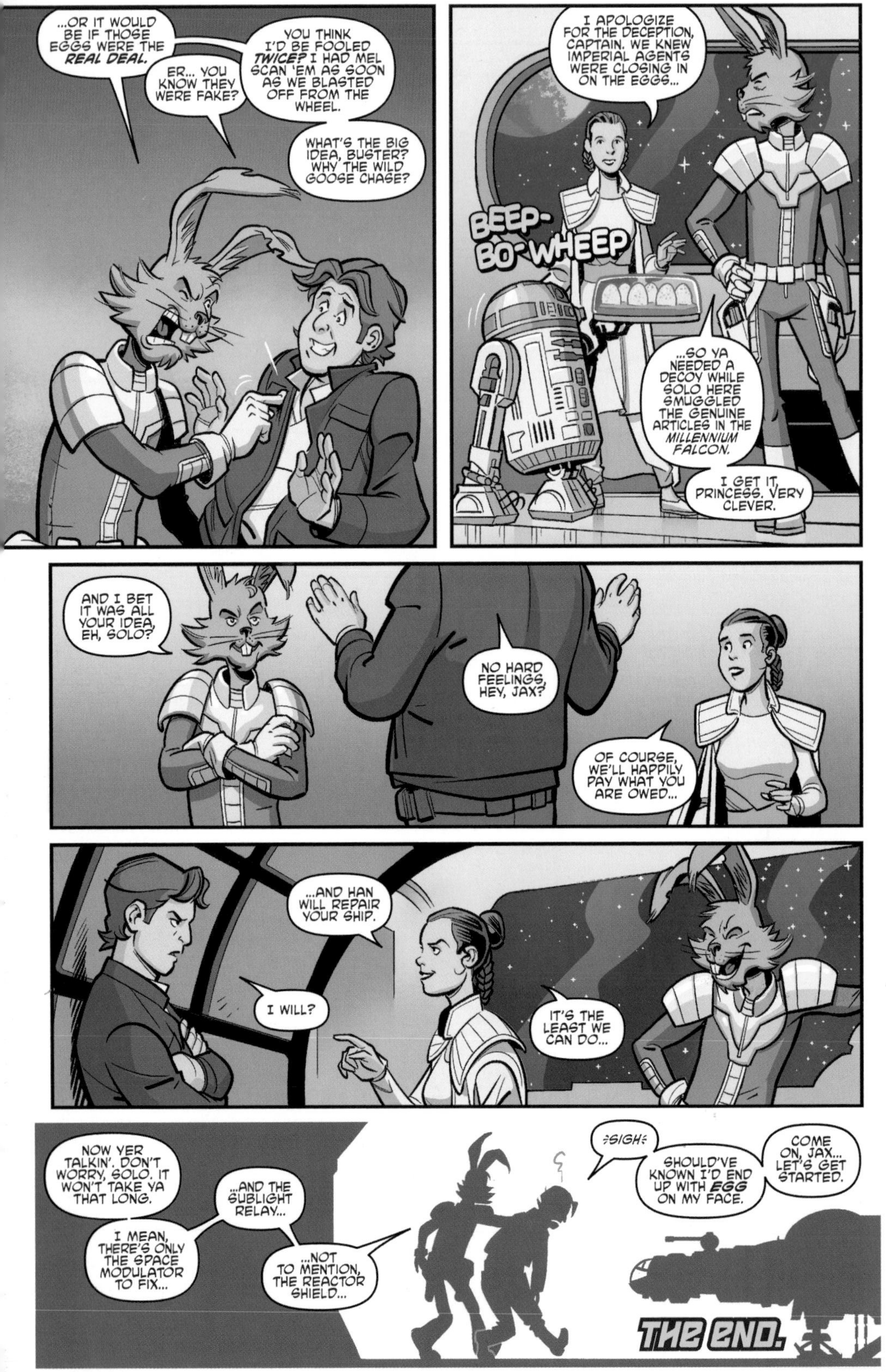
...OR IT WOULD BE IF THOSE EGGS WERE THE REAL DEAL.
ER... YOU KNOW THEY WERE FAKE?
YOU THINK I'D BE FOOLED TWICE? I HAD MEL SCAN 'EM AS SOON AS WE BLASTED OFF FROM THE WHEEL.
WHAT'S THE BIG IDEA, BUSTER? WHY THE WILD GOOSE CHASE?
I APOLOGIZE FOR THE DECEPTION, CAPTAIN. WE KNEW IMPERIAL AGENTS WERE CLOSING IN ON THE EGGS...
BEEP-BO-WHEEP
...SO YA NEEDED A DECOY WHILE SOLO HERE SMUGGLED THE GENUINE ARTICLES IN THE MILLENNIUM FALCON.
I GET IT, PRINCESS. VERY CLEVER.
AND I BET IT WAS ALL YOUR IDEA, EH, SOLO?
NO HARD FEELINGS, HEY, JAX?
OF COURSE, WE'LL HAPPILY PAY WHAT YOU ARE OWED...
...AND HAN WILL REPAIR YOUR SHIP.
I WILL?
IT'S THE LEAST WE CAN DO...
NOW YER TALKIN'. DON'T WORRY, SOLO. IT WON'T TAKE YA THAT LONG.
I MEAN, THERE'S ONLY THE SPACE MODULATOR TO FIX...
...AND THE SUBLIGHT RELAY...
...NOT TO MENTION, THE REACTOR SHIELD...
SIGH
SHOULD'VE KNOWN I'D END UP WITH EGG ON MY FACE.
COME ON, JAX... LET'S GET STARTED.
THE END.

COVER
GALLERY

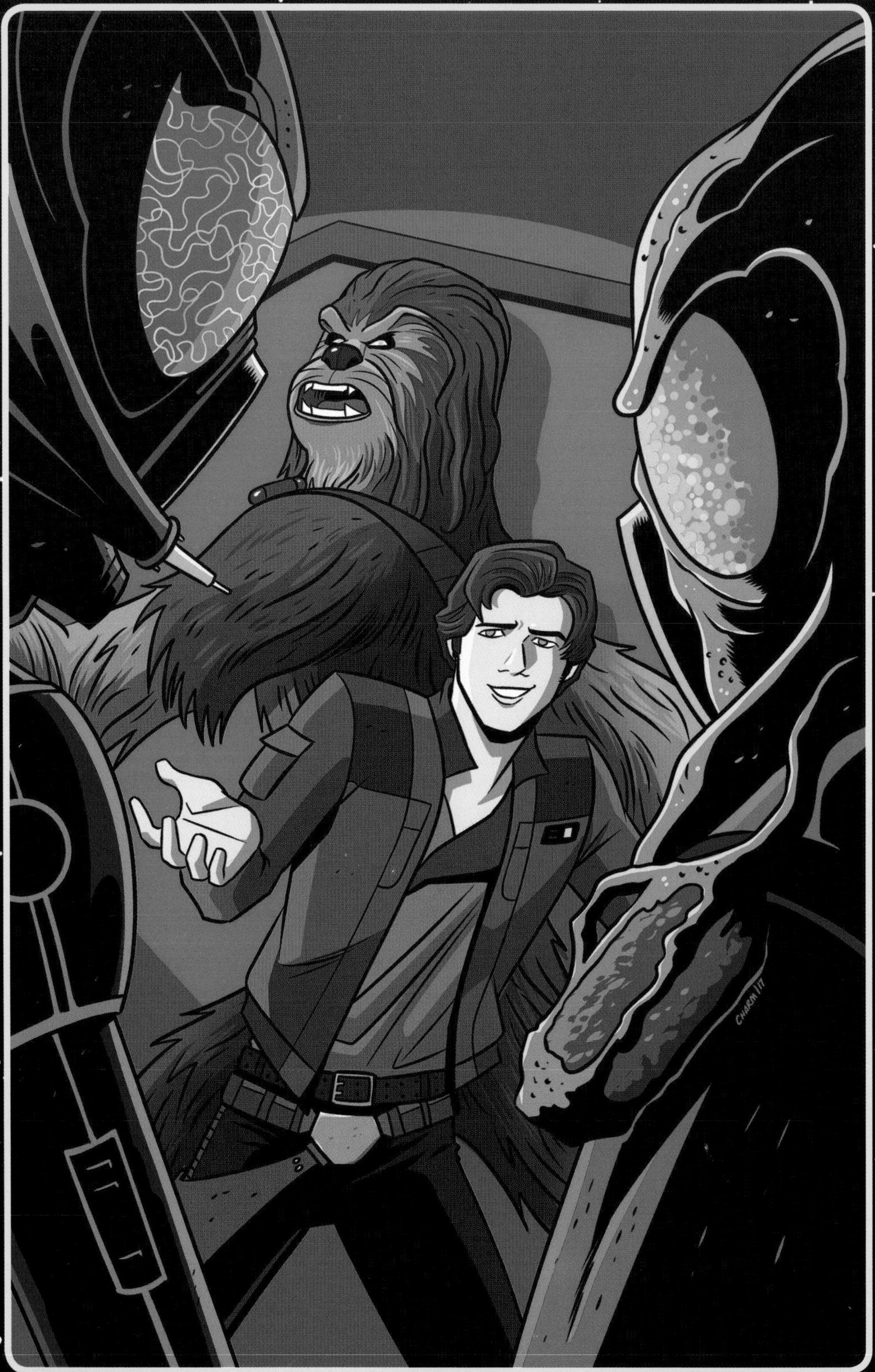

Art by Derek Charm

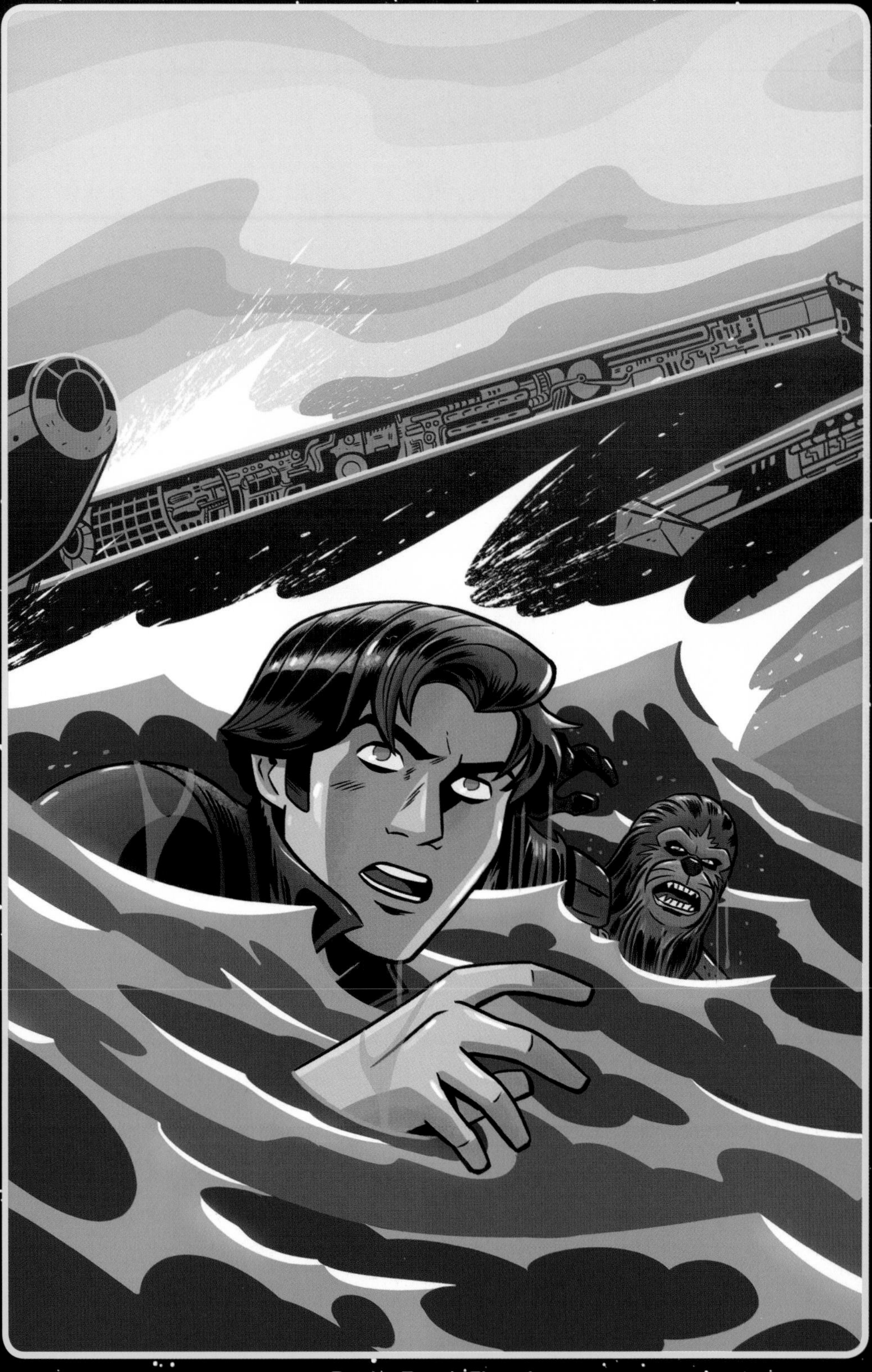

Art by Derek Charm

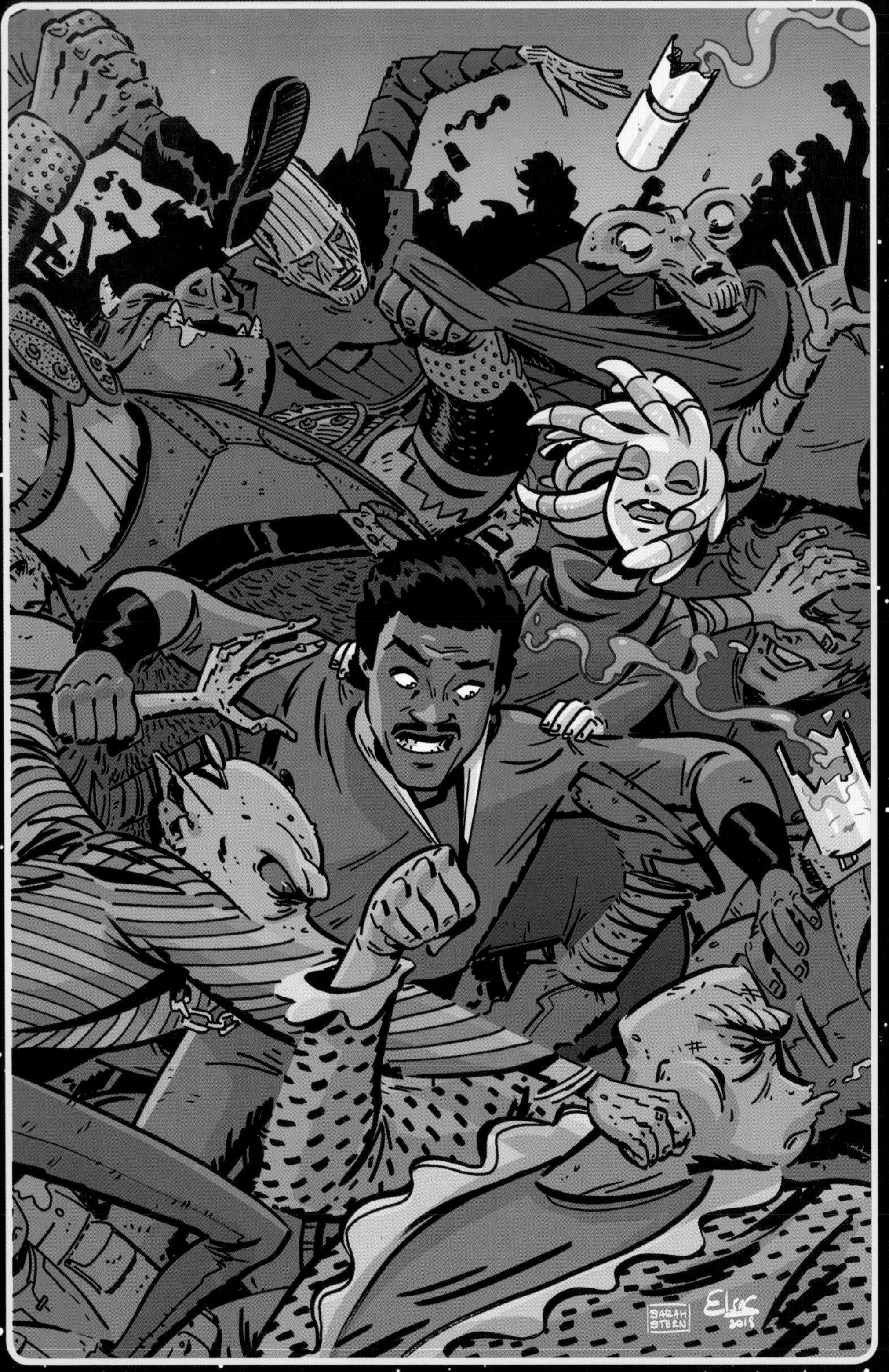
SARAH STERN
Elsa
2018

Art by Elsa Charretier, Colors by Sarah Stern

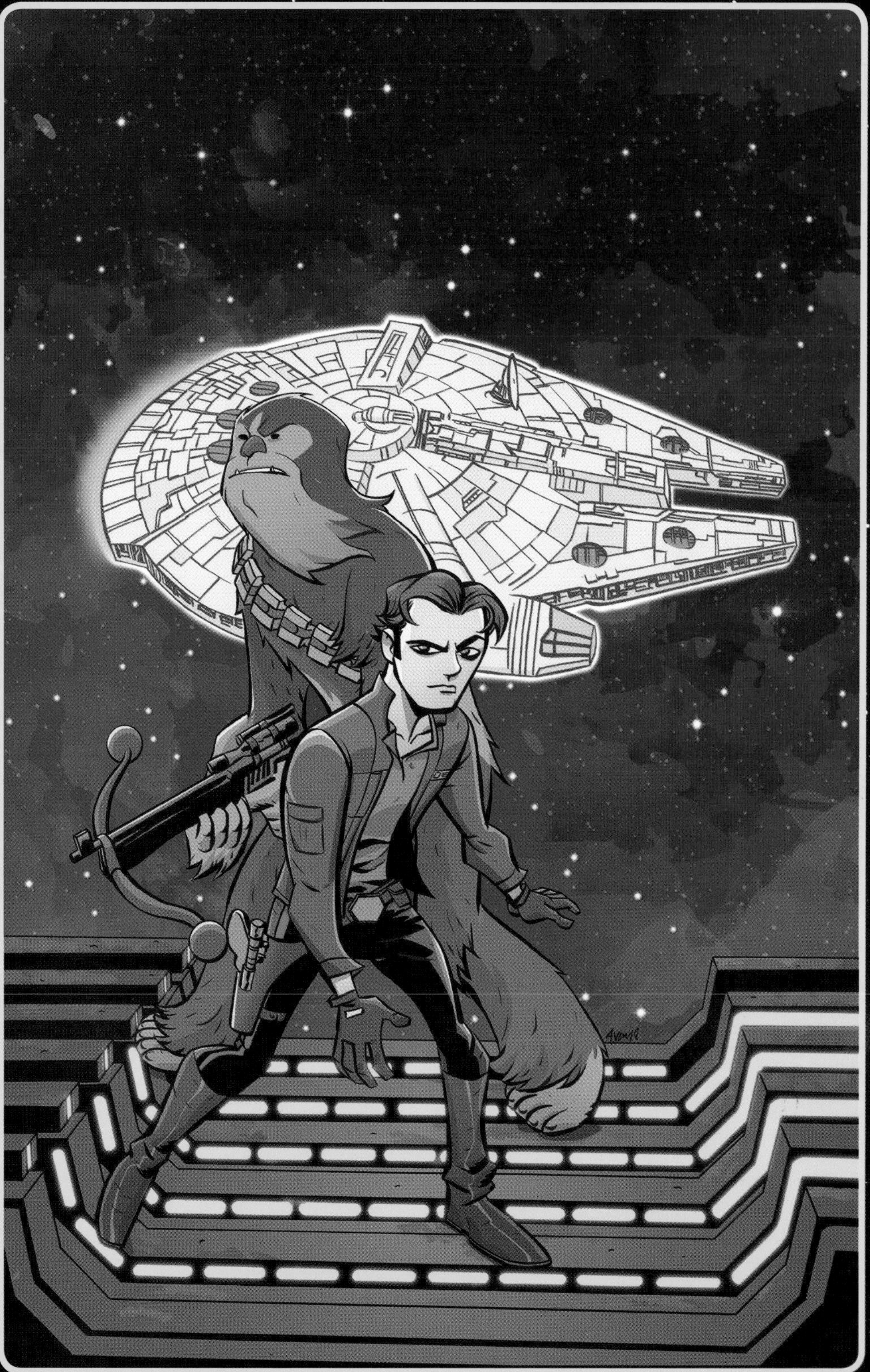

Art by Mike Oeming

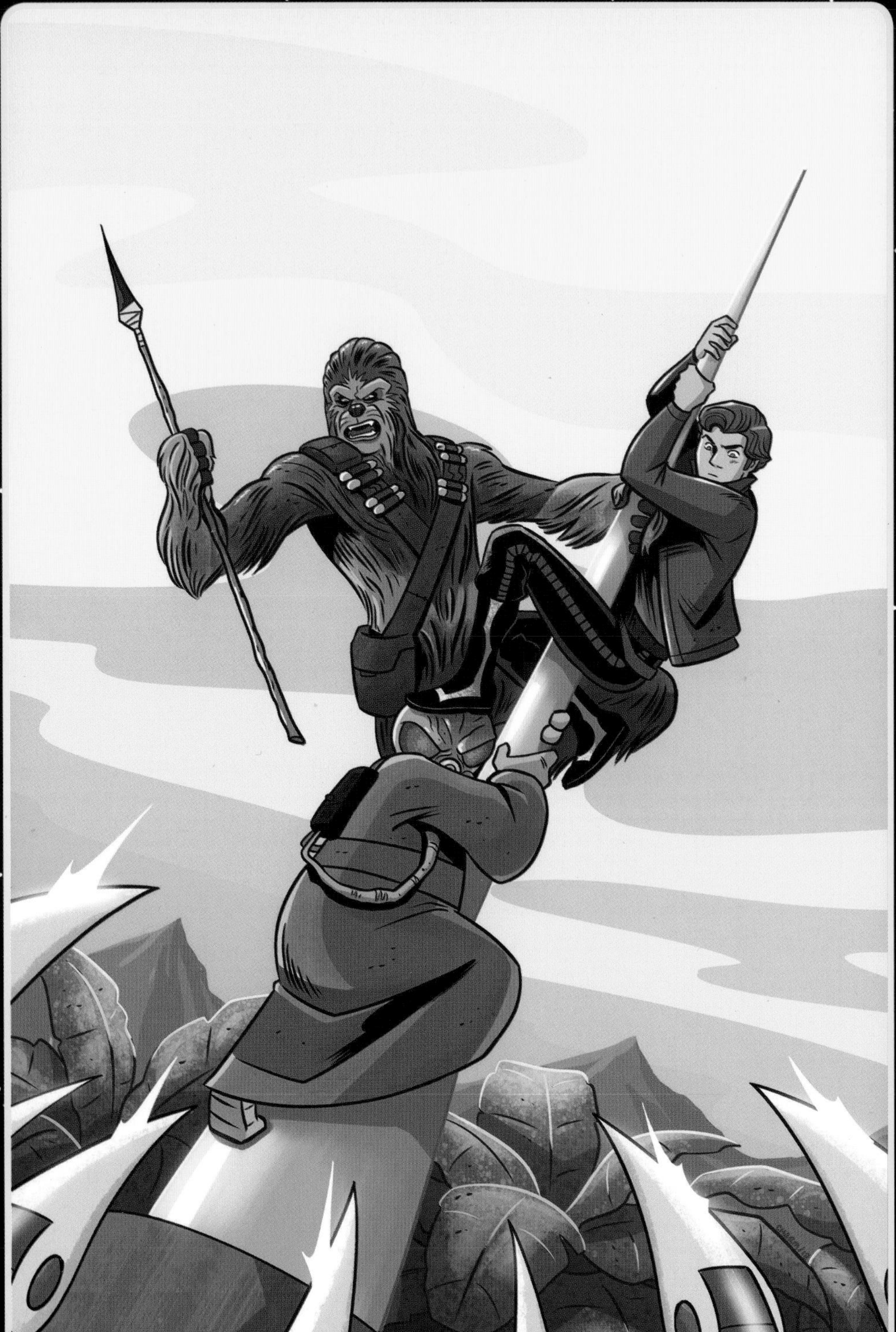

Art by Derek Charm

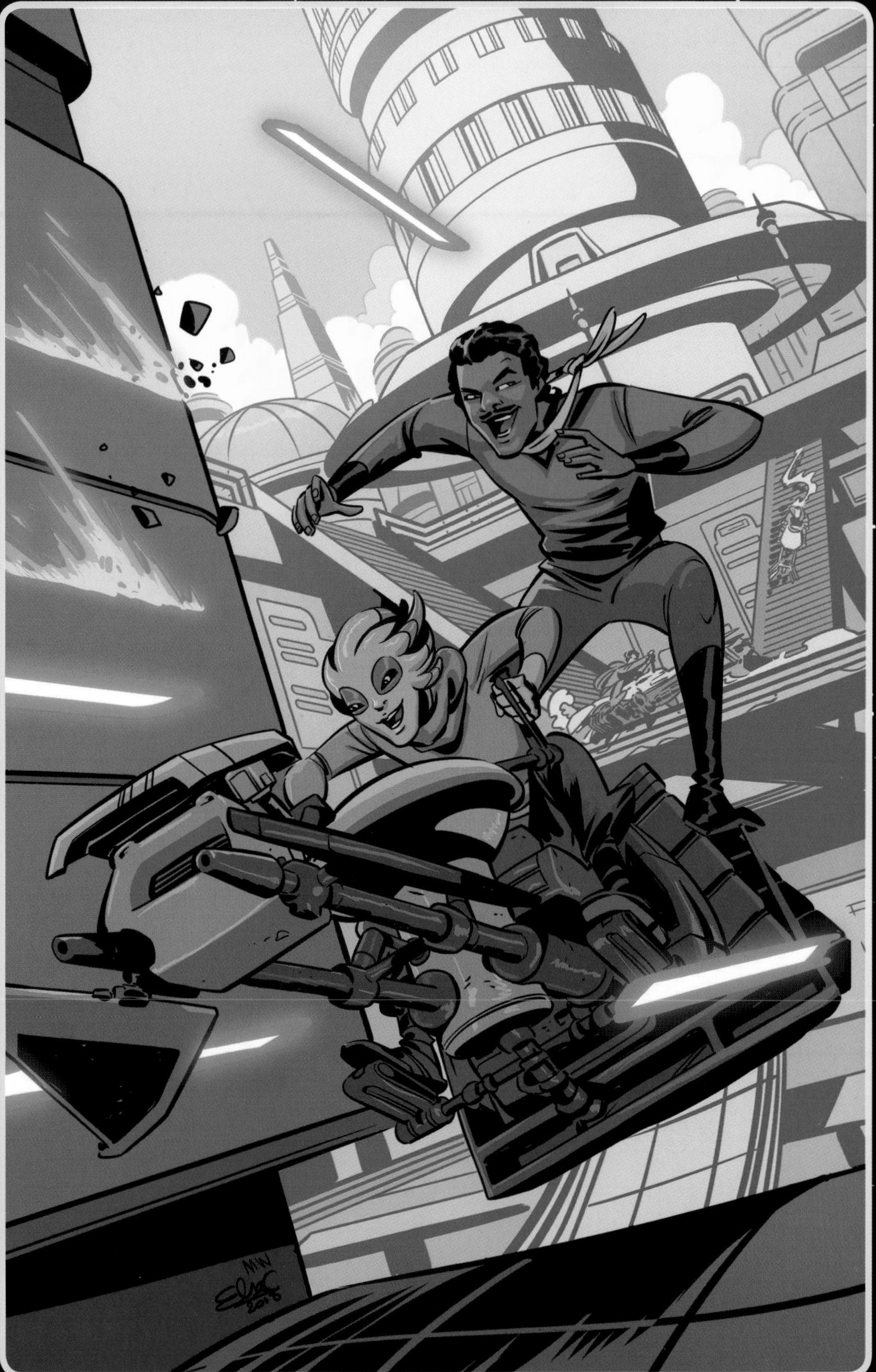

Art by Elsa Charretier, Colors by Sarah Stern

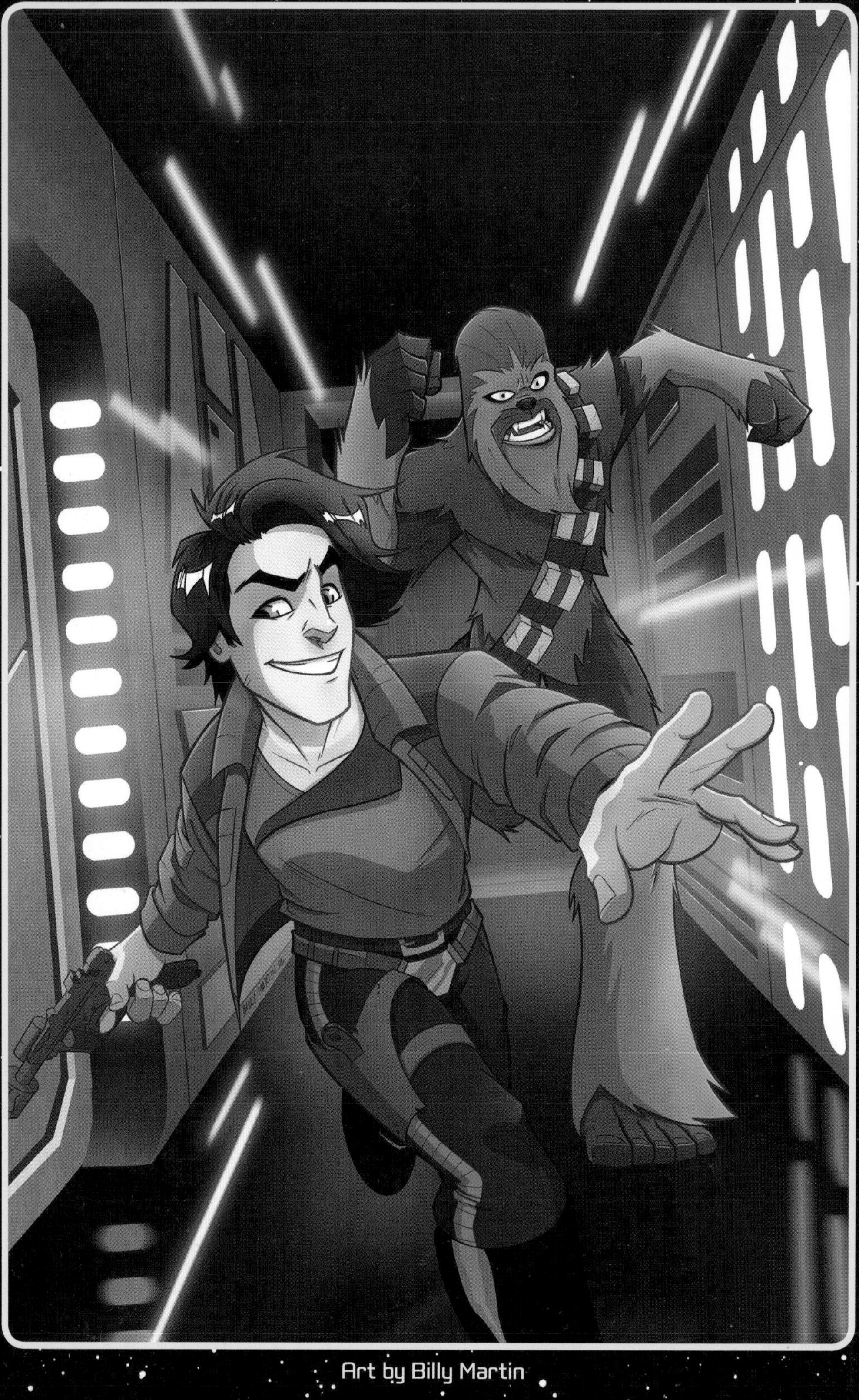

Art by Billy Martin